STRING OF
Pearls

D1091338

STRING OF *Pearls*

MELODY CARLSON

WhiteFire
Publishing

This is a work of fiction. All characters and events portrayed in this novel are either fictitious or used fictitiously.

STRING OF PEARLS

WhiteFire Publishing
13607 Bedford Rd NE
Cumberland, MD 21502

ISBN: 978-1-939023-69-8 (print)
           978-1-939023-70-4 (digital)

One

January 1943

Molly was flying high as the airplane landed in San Francisco, but as she disembarked the sleek silver craft, she felt a definite letdown. It wasn't that she didn't want to see Mam and Dad again, as well as Margaret and the baby, but she wasn't the least bit eager to return to her "normal life." Not that she'd wanted to remain in Hollywood forever...but any excuse not to return to high school seemed a good excuse.

Molly wasn't even excited about seeing her "friend" Dottie anymore. Back in the old days, she would've been eager to tell Dottie all about her Hollywood visit. But Dottie had been dating Bill Brimfield since last fall—she was head over heels for the guy—and Bill was Charlie Stockton's best friend...and Charlie was a dirty rat! As a result, Dottie and Molly had been a bit estranged.

The wind whipped against Molly and, tightening the belt of her wool trench coat, she waved at Margaret, hurrying across the tarmac toward her.

"Welcome home, world traveler!" Margaret hugged Molly, kissing her on the cheek. "I missed you, baby sister."

"Thank you—and thanks for picking me up." She linked her arm in Margaret's as they scurried over to the terminal. Molly couldn't help but wonder whether Margaret had truly missed her or simply missed her help as her part-time nanny. "Where's Baby Peter?"

"With Mam at the store. It was too cold to bring him out." Margaret slowly shook her head. "And I hate to admit it, but I don't mind having a little time off from motherhood. I never knew that babies could be so demanding." She turned to peer at Molly. "But forget about that and tell me everything. How was Hollywood? Did you see anyone famous? Did Colleen let you go to the movie set with her? And has she heard anything from Geoff? Did you—"

"Slow down." Molly held up a hand. "I can't answer everything at once."

"Sorry. It's just been so quiet around here lately. And I'm curious about life down there." She scowled. "To be perfectly honest, I was a little envious over your visit. Just this morning, I found myself wishing I were in your shoes."

"Then you'd be the one sitting in Mr. Barnes' boring old algebra class tomorrow." Molly grimaced. If only she could trade places with Margaret!

As they collected her luggage, Molly described Colleen's compact apartment. But, not wanting to feed her sister's envy, she played down the modern appliances in the kitchen, trying to make the place sound less glamorous than it actually was.

"So it's really tiny then?"

"Yes...although the grounds are pretty. And there's a swimming pool," Molly confessed as they hurried across the parking lot. "But I only used it once. It really wasn't hot enough to enjoy a swim." She shivered. "Although it was a whole lot warmer than here." She smiled at Margaret. "By the way, happy New Year. Did you do anything special last night?"

"We had the Hammonds over. They stayed up until midnight,

playing bridge and merry making like old people do. But I was a party pooper. I went to bed with Baby Peter." Margaret sighed as they put the luggage into the trunk. "My life must sound terribly boring. I bet you and Colleen had fun. What did you girls do last night?"

"We went to the Canteen!" Molly couldn't hide her enthusiasm now. "It was my third time to visit—but it was still absolutely amazing, Margaret."

"You mean the Hollywood Canteen? That's like a USO club, right?"

"Yes. It's for the servicemen down there. But it's so glamorous! So exciting! Naturally, Colleen insisted on dressing me up. I got to wear this dreamy satin gown of midnight blue with silver sequins around the neckline. Someone from her agency gave it to her when she did her screen test. But, honestly, I felt just like a starlet in it. Colleen warned me that since it was New Year's Eve, the Canteen would be crawling with celebrities. Mostly starlets, of course. Although I nearly fell out of my shoes—rather, Colleen's shoes—when James Stewart walked in." Molly fanned herself like she was swooning.

"No kidding? James Stewart was really there?"

"In his air force uniform." Molly let out a loud sigh. "So handsome! And he had Hedy Lamarr on one arm and Judy Garland on the other."

"His costars from *Zigfield Girl*," Margaret said in an awed tone. "Oh my! I just love Jimmy Stewart."

"Colleen begged me not to gape at him." Molly laughed. "Believe me, that was not easy. Oh, you should've seen the lineup of starlets coming through the door, Margaret—all dressed to the nines. Lana Turner, Ava Gardner, Joan Fontaine, just to name a few. Honestly, it was hard not to stare. But I did my best not to embarrass Colleen."

"Oh, my goodness! I'm sure I would've made a complete fool of myself."

"I don't think anyone guessed I'm still in high school. And the servicemen I danced with assumed I was an actress too." She giggled. "And since it made them happy to think that I was famous, I sort of just went along with it. I mean, I didn't lie—I did tell them my real name. But if they acted like they recognized me from the silver screen, I simply kept my mouth shut."

"That must've been so fun!"

"And, oh yeah, I got to meet Miss Bette Davis too. You know she really helped to get the Canteen going in the first place. She's such a nice lady."

"Did you actually speak to her?"

"Well, just barely. She was pretty busy—but she was very polite to me, treated me like I was just as famous as any of them."

"It all sounds like a dream. I still can't believe our own Colleen is really an actress, living in Hollywood...making a motion picture."

"You know what was the most fun about being at the Canteen?"

"What?"

"Just seeing all those servicemen. You know how they always look so strong and capable in their uniforms, so devoted to the war effort. But then I'd catch one of them being star-struck by an actress. It's hard to explain, but it was really sweet. It made them seem so human."

"Well, of course they're human."

"I know. But I usually think of servicemen as being so mature and grown-up. You know how those uniforms make them seem so suave and polished, but last night I got to thinking about how a lot of them were barely older than me. For all we know, they could've been fresh off the farm, barely out of high school, the kid working at the local gas station last week. And now they're getting ready to head off to war."

"That's true."

"But last night, I was watching them more closely. Like when this sailor came in and instantly recognized Rita Hayworth." She chuckled. "It reminded me of a *Loony Tunes* cartoon. Like when Daffy Duck's eyes pop out of his head."

Margaret laughed. "I can just imagine that."

"And last night, I got seriously worried that a young sailor I'd been talking to was about to faint when Judy Garland asked him to dance. The poor guy was totally speechless and barely breathing. I had to practically push him into her arms. Fortunately, she caught him."

They both laughed.

"Did you take any photographs?" Margaret asked.

"Colleen wouldn't let me take my camera to the Canteen, but I got lots of other pictures of Hollywood. I can't wait to get them developed." She let out a happy sigh. "I just loved being down there with her, Margaret. Don't tell Mam and Dad, but I really didn't want to come home today."

Margaret looked slightly alarmed now. "Don't tell me you've got the Hollywood bug now! Are you thinking about becoming an actress too?"

Molly shook her head. "No, of course not. That wasn't it at all. I just liked feeling, well, sort of grown-up...you know?"

Margaret scowled. "Don't be so eager to grow up, Molly. It's not nearly as much fun as you're imagining."

Molly considered this. Maybe adulthood wasn't fun for Margaret, but Molly felt fairly certain that Colleen was having a good time. And the idea of leaving her immature high school peers behind her was extremely enticing.

"What about Geoff, Molly? You haven't mentioned him. Has Colleen heard anything?"

Molly grimly shook her head. "Not a word. And she even called Geoff's mother last night, to wish her Happy New Year...but no news."

"Poor Colleen. As relieved as we were to learn that Geoff survived getting shot down, it's horrible to imagine him in a Japanese prison camp right now. Honestly, I just shudder to think about it."

"I know. And I could tell that, even though Colleen doesn't talk much about it, she's worried for him. I pray for Geoff every night. Actually...I pray for everyone I know that's serving overseas. I hate to admit it, but every time I read the news lately, well, it sounds worse than before. Sometimes it feels like we're fighting the devil himself. I don't understand how there can be so much evil in the world."

"I know. Hard as I try, I still can't take too much news. I don't want to be an ostrich with her head in the sand, but a little bit goes a long way with me."

Molly knew how anxious Margaret could get over the war. Mam too. Certainly it wasn't easy for any of them, knowing their loved ones were right in the thick of the fighting. "Did we get any letters while I was gone?"

"We got a nice one from Bridget. It was short, because she said they'd been very busy."

"I'm sure there must be a lot of wounded servicemen in her area." Molly had just read the newspaper on her flight. There'd been many devastating battles near the Philippines—the number of lives lost, as well as the wounded, was overwhelming.

"Despite the workload, Bridget sounded in good spirits. She really loves nursing."

"What about Brian?" Molly asked tentatively. She knew that

Margaret's greatest anxiety was probably related to her husband. Brian was serving in the army, where his unit, the Mulligans suspected, had been recently relocated to North Africa. According to the news, the fighting there was fierce.

"I haven't heard from him since the V-mail I got before Peter's christening."

"He's probably got his hands full."

"You'll be pleased to know you've got a letter from Patrick waiting for you, Molly. I actually had to control Mrs. Hammond from opening it last night."

Molly blinked. "Really? She would open someone else's mail?"

"Probably not. But she hinted that since it was from her son, she should have the right to read it. Anyway, I put it in your room. Of course, that probably just made her even more curious." Margaret chuckled. "Honestly, she was acting like you and Patrick have some kind of secret romance going on."

"Oh, not—not really!"

"I reminded her that you're not even seventeen yet. And that Patrick is seven years your senior! Of course, Mr. Hammond simply pointed out that he's nine years older than Mrs. Hammond." She glanced at Molly with a slightly suspicious look.

Instead of responding to this, Molly began to tell Margaret about visiting the movie studio with Colleen. "It was so interesting to see the sets and how they make films." She described how the scenery worked. "In person you can easily tell that it's fake, but when you see it on film, it looks real." She explained how a cinematographer actually let her look through his camera lens. "You know, Margaret, if I did get bitten by the Hollywood bug, it would be to control one of those huge movie cameras. Now that would be fun."

"Do you mind if we go straight to the store?" Margaret asked as she turned down Market Street. "I told Mam I would stop by there first."

"Not at all. I'm surprised the store's even open today. Isn't New Year's Day usually a holiday?"

"It always has been for us. But Dad insisted on opening. He got it into his head that we could get some new customers by being open when everyone else was closed. And I have to admit that we've been somewhat busy."

Molly suspected Dad was getting overly concerned about finances again. She knew that, despite Colleen's help with Margaret's hospital bills related to Peter's birth, their family's finances were still in peril. She'd never heard real numbers, but she knew that Dad's long stay in the tuberculosis sanitarium had set them back considerably. "And I can work at the store this afternoon," Molly offered. "So you and Baby Peter can go home."

"No, that's okay. I plan to stay and work on the books this afternoon. But, if you don't mind, I'd like you to take Dad home with you." Margaret frowned as she turned down the back alley behind the store. "I don't want to alarm you, Molly, but Dad didn't seem too well this morning."

"Oh, no—it's not TB again, is it?"

"No, no. I don't think so. I mean, after all, he got a clean bill of health last fall."

"What was wrong then?"

"He just seemed a bit pale." Margaret turned off the engine. "Naturally, he played it down. Dad said he was worn out from staying up too late last night. But I'm not so sure. It seemed he had trouble catching his breath after he carried a case of green beans out of the backroom. Anyway, I don't want to make scene, but I hope you can talk him into going home with you."

"I'll do my best." Molly felt a rush of concern. She had enjoyed getting closer to Dad over the past several months. She relished their chess games and discussions about the war and perusing the atlas together. What if his TB were back? And what if he had to return to the sanitarium?

Two

Following a happy reunion with Mam and a quick cuddle with her infant nephew, Molly turned her full attention to Dad. "Why don't you come home with me?" she said in a teasing tone. "I'm due to beat you in a chess game."

"Oh, I don't know." Dad frowned. "I need to finish cutting that beef and—"

"I'll finish that," Mam said quickly.

"Come on, Dad," Molly urged. "We can catch up. I'll tell you all about Colleen's life down in Hollywood."

"Yes," Margaret eagerly agreed. "Just wait until you hear what your baby girl has been up to, Dad."

"And Margaret and I will be fine," Mom assured him. "You saw how slow it was this past hour."

"All right then." Dad nodded firmly as he untied his grocer's apron. "I'll go home with Molly." He winked at her. "As long as you promise to tell all about your glamorous Hollywood vacation."

"Pick us up around five." Margaret tucked the car keys into Molly's hand.

"And I just used my ration card to fill the tank," Mam told Molly. "Although I still don't understand the need for gas rationing on the West Coast. Goodness knows that California has plenty of gasoline."

"That's not why it's being rationed," Molly pointed out. "I just read an article about it, Mam. It has to do with rubber shortages."

"But why ration gas then?"

"There's a simple reason." Dad pulled on his winter coat. "The government decided the best way to conserve rubber was to limit automobile use. What better way to do that than by limiting our gasoline?"

"But why is there a rubber shortage?" Mam asked absently.

"Because the tropical countries that produce rubber are caught in the middle of this war," Molly reminded her. "In the Pacific and Malaysia."

"Oh, yes, I suppose I hadn't thought of that." Mam nodded. "That does make sense."

Dad put on his hat. "Don't forget to add the right portion of fat when you grind the beef and make—"

"Don't you worry yourself, Riley." Mam gently nudged him toward the back door. "I know how to grind beef, old man. I've been doing it since I was a girl."

Dad kissed Mam good-bye, but he and Molly were barely out the door when he held out his hand for the keys, insisting on driving.

"But I—"

"The doctor never said I can't drive," he said sharply. "That was your mother and sister's doing."

Molly wasn't too sure about this, but deciding that driving the short trip home would do him no harm—and possibly lift his spirits—Molly surrendered the keys. Dad smiled as he got behind the wheel, but when he turned in the opposite direction of their neighborhood, Molly felt a wave of concern. "Are you taking a different route home?"

"Worried about wasting gas?" He continued driving in the wrong direction.

She shrugged. "No. Just curious."

"Do you think your old dad is lost?" His tone was teasing but his expression seemed sober. "Or losing his senses?"

"No, not at all. You know San Francisco better than anyone."

He just nodded and continued driving south.

"Where *are* you going?" she asked cautiously.

"Just a little side trip." His expression grew serious. "Somewhere I need to go."

"Are you feeling all right, Dad?"

"Oh, sure...I just need to pay someone a little visit."

Molly frowned, trying to determine who Dad knew on this side of town—a friend he could pop in on unexpectedly. "Uh...who do you want to visit?"

There was a long silence as he waited at a stoplight before finally he answered. "Your brother."

"Oh..." Molly didn't know what to say as he turned down the street that led toward the Golden Gate National Cemetery.

"I've not been to Peter's gravesite. Not even once. And it's been troubling me." He glanced at her. "Do you know where his stone is located, Molly Girl?"

"Yes." She slowly nodded. "But are you sure you're up for the walk, Dad? It's a little ways to it. And it's pretty cold and windy out today. We could always go another time and—"

"I want to go today," he declared.

As they got out of the car, Molly tried not to consider what Margaret would say to this unplanned expedition. Here she'd expected Molly to get Dad safely home to rest...and now they were outside walking through the damp chilly air through the National

Cemetery. Still, what could Molly do? Weren't children supposed to respect their parents?

"I still find it hard to believe that he's gone sometimes."

"I know." She sighed. "So do I."

"I thought it would help to come here. I'd meant to come here on December seventh, the anniversary of his death, but there was too much going on... And truth be told, I think that was a difficult day for all of us."

"It's only natural you'd want to see his memorial stone." Molly reached for Dad's hand. Then, surprised at how cold it felt, even through her gloves, she wrapped her fingers more snugly around his. She wanted to suggest they walk faster to stay warm, but remembering what Margaret had said about him being tired, she let him set the pace.

"Your brother was a fine young man," Dad said quietly as they strolled down a path.

"I know."

"My only son."

"My only brother," she said softly.

"It's hard to accept that he's really not coming home again."

"Yeah." She sighed, leading him past a tidy row of identical carved stones.

"Parents should never outlive their children, Molly."

She didn't know how to respond to that, and so she simply nodded, grasping his hand more tightly. "It's right over there." She pointed to the section.

"I realize that Peter isn't really here," he said slowly.

"I know. But I've come here too, Dad, hoping to make a connection with him." She paused in front of Peter's stone. It was the same dull gray color as the sky.

Dad stood in front of the marker, just staring down at it...with such a sad expression that Molly felt her own eyes filling with tears. Dad released her hand and, kneeling down before the stone, leaned forward to brush a dead leaf away from Peter's name. Molly knelt beside him, wrapping an arm around Dad's shoulders and wishing for something to say...something to comfort him. But no words came to her. And so she simply waited. But as she waited, she realized how frail her father felt beneath his thin woolen overcoat. A shadow of the big strong man she'd grown up with. But was it any wonder, considering what their family had gone through this past year?

As she listened to Dad's quiet, choked sobs, she realized her own face was wet. Extracting a handkerchief from her coat pocket, she wiped her tears then handed it to him. He blotted his cheeks and then slowly, with her help, got to his feet.

"Thank you," he said in a husky voice. He handed the damp handkerchief back to her.

"I can understand you wanting to come here, to see Peter's stone in person," she said quietly. "But the truth is I can feel Peter's presence more in other places."

"Other places?" Dad's brow creased.

"Like Golden Gate Park...or the Presidio...or the zoo... or even just our neighborhood and home. You know—the places where we spent time with Peter. Places we know he loved."

Dad nodded. "That makes sense." He pulled his coat collar more snugly around his neck.

Molly shivered. "It's really cold out, Dad. Let's get back to the car."

He put an arm around her now. "Yes, we'd best do that."

Neither of them spoke as they walked, a bit more quickly, back to the car. To Molly's relief, Dad didn't argue when she took the keys from him. Fortunately, the car was warmer than the winter air and, after she started the engine, she reached into the backseat for the lap robe. Tucking it around her dad's legs, she noticed that, not only did he look pale, but his lips seemed almost blue. "I think you got colder than you realized out there," she said as she turned up the heater. "Let's get you home."

As she drove through town, Dad sat quietly. To fill the air, she chattered away about her visit in Hollywood, commenting on how much milder the weather down there was compared to San Francisco. "Maybe you and Mam can go down for a visit sometime."

But Dad, leaning back in the seat, said nothing. By the time she got home, Molly agreed with Margaret. Dad was not well.

She felt huge relief to get Dad safely into the house and settled in his easy chair with today's morning paper in his lap. Satisfied that some of the color had returned to his face, she went to the kitchen to put on the tea kettle. She suddenly wished that Bridget wasn't so far away. With her nurse's training and general interest in well-being, she would probably have some helpful suggestions for Dad's healthcare. But Bridget was halfway around the world at the moment, tending to wounded soldiers...some whose lives would be changed forever by their severe injuries.

"Here you go, Dad." Molly set a teacup, as well as a piece of bread and jam, onto the table next to his chair.

"You're too good to me." His pale blue eyes twinkled as he smiled. "It's good to have you home again, Molly Girl."

"The truth is I'm worried about you." She sat on the ottoman across from him.

"Worried about your old dad?" His smile faded. "Whatever for?"

"I know it was hard on you to visit Peter's gravesite...but it's more than that. You don't really look too healthy to me."

"Well, now, I'm not in such good shape anymore, not like I used to be. I get winded more easily and—"

"I think it was more than that, Dad." She reached for his hand. "I think you should have a checkup with your doctor."

He pulled his hand away from her, waving it in a dismissive way. "No need for that, darling. It's just like they told me at the sanatorium. I need to take it easy for a spell. The doctor said it could take up to a year before I get back to my old self. And truth be told—though you don't need to tell Mam or Margaret, since they're the worriers in the family—I've probably been overdoing it lately."

"Is that all this is? *Really?*" She studied his face hopefully. "You just need to take it easier?"

He reached for his teacup. "For sure and for certain, Molly Girl. That's all 'tis. I give you my word."

"And do you promise to take it easier, Dad?"

He nodded solemnly.

"Then I'll make a deal with you." She stood up, placing her hands on her hips and looking down on him in what she hoped was an authoritative stance.

"A deal, you say?" He set down his teacup with amused interest.

"You promise to take it easier, and I promise not to nag you to go to the doctor."

He rubbed his chin, nodded, and stretched out his hand to grasp hers. "You drive a hard bargain, Molly Girl. You'd make a formidable businesswoman."

She chuckled. "Wonder where I got that trait from."

Dad pointed to the nearby chess set. "So...you still think you can beat your old dad?"

Molly grinned as she reached for the small table, setting it between them. "I don't know, but I'll give it my best shot."

The game started out with the usual competitive bantering, but after just a few moves, she could see that Dad was tiring. And when he left his queen wide open to her bishop, she knew it was time to quit. "You know, Dad, I'm a little worn out from my trip." She made a weary stretch. "Mind if we finish this later?"

"Not at all." He leaned back in his chair with a sigh. "I might grab forty winks myself—good to be home when the house is nice and quiet."

After she put the chess table aside, Molly picked up the afghan and gently laid it on Dad's lap. His eyes were already closed, but he mumbled his thanks as she tiptoed away. Still concerned for his health, she reminded herself of their agreement. If Dad didn't take it easy, she would insist on calling his doctor herself. And that was that.

As Molly unpacked her suitcase, which—thanks to Colleen's generosity—had come back fuller than when she'd left home a week ago, she felt slightly glad to be back in her old room again. Although she and Colleen had shared this room for most of Molly's life, she had enjoyed having it all to herself this past year. One of the only perks for a family that had changed so drastically thanks to the war.

Spying a corner of a V-mail letter tucked beneath her jewelry box on her bureau, Molly realized that was the letter from Patrick. Feeling even more grateful for this private space, she eagerly but carefully slit it open and started to read, but to her dismay—and what would probably be Mrs. Hammond's relief—the letter was rather impersonal and brief.

The letter had been written in mid-December, and Patrick blamed the brevity on the increased activity in the Pacific region. Probably related to the disturbing newspaper article she'd read on the plane. But, as usual, Patrick went into no detail about military activities. As a naval officer, he knew the importance of withholding vital information from loved ones at home. In his line of work, loose lips really could sink ships. And Molly respected this.

She put the letter in the old hat box where she kept the rest of her correspondence from overseas. But as she tied the box closed, she wondered why she hadn't received a letter from Tommy Foster during her absence. Tommy usually wrote at least once a week, but the last she'd heard from him was early December. As she continued to unpack and put things away, she prayed that Tommy was okay. And, even though he hadn't written, she was determined to send him a letter before the end of the week. Thanks to her recent visit with Colleen, she should have plenty to write about—to everyone.

Molly put her camera case on the bureau. If it weren't New Year's Day, she'd brave the chilly weather and run her undeveloped films down to the drugstore. But suspecting they—unlike her family's grocery store—were closed today, she decided not to waste her time.

Instead, she would answer Patrick's letter. But unlike his short memo, hers would be a long one, complete with lots of colorful details about her recent and exciting visit to Hollywood. And updates on Colleen. And the good news about Geoff. She wished she could put some photos in with it, but that would have to come later.

Three

Margaret didn't think it possible to love Baby Peter any more than she already did. He was adorably sweet and, according to his doting grandmothers, "the perfect baby." And Margaret couldn't agree more—Peter Brian was a peach. This only made it harder to understand why she had moments when she longed to escape her darling little bundle of joy. More so lately than usual. Of course, this remained her dark, shameful secret. Because, really, who would understand? Even young Molly had looked somewhat askance when Margaret had hinted at her true feelings.

Truth be told, it was something she could barely admit to...an admission she couldn't even share with Father McMurphey during her latest confession. It felt unmotherly, selfish...abominable. How was it possible to love a child more than she loved her own life and yet still long for something more? She honestly didn't understand it.

As she sat in the dreary, windowless store office, poring over last year's accounting books with Peter peacefully sleeping in the wicker laundry basket that she'd set up in the corner, she felt that familiar yet irrational stirring of deep-down discontentment. It was all so very disturbing—not to mention humiliating. Good grief, she was a mother! Why was she filled with such unmaternal feelings? What in heaven's name was wrong with her?

Margaret laid down her pencil and tried to think clearly. Oh, she knew that hearing Molly going on about Colleen's exciting Hollywood life had not helped her situation one bit. But then Margaret had begged her baby sister for more information. Like a glutton for punishment, she'd wanted all the glamorous details, but now that she'd heard them, she felt more miserable than ever.

To be fair, Margaret had already felt restless and uneasy these past few days. She partially blamed it on being stuck, day in and day out, with Mam and Dad and the baby and the store...especially when it seemed everyone else was out having a great time. And yet, she appreciated having her parents' company and support. She had to admit that having family around to help with the baby really did make her life easier.

It was just that none of this had been what Margaret had planned. Not really. This was not how she'd ever imagined she would be spending her adult life. Although she should know by now that her life was never going to proceed as planned. It never had, and she suspected that it never would. Perhaps she'd been born beneath an unlucky star. In contrast with Colleen, who must've been born under a lucky one.

Margaret noticed the corner of a new war bond poster still on her desk. She had meant to hang it last week. She removed the newspaper that she'd laid across it the other day. She had no doubts that she'd covered the poster simply because the image on it had disturbed her. She stared at the depiction. It was a soldier serving overseas, but the young man's facial expression looked distraught and slightly desperate. Clutching a rifle, he was running in the night—clearly in distress—as if the enemy were right on his heels. She read the slogan so familiar to those on the home front.

Bring Him Home Sooner—Buy War Bonds.

Well, Margaret had been buying war bonds...when she could afford to. But, really, would that bring Brian home sooner? She had absolutely no idea. For all she knew, those horrible Axis powers were about to overcome the entire earth with their awful ideals and regimes. Didn't the headlines hint at this very thing almost every single day? She glanced at her slumbering baby. What would become of them if that happened? And why was she feeling so negative and pessimistic about everything?

Margaret laid the poster back down with a loud sigh. She had no doubts that this stupid war was greatly responsible for a lot of her personal disappointment and heartache. Sometimes—though not often—she would try to imagine what life would've been like if those three psychotic monsters, Hitler and Hirohito and Mussolini, had never been born. How different things might've been.

Margaret leaned back in the office chair, trying to remember what her dreams had actually been like back before the war changed everything. She didn't often allow herself to go down this frustrating trail, but she was already feeling so blue...and weary of bookkeeping. Plus the baby was asleep and the store seemed quiet. And, well, after feeling envious of Colleen...maybe this was a good time for a sentimental journey. Margaret glanced down at last year's calendar, now occupying the waste basket. What a year it had been. She tried to recalculate the time...wondering how their lives would be different if the war hadn't interfered.

For starters, Peter would still be alive. He wouldn't have enlisted in the navy and been killed at Pearl Harbor. Instead of her, he'd be the one sitting in this chair right now. He'd be carrying this load, managing the store, balancing the books. Not only that, but if not for the war, Brian would've graduated from law school last spring. He'd probably be practicing with his uncle like he'd planned. And they would've gotten married last summer—Margaret had always dreamed of a beautiful June wedding. Not a rushed one like they'd had last year.

The happy newlyweds would be living in a sweet little apartment, maybe even in the North Beach area. Margaret would be contentedly keeping house, surrounded by her own lovely things—including the wedding gifts that were still in boxes and stored in her parents' attic. Brian would arrive home after work each evening, greeted by a pleasant wife and a deliciously prepared meal. They would sit and visit about their day. Perhaps they'd take in a movie afterward. Or maybe they'd meet with friends and play cards and share laughs. She definitely would not have a baby yet. She doubted that she'd even be pregnant. Without a war breathing down their necks, there would be no hurry to have children—"war babies."

With no war raging and changing everything, there would be time to be young and free and happy and in love! There would be no blackout curtains, no rationing, no shortages. There would be no living with one's parents, no working a job that she didn't want, no trembling in fear whenever she turned on the radio or glanced at a headline. And perhaps best of all, if there were no war, thousands of young men—not to mention some women—would still be alive. Margaret felt a lump in her throat.

This stupid, stupid war! She hated it—hated it—hated it! Everyone else could go around acting patriotic and brave, making noble sacrifices to contribute to the war effort, but Margaret would continue to resent this war to the core of her being. It had ruined everything for her. But could she make such confessions to anyone? Not without looking like a selfish, dissatisfied shrew. And since that was not an image she relished, she knew she would have to continue to keep her feelings of discontent to herself. But it wasn't easy. She retrieved a hanky from her skirt pocket, using it to blot her tears.

"Margaret?" Mam poked her head into the office then frowned. "Oh, no. What's wrong?" She glanced over to the basket where Peter was still sweetly slumbering. "Not the baby, I hope."

"No," Margaret said quietly. "Just me...acting like a baby."

"What is it, dear?" Mam came over to the desk, leaning over to peer curiously at Margaret. "Are you unwell?"

"Only in spirit, Mam." Margaret blew her nose. "I was just feeling sorry for myself...again. Silly me."

Mam came closer, putting an arm around Margaret's shoulders. "Oh, honey. I think you have every right to feel sorry for yourself. At least you do today."

"Really?"

"Of course. I didn't forget that yesterday was your one-year anniversary, darling. Dad and I and the Hammonds all agreed not to mention it to you. We didn't want to make you feel worse. But we all suspected that was why you went to bed so early last night."

Margaret shrugged. "I didn't feel much like celebrating."

"I understand. And yet you have so much to celebrate, Margaret."

Margaret blinked. "Such as?"

"You're married to a wonderful man. And such a scholarly one too. Goodness, Brian was very nearly finished with law school. That is no small accomplishment." She nodded to the laundry basket. "And you have a perfect baby." Mam smiled at Margaret. "And you are a beautiful, strong, intelligent young woman with a fabulously bright future ahead of her."

Margaret frowned doubtfully. "Really, Mam, you must've been kissing the blarney stone lately."

Mam chuckled then squeezed her. "It's all true, Margaret. Every word. I should've said as much yesterday, darling. But it was a busy day for everyone."

Margaret sniffed. "Well, thank you anyway."

"I just wanted to let you know it's closing time. Molly's out there now, locking up and turning off the lights. Are you ready to go home?"

Margaret picked up the poster and a roll of scotch tape. "I just want to hang this first. I keep forgetting to put it up."

Colleen had been relieved to have New Year's Day off, but now, sitting alone in her little Beverly Hills apartment, she felt inexplicably lonely. Oh, it was probably her own fault since she'd turned down an invitation to join some of her younger actor cohorts at a borrowed beach house in Malibu. But then she'd heard tales of these impromptu gatherings—along with some cautious warnings from her agency—and consequently she'd made the mature decision not to participate in the shenanigans.

The BG Colleen—meaning before Geoff—would've leaped at the chance to socialize with such exciting young people. The beach house would be crawling with actors, writers, musicians...interesting creative types, all linked with the motion picture industry. But somehow—probably a result of her fiancé's subjection to the cruel deprivations of a Japanese prison camp—Colleen had grown up. Even Molly had noticed that Colleen was changing. That alone was encouraging. So much so that Colleen didn't even feel bad that she'd declined the invitation. She'd used Molly as her excuse, but that wasn't exactly true.

Colleen had thoroughly enjoyed her baby sister's company this past week. Showing her the local sights, seeing Molly's enthusiasm for everything, had been a tonic for Colleen. Molly's optimism was contagious. After just a few days, Colleen had become re-enchanted with the Los Angeles area. But Molly was back in San Francisco now. Already Colleen missed her. She knew that Molly had been reluctant to go home this morning. And, although they hadn't talked about it too much, Colleen felt she knew the reason why.

She glanced at the clock and, without questioning the hour, decided to place a long-distance call to her parents' home. To her relief, Molly answered.

"Oh, good," Colleen told her. "You're just who I wanted to—"

"Colleen!" Molly exclaimed. "What are you—"

"Shh." Colleen hushed her. "Don't tell the whole house it's me. I mainly wanted to talk to you. Is anyone else around?"

"Dad's asleep in his chair," Molly whispered. "Mam and Margaret are in the kitchen with Baby Peter. What's going on?"

"Well, I was just thinking about you, Molly."

"Me? Really?"

"Yes. I was thinking about the problems you've had at school recently. You know...what you told me about Charlie and how the mean girls are gossiping about you and how miserable you've been."

"Oh...yeah." Molly's voice grew flat.

"And I suddenly remembered something."

"Huh?"

"A friend of mine—you probably don't remember her, but Claudia Mason was in my class and—"

"I do remember her. She was really nice. And smart too. I admired her."

"Yes, well, Claudia was very smart. So smart that she decided to graduate high school a whole year early. I kind of resented it at the time, but I understand why she wanted out. It was like she'd outgrown high school. She needed to move on."

"Really?" Molly sounded very interested now.

"Yes. She had really good grades, Molly. Kind of like you. And she took some sort of tests, along with some classes at the college. And she wound up getting out of school a whole year early."

"Interesting."

"For what it's worth, I wondered if you might want to do something like that. Not that I'm encouraging you to do it. I mean, I really do think you should enjoy your teen years as much as possible. That is, if you are enjoying them."

"Which I'm not. Not at school anyway."

"So, for what it's worth, I remember that Claudia talked to the dean of girls a lot. Mrs. Evans." Colleen laughed. "The only times I talked to Mrs. Evans was when I was in hot water, but that's another story. And, really, she was pretty nice and understanding. So, anyway, I was thinking maybe you should talk to her."

"Oh, Colleen!" Molly exclaimed then quickly lowered her voice. "Thank you so much for telling me that. It gives me hope. I didn't want to tell anyone, but I've really been dreading going back to school."

"That's kind of what I thought." Colleen sighed. "Keep me informed of how it goes...if you decide to pursue that."

"Definitely, I will. I'll write you about it," Molly promised.

"Well, I should probably go now...since it's long distance...and dinnertime."

"Yeah, I guess so. It sure is good to hear your voice." Molly giggled. "I know I just talked to you this morning, but I was already missing you."

Colleen chuckled. "So what's for dinner?"

30

"Just meat loaf and mashed potatoes and green beans."

"Mmm. Sounds good."

Molly snickered. "Yeah, they probably don't serve that at your fancy Beverly Hills restaurants."

"It's just one of those things," Colleen admitted. "You don't miss it until it's gone. Anyway, be sure to tell everyone hello for me. But you don't have to mention this conversation specifically. I mean, unless you want to."

"Right." Molly thanked her again, and after they said good-bye, Colleen hung up the pretty white telephone with a sense of satisfaction. It was fun playing the role of older sister with Molly. Hopefully her sisterly advice would be helpful. And if Molly really did graduate high school early, maybe she'd want to come down here to live with Colleen. That would be fun!

Four

Molly wasted no time making an appointment with Mrs. Evans the next morning and, after presenting the whole situation— and honestly explaining everything—she found Mrs. Evans to be surprisingly sympathetic.

"You do seem quite mature for your age," Mrs. Evans finally said. "If you're absolutely certain that this is what you want to do." She held up a file that Molly assumed contained her school records. "You certainly have the academic achievements to accomplish it." She peered curiously at Molly. "But are you sure this is what you want? Sometimes girls go through a rough spell, but it smooths over and life returns to normal."

"I'm sure that's true enough," Molly admitted. "Although my situation started last fall and, really, it hasn't seemed to improve much. But even if it gets better, I really would love to move on with my life." Now she told Mrs. Evans about being down in Beverly Hills with her sister. "It wasn't that I wanted to be like her or live down there, but the feeling of being grown-up and able to make my own decisions was exciting."

"What would you do if you were out of high school?"

"Well, I'd definitely want to continue my education," Molly told her. "I would love to pursue a career in journalism or photography."

She explained her increased interest in photography during the past year.

"That makes sense." Mrs. Evans nodded. "And your contributions to the school paper are proof of your interest in journalism."

"And I may need to help my family with our store. We've been a little shorthanded lately. And my father's health is still not good. I might need to attend college part-time and help in the store part-time."

Mrs. Evans smiled. "Your family is lucky to have you, Molly."

Molly shrugged. "I feel that I'm lucky to have them. Or as Mam would say, I'm blessed."

"Well, if you decide to go through with this, you won't be the only early graduate this year. Gloria Collier and Prudence McCullough are both graduating early too. I hear that Gloria is doing it in order to marry a sailor, but Prudence's case is similar to yours in that she needs to help with her family's business." Mrs. Evans sighed. "She lost a brother in the war too."

"Oh, I hadn't heard that."

Mrs. Evans handed Molly a manila envelope. "Here are some things for you and your parents to read and some papers that must be signed if you decide to pursue this."

Molly thanked her, but as she was leaving the office area, she felt somewhat stunned. Was it really that easy to graduate early—or at least get the wheels rolling? Just talk to the dean then read and sign some paperwork? It was a wonder everyone didn't choose to do this. Oh, she knew it would probably require a lot more effort, but Molly didn't think it was anything she couldn't handle. At least, she hoped not. Because now, more than ever, she wanted to do this.

Colleen still wasn't completely comfortable with the amount of time she spent just sitting around at the studio. Oh, it wasn't that she didn't enjoy this leisure downtime, but having grown up in a hardworking family, it seemed strange to get paid for doing nothing. To be fair, sitting through hair and makeup and costume fittings wasn't as easy as some people assumed, but it wasn't nearly as hard as her previous job at the airplane factory either.

She'd arrived at the studio early this morning—even before Darla Devon and Robert Miller, the real stars. Finished with hair and makeup for more than an hour, she was already in costume and ready for her first scene, which she'd been informed that it wouldn't be shot until noon...or later. And so she was killing time by writing a letter to Geoff. But as she wrote, she felt somewhat irked that she'd been the first one ready this morning but wouldn't be needed for hours. What a crazy way to work.

Of course, Colleen knew that she was far too low on the totem pole to complain about such things. And she fully understood that Darla Devon, the queen bee, was the one in high demand for this film. Essential to almost every scene, Darla was allowed to complain about every and almost any thing—and yet she was still treated with the utmost respect. Colleen knew this was due to being a film star of Darla's caliber. She had worked hard to get to this place in the motion picture industry. A fact that Darla was sure to remind Colleen of whenever the opportunity presented itself, which was quite often.

As a result, Colleen tried to maintain a low profile around Darla. She'd long since heeded the warnings of Diane and Stella— her hairdresser and makeup artist—and she knew from personal experience that Darla was subject to unexplainable bouts of extreme jealousy for both real and imagined rivals. Unfortunately, this meant Colleen not only avoided crossing Darla's path, but her costar's as well. Because everyone knew, even though Robert Miller was married with children, Darla's sights were set on him. Rumors about Darla and Robert being romantically involved in their previous film had been squelched by the agency and the studio, but according to Diane and Stella, such rumors had been true.

For some reason, Robert's private attentions toward Darla had been waning during this film. Although that seemed a good sign to Colleen, who hoped that the picture would do better without that innuendo circulating about, she was starting to feel increasingly uneasy about Robert's effusive compliments toward her. And seeing him coming directly toward her now made her want to turn and run. Instead, she leaned down, focusing her attention on the letter she was attempting to write to Geoff. It was the third one she'd penned since hearing the news that he was alive.

"Maureen," Robert said warmly. "How are you doing today?"

Caught off guard at being addressed by her stage name—actually her middle name—Colleen looked up with curiosity. "Good morning, Robert."

He pulled a director's chair over to the table that she'd been using as her writing desk. "I just had to tell you that you were absolutely brilliant in that barnyard scene yesterday." He beamed at her.

She smiled politely. "Thank you, Robert." That was actually high praise coming from someone like him. Not that she intended to show him how much it meant to her. She did not want to encourage him. "It was a challenging scene, but I did my best."

"I mean it, Maureen. You were spot-on in the song and dance number." He lowered his voice. "Don't say I said so, but you outshone Darla in that scene."

She felt her brows arch with concern. "Oh, dear...I hope not."

"I mean in a good way. It wasn't as if you were trying to

upstage her." He pointed to her half-written letter. "Writing to your boyfriend?" His tone was teasing.

"My fiancé," she clarified. Perhaps this was her opportunity to show Robert that she had absolutely no interest in any romantic relationships...besides with Geoff. "He's a navy pilot," she told him.

"Oh, yes." Robert frowned. "I remember hearing that now. But I, uh, I thought he was killed in the Pacific."

Colleen solemnly filled him in on Geoff's status as a prisoner of war. "I only found out a couple weeks ago. And although it's fabulous news, it's still difficult to think of him in a Japanese prison camp." She shuddered.

Robert nodded grimly.

"This is the third letter I've written him since Christmas," she explained. "His mother told me the address where we can send them, in care of his commander. When he's released, I hope he'll be surprised by how many I've written."

"What a faithful fiancée you are." His eyes twinkled with mischief, as if he didn't quite believe any of this.

"I do my best." She smiled stiffly. Then, seeing Darla and her entourage approaching the set, she suddenly wished that Robert would take his attentions elsewhere. "Looks like they're getting ready to shoot your next scene." Colleen picked up her pen, focusing back on her letter, relieved that she wasn't part of this morning's first couple of scenes.

"I'll see you around." Robert slowly stood. "Give my regards to your fiancé."

She looked up. "Really?"

"Absolutely."

Colleen nodded. "Okay, I will." Of course, this presented a whole new problem...and something Colleen had not been able to quite face as of yet. She still had to tell Geoff about her Hollywood career. She hadn't expected it to be this big of a challenge. After all, Geoff had been aware of her interest in an acting career. He'd even encouraged her to chase her dreams. Certainly, he'd had no problem chasing his own dream of being a pilot. Despite his mother's disapproval, he'd gone after it with gusto since he was a teenager. Then, when the war started, the navy had eagerly swooped him into their arms. According to Geoff, a pilot enlistee who actually knew how to fly was a bit of a novelty in the armed forces.

She reread the first paragraph of her letter, wondering about how she'd managed to write two letters already without one reference to film making. Even in this one, she was skirting around her real life, chatting about this and that...and how much she missed him...how she hoped and prayed that he would be safe. The other letters had been similar. Oh, she'd updated him on all of her family's doings, and certainly, there'd been plenty to tell. In this letter, she'd described some of her recent visit with Molly in Southern California without even mentioning why she was down here.

"This is ridiculous," she exclaimed.

"Quiet on the set!" the assistant director growled over his shoulder.

She glanced up in time to see that they were getting ready to shoot. Embarrassed for her little outburst, she looked back down at her letter. It was time to tell Geoff the truth. But how? Pulling out a fresh piece of stationary, she decided to begin again. This letter would be honest. Geoff would understand. And he would be proud of her. Wouldn't he?

As she started to write, she tried to block out Geoff's mother. Ellen had reacted in a reserved yet negative manner when Colleen had confessed to her recent career change. Although Geoff's grandparents had been excited and supportive, Ellen had been generally unimpressed. If Ellen had her druthers, Colleen would be sitting at home with her family right now. She'd be knitting socks for servicemen, volunteering for the American Red Cross, and living a quiet, "respectable" life. But that wasn't Colleen. And anyone who really knew her was fully aware of it, including Geoff.

> *Dearest Geoff,*
>
> *I have something very important to tell you, but first I want to tell you how much I love you and how much I miss you, and how I would give or do anything to get you safely home again. Now brace yourself, darling, because I have some rather dramatic news....*

Colleen continued to write, her pen moving faster than ever as she confessed all about the promotional film she'd participated in last year. By page two she was explaining about the talent agency calling, and her screen test and subsequent movie contract. As she wrote, she was unreservedly frank, even describing her volunteer work at the Hollywood Canteen and dancing with soldiers and sailors. Although she made it clear that there was no chance for romance with these sometimes lonely servicemen. Her heart belonged to Geoff.

But she knew that this letter—if and when he got it—could be the undoing of their relationship. Still, she knew it was best to be honest. Let the chips fall where they may. If Geoff disapproved... well, so be it. There was no point in pretending to be something she was not, no point in deceiving him. Geoff deserved the truth—and it was a relief to tell it.

Molly's plan for graduating a year early from high school was solidly underway. She and her new friends, Gloria and Prudence, were enrolled in two night classes at San Francisco College. Mam and Dad had been a bit concerned about this development at first, but after listening to Molly's reasoning, followed by an appointment with Mrs. Evans, they had both agreed it was a good idea. And Molly couldn't be happier.

She had always loved history, but her college history class was by far the best one she'd ever taken. Professor Blackstone wasn't only a superb teacher, he obviously loved history as much as Molly. Probably more. So when he walked up to the podium with a very grim expression, Molly grew concerned. This was only her third class with Professor Blackstone, but she'd been looking forward to it all day. Yet when he began to drone on about the Battle of Lexington, she felt seriously dismayed. Had his enthusiasm for teaching already worn thin? She glanced around to see if any other students had noticed and was further dismayed to see that most of them seemed half asleep. What was wrong with everyone?

When Professor Blackstone stopped talking altogether, simply gazing out over the lecture hall with a sad, blank expression, Molly felt serious concern for the man's health. Was he about to suffer a stroke? And so she raised her hand.

"A question?" he asked glumly.

Thinking fast, Molly suddenly remembered a poem that Dad had read to her before. "Yes. I'm curious, was the Battle of Lexington the same battle that later became known for that saying, 'the shot heard round the world'?"

Professor Blackstone perked up slightly. "As a matter of fact, yes." He nodded slowly. "Thank you for asking that." He looked directly at her. "And I must apologize for what probably appears to be a lack

of interest in today's lesson. In fact, I have a confession to make."
Suddenly the lecture hall seemed to come awake, as if everyone was
at instant attention. What was he going to confess?

"Right before coming to class, I read a news story in the evening
paper—a story that has shaken me to the core," he spoke slowly. "The
article was about the Sullivan brothers. Have any of you heard about
this yet?" When no one responded, he continued. "Well, this story
isn't history yet, but mark my word, someday it will be. So I'll make
no apology for sharing it now, especially since I can't seem to think
of anything else at the moment. Perhaps we can have discussion
about it afterward." He cleared his throat.

"Like many other brave young men, five patriotic brothers by
the name of Sullivan enlisted in the navy shortly after the Japanese
attacked Pearl Harbor. All five brothers were assigned to the same
ship—the USS *Juneau*. I'm sure that must've been exciting for
these young men, serving together on the same ship. Apparently
the *Juneau* was a light cruiser that participated in the Guadalcanal
Campaign this past year. Well, it seems the *Juneau* was struck
by a Japanese torpedo during a battle in the Solomon Islands last
November. As a result, the ship exploded and sank. For security
reasons, the military didn't allow the navy to disclose the loss of
the USS *Juneau*." He sadly shook his head.

"Back in Iowa, the Sullivan family began to notice that letters
from their five sons were no longer coming like they used to.
Naturally, they grew worried. Eventually, the mother wrote to the
War Department to inquire." He picked up a newspaper from the
podium. "I'll just read this."

"'Yesterday morning, when Mr. Thomas Sullivan prepared to
leave for work, three officers in uniform appeared at his door.
"I have some news about your boys," the lieutenant commander

announced. "Which one?" Thomas Sullivan asked. "I'm sorry," the officer replied, "All five.""

As the professor laid down the newspaper, the lecture hall grew deathly quiet. "I cannot begin to imagine the pain the Sullivan family is feeling right now, but my heart goes out to them. And that is why I've had difficulty focusing this evening."

Molly felt a lump growing in her throat as she reached for her handkerchief. Several others began to sniffle and wipe their eyes as well. "War has always been an integral part of history," the professor said solemnly, "but I hope and pray the day comes when history will not be defined by war." He picked up his notes. "And now, back to the American Revolution."

Five

For the past month, Molly and Prudence and Gloria had been sharing rides to the college campus in the evenings. Molly welcomed these new friendship, especially since Dottie had continued to give her the cold shoulder. Prudence, like Molly, was very serious about her studies. But Gloria seemed more interested in her upcoming marriage than attaining her high school diploma. So when Gloria suddenly dropped out of both the college classes and high school this week, Molly wasn't too surprised.

"Gloria told me she wants to get married on Valentine's Day," Prudence confided to Molly as they walked through the parking lot after their history class. "That is, if Henry can get his leave in time for a wedding."

"I hope Gloria doesn't regret quitting school like this." Molly couldn't imagine sacrificing her education just to get married.

"If you ask me, Gloria is completely oblivious." Prudence chuckled as they got into the car. "She thinks life is a fairy tale and that becoming a wife will be her happily ever after. As if marriage is the ultimate end-all for any female. Can you imagine?"

"My older sister was like that—Margaret was always talking about getting married, planning her wedding." Molly started the engine.

"And I hate to say it, but now that she's a wife and mother, well, I think she might have some regrets."

"She wishes she wasn't married?"

"Oh, I don't know that for sure. But I do know it hasn't turned out how she'd hoped it would. And Margaret didn't get married until she was twenty, which she claimed was almost an old maid." Molly shook her head. "And her husband Brian is even older. He was nearly finished with law school when they married, but he enlisted as an officer in the army. So it's not as if they were young and foolish when they married."

"Well, Gloria is only sixteen," Prudence declared. "I wonder how she'll feel about her decision when she's twenty."

"I don't know, but I wish her well." Molly turned to Prudence as she waited for a traffic light to change. "And I'm glad that you're still onboard with this. It's so much nicer having a friend to go to night classes with. I'm not sure I could do this alone."

"I know what you mean." Prudence adjusted her glasses. "And based on Professor Blackstone's interest in you, I'm glad you're not alone, Molly."

Molly blinked as the light turned green. "What on earth do you mean?"

Prudence laughed. "Don't tell me you haven't noticed."

"Noticed what?"

"How solicitous Professor Blackstone is toward you."

"You can't be serious." Molly laughed.

"Perfectly serious. Professor Blackstone clearly favors you."

"Oh, Prudence, you're imagining things. Professor Blackstone simply likes that I'm interested in history. I ask more questions than anyone in the class. I probably help to keep the other students awake." She giggled. "The professor probably appreciates that."

"I don't know. I think there's more to it than that, Molly."

Molly just shook her head.

"The professor was taken with you from our first day of class. Even Gloria noticed it. And then that time when you asked him a question and he told us about the Sullivan brothers—well, you instantly became teacher's pet."

"You're letting your imagination run away with you, Prudence. Good grief, Professor Blackstone is old enough to be my father."

Prudence chuckled. "He'd have to have been a pretty young father. I doubt he's even in his mid-thirties yet."

"Even so."

"Well, just the same, you'd better watch out. I'm pretty sure he's got his eye on you...and for more than just academic purposes." Prudence folded her arms across her front. "Fortunately, that's not a problem I have with the opposite sex. Not like some girls anyway."

Molly wasn't sure how to respond to that. On one hand, it was somewhat complimentary...but on the other hand, well, it was disturbing. Molly glanced at Prudence. Maybe Molly should imitate the serious-minded girl and pull her hair tightly back and wear some heavy-framed glasses. Wouldn't Colleen throw a fit?

"So what do you hear from your nurse sister?" Prudence asked. "The one in the ANC? What's her name again?"

"Bridget." Molly was relieved for the topic change. "She's been so busy that her last two letters have been pretty short. She sounds happy enough, but I'm worried she's worn out. Mam's afraid she's going to get sick with some tropical disease."

"But is she still glad to be a nurse?"

"Of course. She loves helping servicemen." Molly knew that Prudence was interested in a similar career. "But it sounds like very hard work. I've heard that army nurses work even harder than army doctors."

"Maybe I'll become a doctor," Prudence declared.

Molly grinned. "I'll bet you'd be a good one."

"Anyway, it's good to dream." Prudence sighed. "Jerry used to dream of becoming a doctor."

Molly knew that Jerry was Prudence's older brother. Like Peter, he'd been killed in the war. Not at Pearl Harbor, but not that long afterward. "I'll bet Jerry would be proud to have his little sister become a doctor," she said quietly. "And I'm sure you've got the brains for it, Prudence."

"Thanks."

"I used to think I wanted to be a nurse," Molly admitted. "But then I got interested in photography...and journalism. That's what I want to pursue. Besides, I think one nurse in the family is enough."

"You're lucky to have a big family."

"I used to think so...but it feels like it's shrunk these last couple of years."

"How's your actress sister doing? Colleen, right?"

"Yes. But her stage name is Maureen Mulligan. Maureen's her middle name. I just got a letter from her, and she sounds fairly happy. Her movie is supposed to wrap up in a couple of weeks and she promised to come home."

"For good?"

"No. Just for a visit. Her agents are working on another movie deal for her. A supportive role again."

"Still no word from her fiancé? The guy who's in the Japanese prison camp?"

Molly shook her head. "But Colleen keeps writing to him."

"Do they deliver letters to the prison?"

"I don't think so, but Colleen writes him anyway. She said that Geoff's mother got a letter from another pilot who was shot down the same day as Geoff. Apparently this guy was swimming to shore when he witnessed Geoff's raft getting picked up by the Japanese. Somehow the other pilot avoided getting captured. He was eventually rescued, but in such bad condition that he was in the hospital for several months before he was well enough to report on Geoff and his flight crew."

"That's amazing—like something out of a movie."

"There are lots of remarkable stories," Molly told her. "It seems like every time I pick up a newspaper, I read a new one. That's the main reason I want to be a journalist. I'd love to report those kinds of stories—both in writing and with photographs. It would be so exciting."

"Do you think they even allow female reporters over there? I mean, to cover the war?"

"I don't know why not. Women are allowed to serve as nurses and military support personnel. Why not as reporters?"

"Why not!" Prudence declared. "You'll be a journalist, Molly. And I'll be a doctor—and we'll both do everything we can to set the world on fire."

Although Margaret had only planned to work part-time at the store—and only after her doctor agreed she was ready—that had quickly changed to full-time with Dad's health issues. Molly had confirmed what Margaret had feared—Dad was not well, but because neither of them wanted to worry Mam, they kept their concerns to themselves. To this end, Margaret had insisted that she was ready to return to work full-time. So every day, she and Mam, with Baby Peter in tow, would head to the store.

With the help of two part-time employees, Dirk and Jimmy, plus Molly on weekends, they kept the shelves filled, customers served, and books balanced. At least for the most part. But Margaret was tired. Still, she knew better than to complain since Mam was probably equally tired.

"I do not see why you women won't let me come to the store with you," Dad growled in a grumpy tone as Margaret, Molly, and Mam were preparing to leave. "I am not an invalid."

"Your doctor told you that you need a year to recover." Molly reached for her book bag, dropping a kiss on his cheek. "And you promised to take it easy, remember?"

He scowled darkly as he set down his coffee cup. "You females think you rule the world nowadays."

"Isn't that what they say about the hand that rocks the cradle?" Margaret rolled her eyes as she pulled a knit cap onto Peter's head. "We rule the world." She let out a sarcastic laugh. "So this is what it feels like to be rulers, eh? Where's your crown, Mam?"

Mam snickered. "I think I left it in the oven with the pot roast." She leaned down to kiss Dad. "Don't forget to check on it for me."

"Yes, yes…leave me behind to keep the home fires burning… that's all I'm good for."

"Oh, Riley." Mam frowned as she pulled on her coat.

"Maybe you'd like to call your doctor," Molly suggested. "If you're well enough, I'm sure he'll permit you to return to work."

"Off with you." Dad waved his hand. "Women!"

Margaret had to bite her tongue as she went outside. She'd happily trade places with Dad. Let him go to work, and she and Baby

Peter would stay home and keep the home fires burning. That'd be just peachy!

"Poor Dad," Molly said as they got into the car. "He feels so useless."

"At least he's not useless in the sanatorium," Mam said.

"I wish he was well enough to go to work," Margaret added.

"You could bring the books home for him to work on," Mam said tentatively. "That might make him feel useful."

Margaret had considered this more than once. But that would mean giving up her one quiet time of the day—when she went to the office to work on them. "I think it's best for only one person to keep the books," she told them. "Plus, I do it the way Peter taught me. Dad does it a different way, and it usually gets messed up when we both try to do it."

"Maybe you could teach Dad to do it your way," Molly suggested as they neared her school.

"Good grief, do you really think it's possible to teach Dad anything?" Margaret said with irritation. "Have you ever tried?"

Mam chuckled. "He can be a mite stubborn."

"Have a good day," Molly called as she got out of the car.

"Lucky her," Margaret said as she continued to drive.

"Why is she lucky?"

"No responsibilities."

"Molly has responsibilities. She has school and—"

"I mean no grown-up responsibilities," Margaret countered. "And I honestly do not understand why she's in such a doggone hurry to graduate high school and become an adult. It's not as if we're all out here having a grand old time."

"It's true we all have our challenges, Margaret. What with the state of this world and the war raging all over. But we also have plenty to be thankful for, don't you think?"

"Yes, Mam. You're right. I'm sorry to be such a complainer this morning. I honestly don't know what's wrong with me. Every morning I get up and say my prayers. And then I tell myself that today is going to be a good day and that I'm not going to grumble or complain or fret or worry." She sighed. "And the next thing I know, well, I'm going off on everyone."

"Maybe you're tired from getting up for the baby's three o'clock feedings," Mam suggested. "Having your sleep interrupted can take its toll on a young mother."

"Maybe. And last night, it took so long to get him back to sleep."

"I know." Mam sounded weary.

"Did he disturb your sleep too?"

"Oh, not so much...perhaps a little."

"I'm sorry, Mam. I suppose it wakes Dad too."

Mam waved a hand. "It won't be long until Peter sleeps through the night."

Margaret hoped she was right, but as she remembered how loudly he had wailed last night, impatiently waiting for her to warm his formula, she wasn't so sure. "I remember you telling me about how you lived above your parents' store when you were a young mother," she said wistfully.

"I wish we still had the old store," Mam said. "But it burned down many years ago."

"I know." Margaret frowned. "But we do have that attic storage space. I wonder if I could turn that into an apartment."

"I don't see how."

"But what if I could?" Margaret considered this.

"Oh, darling, that space is not fit for human habitation."

Margaret wasn't so sure. "But if it could be—would you care if I used it?"

"Not if it was safe...but I can't imagine how it could be."

"You know I wouldn't dream of using it if I thought it was unsafe, Mam. Not with a dependent child to consider."

"No, I'm sure you wouldn't. I'll leave it to you, Margaret. But I'm sure once you see what it's really like up there...well, you won't be so interested."

Margaret wasn't so sure. And for the first time in a long time, she felt a tiny glimmer of hope. Perhaps this was the first step to getting some control over her life. It would be so wonderful to have her own little apartment—for just her and her baby. And for Brian when he came home on leave. If only she could make it work!

Colleen flipped through a fashion magazine as she waited for the crew to set up for the next scene. From the corner of her eye, she could see Darla still in makeup. Although Colleen couldn't actually hear what Darla was saying, she could tell by the tone of her voice and the waving of her hands that the diva was in a foul mood. Good to know.

"Hello, Maureen." Robert scooted a director's chair next to her, sitting down with comfortable familiarity. "How are you doing?"

Colleen smiled politely. "I'm fine, thank you. How are you?"

"I'm not sure just yet." He glanced over to Darla. "Guess I will soon find out." He chuckled. "Did you do something to ruffle her feathers?"

"Not that I know of." Colleen bristled to think it might be her fault. "I hope not."

"Never mind her." Robert removed a folded newspaper from

beneath his elbow with a grim expression. "I just read an article in the *Times*...made me think of you."

"What's that?" She glanced down at the paper.

He solemnly pointed to the headline. JAPANESE POW CAMPS IGNORE GENEVA CONVENTIONS. "It's not good news, Maureen, and I'm not suggesting you read it, but it reminded me of your fiancé."

"I've heard that their prison camps are pretty bad." She reached for the paper, scanning the subtitle: ESCAPED MARINE TELLS ALL. The mere idea that a serviceman had actually escaped a Japanese POW camp compelled her to read more. Maybe Geoff would be able to escape too.

But this marine sergeant, who asked to remain anonymous, described in detail the atrocious treatment during his eight months of internment in a Japanese camp in Malaya. Sure, it wasn't all news to Colleen. She'd heard of severe beatings, brutal starvation, and cruel deprivations before. But according to this man, although many of the internment camps were not very secure, it was extremely dangerous for an internee to attempt escape. If caught, the failed escapee was executed on sight—usually by public beheading. Not only that, but ten or more of his unfortunate fellow inmates would be executed as well. In the same manner. It sounded almost worse if the escapee actually managed to flee, like in this marine's case. Then his fellow inmates—the ones left behind—would be tortured in the most inhumane ways before they were executed. Horrifying.

This, he explained, is why few inmates would try to escape. The Japanese used this evil incentive to keep the captives in their place. And this was probably why the sergeant wanted anonymity. She wondered if a bunch of his buddies had been executed for his freedom. And what if Geoff was one of them? She cringed to think of that. She didn't want to judge the marine sergeant, and he made it sound as if he'd had no choice but to make a run for it, but it was clear that he felt guilty...and sad for his friends who didn't make it out. He finally explained that the only reason he wanted his story told was so that Americans would grasp how dire the situation was over there—so that everyone would keep doing their part, that everyone would work together to win and end this war.

Six

Colleen shuddered as she shoved the newspaper back to Robert. "That is awful." She closed her eyes and shook her head, trying to block out what she'd just read. "Just horrifying."

"I didn't really want you to read it," he said quietly. "But I suppose it's good to know the truth. It's a terrible situation for some of our boys over there."

"Yeah," she said gruffly, swallowing hard over the lump now growing in her throat and wishing she were stronger. "I know we need to be aware, but it's not easy to hear." She fought to hold back tears. "I just hope I can pull it together for our next scene." She couldn't imagine smiling and singing just now. Never mind that this was a war movie, it was supposed to be a happy victorious story, to make audiences cheer in the end. But at the moment she felt like crying. She swiped at a stray tear streaking down her cheek. Great, her makeup was probably ruined.

"I'm so sorry, Maureen." Robert slipped his arm around her shoulders. "I never should've shown that to you. Bad timing on my part."

"No, no," she said quickly. "I'll be okay. And I don't want to be in the dark."

"It just makes me so angry to read how our servicemen are being mistreated...to hear how those Japanese savages can completely ignore the Geneva Conventions. It makes me wish that I was in good enough condition to enlist myself."

"You're not?" She considered how tall and strong and fit he seemed. And she knew, although he was in his early thirties, he wasn't over the enlistment age limit.

"Bad knees." He glumly shook his head.

"I'm sorry." As another tear slip out, Colleen noticed Darla staring at them. Done with makeup, she was coming directly toward them.

"I'm the one who should be sorry." Robert whipped out a handkerchief and carefully blotted her tear. "Maybe you should head back to makeup."

"Yes." Colleen was about to stand, but Darla was in front of her now, blocking her as she stared down with pure disdain. "What a tender scene." Darla glared at Robert. "Oh, my, am I interrupting something?"

"No. Not at all." Colleen pushed her chair back and turned away, hurrying to her makeup station.

"Well!" Darla made a *humph* noise and some other comments that Colleen wasn't eager to hear.

"What's the trouble?" Stella asked as Colleen flopped into the makeup chair.

"Just a quick touch up." Colleen reached for a tissue, blotting another tear.

"Oh, doll." Stella peered closely. "Did someone upset you?"

"Not really. Just a sad article in the *Times*." She quickly explained it as Stella retouched her foundation.

"And it made you think of your beloved fiancé." Stella made a tsk-tsk sound as she reached for the eyeliner. Colleen had already told her all about Geoff. "Well, I have a good feeling about your man, doll. Every time I pray for him, I feel like he's going to be just fine. I can't even explain it. But I do believe it."

"Thanks, Stella." Colleen glanced over to where Robert and Darla were still talking—and Darla was dramatically flailing her arms. "Is it my imagination or is Darla about to blow?"

Stella nodded. "Sounds like it to me. Not a good way to start a day."

"I'm so glad this film is about to wrap," Colleen said quietly.

"You're not the only one, doll."

Now Diane, the hairdresser, came over to join them, pretending to be working with Colleen's hair, although it was already perfectly in place. "What did you say to her?" Diane asked Colleen in a hushed tone.

"Nothing." Colleen held still as Stella retouched her eye makeup.

As she worked, Stella quietly explained the little dilemma to Diane. "Tempest in a teapot." She now used the face powder to expertly brush all traces of tears away. "Darla just wanted an excuse to rail at our girl. You know how angry she's been at Robert lately."

"Just because he finally realized he was a married man." Diane lowered her voice. "And figured out that Darla was poison."

"Not in the box office," Colleen reminded them.

"Not yet." Diane frowned. "Someday she'll show her true colors and her fans will find out."

Colleen wasn't sure that would change anything, but since Stella was retouching her lipstick, she kept her mouth closed.

"There you go, doll. Just as pretty as ever."

"Prettier than Darla," Diane whispered. "Just don't say you heard it here."

Colleen thanked them and, hearing the director calling them to the set, braced herself for what was probably going to be a long day of retakes. Darla had a way of punishing everyone when she was in a snit. As she walked past the camera crew, Colleen suddenly longed to go home. Not to her pretty little apartment, but home... to her family.

Margaret's dream of carving a habitat from the store's storage attic had been steadily moving forward—one baby step at a time. Of course, it was more work than Margaret had originally imagined, but she controlled herself from complaining to anyone. Instead, she acted as if it were all going perfectly smoothly—as if she weren't exhausted every night when she fell into bed. For the first couple of weeks, Mam cared for Baby Peter in the evenings, allowing Margaret to work without distraction on the overwhelming project.

To start with, Margaret had to find new places for what little dry goods had been stored up there. And then she spent several evenings thoroughly cleaning the space. Removing curtains of cobwebs, sweeping up mounds of dust, disposing of what seemed like years' worth of mouse debris. Then she scrubbed every square inch of the place until it smelled clean and fresh. She used steel wool to stuff into the cracks and crevices that had probably provided entry to rodents, and she set up a multitude of mouse traps along the exterior walls.

After that, with Molly's help on the weekend, Margaret managed to whitewash all the walls and ceiling as well as paint the floor planks creamy white. The result was a spacious, albeit slightly rustic, room that looked surprisingly clean and fresh.

"This almost looks habitable." Molly swished her paintbrush in the jar of turpentine to clean it.

"Almost?" Margaret frowned.

"Well, it needs a few things." Molly waved a hand. "Something to sit on for instance."

"Naturally, I'll have furnishings." Margaret smiled to imagine how she would arrange it. "Brian's parents have offered me a few old pieces, including a big old rug that belonged to Louise's mother. And Mam said there are some old furniture pieces in the attic that I can have. And, of course, I have my bedroom things and Peter's nursery items." She pointed to the back end of the room. "They'll go down there." She sighed. "And for the first time I'll be able to use all the pretty wedding presents that have been in storage all this time."

"That'll be nice for you. And this will probably turn out to be a lovely apartment." Molly frowned as she wiped the brush on a rag. "But won't you miss all of us at home?"

"Of course. You know, I've never lived away from home. And you and Mam have helped me so much with Peter. I'm sure I'll miss that."

"I can still help you with him on weekends," Molly offered. "I can baby-sit for you sometimes if you want. It'd be fun to come up here to visit you."

"That'd be great, Molly." Margaret sighed happily as she set the cleaned paintbrushes in the bucket. "I have such a hopeful feeling about this. It's like I'm finally able to grow up. Being on my own with my baby. Responsible for myself and for him. Do you know how freeing that's going to feel?"

Molly smiled. "I'll admit it does sound fun. Kind of like playing house."

Margaret nodded eagerly. "Yes, that's how it seems—like I finally get to play house. But besides that, I know it'll be good for our family. I'm well aware that we've disrupted everyone's sleep during Peter's late-night feedings. And it's stressful for me too. I'm trying to hush him and worrying about waking Dad, then I start fretting about Dad not getting good rest...and how it might affect his health."

"You could be right about that. The doctor did say he needs to get lots of good rest."

"And I worry about Mam too. Even though she acts like we're no trouble, I think it wears her out. And sometimes she gets those headaches. Really, I feel it's time for me to move on."

Molly patted her on the back. "I just don't want you to be lonely up here, Margaret. And I hope...well, in case it doesn't work out here, I hope you'll feel free to come home. You will, won't you?"

"Of course. But I really don't think that'll happen."

"What about food and cooking?" Molly glanced around the spacious room. "There's no kitchen."

"I'll set up a table with a hotplate right there." She pointed to the center of the room. "I found an old bureau that I can use for storage, and I'll equip it with kitchen stuff. And I can use the refrigerators down in the store for perishable foods. Or maybe even get an old icebox to put up here."

"You won't ever run out of food with the store below," Molly joked.

"I realize that I'll have to carry up my water for cooking and washing, but I have a plan for that too. It'll be a little bit like camping or like being a pioneer. But I'm looking forward to it. I think it will be an adventure." She grinned. "And it'll be good for me."

"I hope so." Molly still looked doubtful. "At least you have a bathroom downstairs. Aren't you glad that Dad had that shower installed before he got sick? I remember Mam saying how it was a waste of money."

"Yes, I'm very grateful for that."

Molly slowly shook her head, looking like she still wasn't quite convinced. Or perhaps she just questioned Margaret's tenacity. After all, everyone knew how Margaret was given to complaining, worrying, and general negativity. But maybe this was her chance to show them. She was growing up!

"Just you wait and see," Margaret reassured her. "When I get all my furnishings and everything up here, it'll be very homey. In fact, I think I'll invite you all up here for an open house when it's all done."

"I can't wait."

By the end of February, Margaret's apartment was finally ready for visitors. Throughout the previous week, she'd engaged Dirk and Jimmy to help her when the store wasn't too busy. They used the store's truck to pick up her furniture then hauled everything up the stairs for her.

By Sunday afternoon, everything was in perfect place and Margaret couldn't be happier. The oriental rug from the Hammonds was laid out on the front end of the space, the area that got the best light during the daytime. Mam's rocking chair and a well-worn easy chair that Margaret had slip-covered with an old set of drapes were positioned opposite a dark green horsehair settee donated from the Hammonds. Two apple crates with a print floral tablecloth laid over them made for a coffee table. And a compact radio set, a wedding gift, sat atop a narrow oak table beneath the window and was quietly tuned to a classical music program. Adorning the window was a set of pale green ruffle-trimmed curtains that Margaret had sewn herself. Although she had to cover them with the ugly blackout curtains every night.

At the other end of the spacious room, she'd carved out a bedroom and nursery area, filling it with familiar items from home. She'd even created a closet by hanging a closet rod, concealing behind it with a curtain she'd sewn out of pink and blue calico. She'd even splurged on another rug for the bedroom area. It was secondhand, but in good condition, and the soft shades of pink and blue looked perfect. She went over to check on Peter, relieved to see that he was still napping in his crib. Hopefully he wouldn't wake up until she finished preparing the snacks she planned to serve for her open house.

In between the living room and bedroom space, adjacent from where the stairs came up, she'd set up her makeshift kitchen. She'd covered a board with gingham oil cloth, setting it on stacks of fruit crates to serve as a work area. Complete with a hotplate, a water pitcher, dishpan, and a few other necessities, it seemed quite efficient. She'd found an old pine table in her parents' attic which, with a pair of wooden chairs borrowed from her office downstairs, now served as her dining area. To make her kitchen complete, she'd utilized an old bureau that had already been up here. She'd covered its top with more gingham oil cloth and used its drawers to store random kitchenware. On top of the bureau, she'd set an old bookshelf. Topping the shelves with shelf paper, it became her makeshift china hutch. Now, filled with dishes and wedding gifts, it looked festive and pretty.

There was no denying that her wedding gifts, a variety of things that she and Brian had received more than a year ago, really added to the apartment's ambiance. At first she'd felt a bit guilty to think she was going to enjoy these items without her husband by her side. But then she realized that Brian would be glad that his wife and son were comfortable. And when he came home for leave, hopefully before long, he would get to enjoy all of this too.

As she made little sandwiches, she felt grateful to her parents. After she'd convinced them that it was safe for her and Peter, Mam and Dad had been supportive of her plan. They seemed to approve of her longing for independence. Dad had even suggested that she should start using all of Brian's military pay to support herself and the baby—the contribution she'd been making to their household. And while she knew she'd have some additional expenses, she also knew that Mam and Dad would still need financial help too. For that reason, she insisted that it was only fair that she should pay rent for her space. It wasn't much, but it would help them make ends meet, and it would cover the additional cost of water and electricity in her apartment.

As she placed the last sandwich on the platter, she glanced at her watch. It was nearly time for her guests, the Hammonds and her family, to arrive. She couldn't wait to see their reaction to her new home. She didn't expect them to love it as much as she did, but hopefully they would like it.

Seven

Late March 1943

Molly's seventeenth birthday came and went without much ado, and that was fine with her. She knew everyone was busy—including herself. Taking a full load of high school classes, taking night classes with Prudence at the college, working on the newspaper and yearbook, and helping out in the store on weekends was almost too much. Not that she planned to admit this to anyone. Although Mrs. Bartley next door seemed suspicious.

"I think you're working yourself too hard," she told Molly on a sunny Sunday afternoon.

Molly looked up from where she was digging in the victory garden. "Oh, it's not that hard," she assured her elderly neighbor. "After that rain we had last week, the soil is fairly soft and malleable."

"I don't mean working too hard in the garden," Mrs. Bartley clarified. "I mean working too hard in general. I fear you're burning your candle at both ends, my dear."

Molly grinned. "Really? What does that mean anyway?"

"That you are overdoing it—and in danger of burning out." Mrs. Bartley frowned. "And I care too much about you to see that happen, Molly."

Molly considered her warning. "I appreciate your concern, but think about it...in two months I will graduate high school...that is, if I finish all my classes, which I plan to do. And then my life will slow down a lot."

"Two months?" Mrs. Bartley picked up a hoe, using it to dig out a weed.

Molly nodded eagerly. "Yes! And I can hardly describe how glad I'll be to be finished with high school. I feel it's completely worth the effort now."

"So you aren't finding your college night classes to be too difficult?"

"Not at all. Prudence and I just started with our new spring term classes, and it's so exciting. Of course, it's harder than high school. But I love the challenge. It makes me so eager to start college properly."

"Will you do that in the fall—go full-time to college?"

"I'm not sure about full-time." Molly frowned. "My parents might need my help in the store."

"How is your father doing?" Mrs. Bartley asked quietly.

Molly had confided in her about Dad's health. "I wrote a long letter to Bridget about it," she admitted. "I described all his symptoms, and she wrote back saying that it's probably his heart. It may have been damaged from his tuberculosis."

"That Bridget. Maybe she should consider becoming a doctor instead of a nurse."

"Wouldn't that be something." Molly plunged the shovel into the soil.

"Has your father been seen by his doctor yet?"

"He refuses to go." Molly dug the shovel deeper, giving it a twist.

"But at least he's still taking it easy?"

"For the most part." She turned the soil, careful not to disturb the earthworm nearby.

"But sometimes I catch him doing something he shouldn't. And I warn him that if he doesn't stop, I'll call the doctor." Molly smiled. "That usually works."

"And how is your movie star sister doing? Didn't you say that her film project was finished? What will she do next?"

"Her movie wrapped up a few weeks ago. She's hoping she'll get cast in another one. She's had several auditions but no offers so far."

"When will her movie be in theaters? I don't go to the cinema much anymore, but I'd certainly make an exception to see Colleen."

"She told me that the movie will premiere in Hollywood in mid-April. She and the other actors will all dress up and attend the big event. It won't be in our theaters until May. I can't wait to see it."

"Well, do keep me posted."

"I've been begging Colleen to come home for a visit." Molly sighed as she continued to work the soil. "It's been kind of lonely lately. Just Mam and Dad and me. So different from how it used to be."

Mrs. Bartley nodded as if she understood, reminding Molly that she lived alone. "So tell me, how are Margaret and the little one getting along?"

"Oh, their apartment is so sweet. Margaret did a lovely job fixing it all up. Someday when you're at the store, you should go up there and see it. I know Margaret wouldn't mind. She loves to show it off."

"And how is her baby?"

"Peter isn't quite six months old yet, but he's trying to crawl. It's so cute to see him squiggling around on his belly." She pointed her shovel at the earthworm that was trying to escape back under the dirt. "Kind of like that."

Mrs. Bartley laughed. "I can just imagine. And what does

Margaret hear from her husband? According to Mrs. Hammond, he hasn't been writing as much as he used to. In fact, she said that both her boys have slowed down with letter writing."

"I'm sure that's because the war is keeping them so busy. Although I did just get a letter from Patrick. He doesn't usually share anything very specific about the war, but he did hint that his battleship was involved in the Battle of the Bismarck Sea earlier this month. I guess that was okay since the battle was over and done with."

"That was such a great victory for our boys." Mrs. Bartley shook her head. "If only this whole war could be over and done with."

"If only!"

Margaret tried not to show how concerned she was for Brian's welfare. If anyone asked—and they always did—she'd just give a pat answer, pretending that all was well, acting as if they'd been in close contact. But the truth was that, other than one very brief—and what seemed impersonal—letter in early February, she hadn't heard a word from him.

Of course, as Mam liked to say, "no news was good news,"—meaning that the War Department hadn't sent a telegram—but Margaret wasn't so sure. Sometimes she'd wake up in a cold sweat, with an image similar to the war bond poster racing through her mind. And then she'd be plagued with questions. Was Brian in trouble? Wounded? Or worse? After a bit, she would remember Mam's advice and reach for her rosary and automatically pray a Hail Mary until she finally calmed down. Sometimes it took awhile.

It didn't help that thanks to store customers—the ones who loved discussing the war with anyone who would listen—Margaret had recently heard that North Africa was quite a hot spot for battles. She'd also heard that some of the American troops had taken a beating. Knowing that was the region where Brian was serving only made it worse.

As Margaret tried to focus on writing him a letter, the second one this week, she couldn't help but remember the movie *Casablanca*. She'd loved the film, except the implication that Americans in that region were in great danger. Naturally, the movie had made it all seem romantic and exciting and patriotic, playing down the killings going on all around them.

Margaret set down her pen, getting up from the table where she'd been writing. Her excuse was to check on the baby since he'd gotten into the habit of kicking off his covers at night. She quietly tucked the soft blanket back around him, kissed her fingertips, then touched his head. Feeling somewhat soothed, she tiptoed over to the radio, tuning it to a music program with the volume turned low. For a long moment she stood in front of the window, just listening and staring blankly at the blackout drape. It felt symbolic of her life. Dark and dreary and heavy.

Oh, Margaret tried to appear happy while waiting on customers or chatting with family members. She was becoming expert at painting a smile on her face. In fact, her acting skills were so polished that even Colleen should be impressed. Margaret maintained the pretense that having her own apartment was the most wonderful thing in the world. And, really, it had been...at first. But carrying water up and down the narrow stairs, cooking on a hotplate, doing her laundry by hand in the bathroom downstairs...well, it had gotten old. Being a pioneer woman was fun for a while, but eventually the comforts of home started calling.

The hardest part of her new living arrangement was that

Margaret was lonely. Very, very lonely. Having grown up in such a large, boisterous family, she'd never spent much time on her own before. And nights were long. As dearly as she loved Baby Peter, it wasn't as if he could carry on a conversation. Oh, certainly, she would talk to him. She chattered constantly at him while caring for him in the evening after work. But although he could smile and twinkle those big blue eyes, he was a bit short on words.

To make matters worse, Margaret was determined not to complain about her situation. She'd fought so hard to get Mam and Dad to agree to her plan. She'd worked to convince everyone it was a good idea to live up here. There was no way she was going to admit that it had possibly been a mistake. Besides, she reminded herself, maybe she just needed to get used to it. Compared to the deprivations and threats Brian was facing...well, she knew it was childish to grumble.

Mid-April 1943

Colleen was fed up with Hollywood. Despite being called back on a couple of auditions, she still hadn't heard anything. If not for tonight's premiere, she would've gladly gone home by now—like Molly had been encouraging her to do. As Colleen dressed, slipping into the sparkly silver gown that the Knight Agency had provided her with—Darla had specifically warned her not to show up in anything blue—Colleen wished that she felt more enthusiastic about tonight's event. But thanks to Darla's acting like a temperamental shrew the last two weeks on the set, Colleen felt nothing but dread for this evening.

"Just hold your head high," Colleen's agent had told her on the phone this morning. "You have every right to be there. You did an excellent job in the film. Leon has been singing your praises to everyone."

"Really?" Colleen wasn't so sure. It was possible Georgina's pep talk was just that...a pep talk.

"Even Robert Miller has spoken favorably about you. And I fully expect to hear from the studio about your audition for the Barry Coltaire film. It's not a huge part, but it's a much bigger film."

"That would be wonderful." Colleen lit a cigarette, taking in a slow drag. "I think I might run home for a few days, you know, after the premiere. But I'm just a phone call away."

"Sure, honey. You deserve a break. Just as long as you promise to drop everything and come back down here if we need you for anything."

Colleen wondered if that would ever happen again. What if tonight's premiere revealed her big fear—that she was a complete and utter flop? She remembered seeing herself on the big screen in the promotional film about women on the home front. She'd felt like a total failure then. What if everyone hated her in this picture? What if no one ever wanted her to be in another film?

Colleen studied her image in the full-length mirror. This silver dress was really stunning. Much better than the sapphire blue one she'd planned to wear. She'd wanted to wear blue because it reminded her of Geoff's navy officer's dress uniform—and because this was a patriotic film. But as she turned around to admire the low back of the stylish gown, she told herself that Geoff would prefer this one. Not only did it show off her figure, it would probably remind him of his silver plane. She closed her eyes, sending loving thoughts in his direction and whispering a simple prayer. Colleen had never been much at praying...not until she'd learned that Geoff was still alive. Now she regularly prayed for his daily safety, good health, and most importantly his deliverance from the POW camp.

"Hello there?" Rory Knight's voice floated through her opened front window. "Ready to go?"

She grabbed her evening bag and the white fur stole that Georgina had given to her a few days ago then hurried out to greet him. "It's so nice of you and Georgina to be my escorts tonight," she said as they walked out to the limousine.

"We just want to show you off," he told her as the driver opened the door for them.

"Oh, Maureen, you look fabulous," Georgina said as Colleen slid into the spacious seat.

"Thanks." Colleen nodded. "I'm feeling a little nervous—I mean about the press. I know how they shout out questions, and I want to handle it right."

"Well, don't worry," Georgina told her. "The press will be primarily focused on Robert and Darla for questions. But we want to make sure they get some great shots of you." She coached Colleen on how they would slowly exit the car, and how they would take their time walking up to the theater. "Imagine being in a pageant. Hold your head high and smile pleasantly. But stay cool."

"As a cucumber." Rory winked at her.

"I can do that."

There was a good-sized crowd gathered in front of Grauman's Chinese Theatre. Colleen took a deep breath as she gracefully emerged from the car. Flashbulbs popped, just like she'd imagined they would, as she waved and smiled in what she hoped was a friendly yet controlled manner.

"Miss Mulligan?" a reporter called out. "Is it true that your fiancé is a navy pilot?"

She smiled at the man. "Yes, that's true."

"And his plane was shot down in the Pacific?" a female reporter called out.

Colleen's smile faded ever so slightly as she nodded. "Unfortunately, that's true as well. It happened more than a year ago."

"And he's in a prisoner of war camp?" the first man asked eagerly.

"Yes." She continued to move forward, but several of the reporters were clustered around her, peppering her with more questions about Geoff and making it impossible to walk more than a few baby steps. She glanced over her shoulder at Rory and Georgina, but they both simply nodded and smiled, as if this were a good thing. And so she continued to answer the press's questions.

"It's interesting that your first major motion picture is a war story," the woman reporter said in a friendly tone.

"Yes," Colleen agreed. "It's a bit like art imitating life."

"Oh, that's good," a reporter said. "We'll quote you on that."

"Do you expect your young man to be released soon?" the woman reporter asked with concerned eyes.

"I pray he will be." She nodded solemnly. "It's always on my mind."

"And when he comes home, will you get married?"

Colleen's face lit up. "He can name the time and place, and I will be there with bells on."

The reporters all let out a cheer, but they continued asking her questions. About where she'd grown up, her family's Irish heritage, all sorts of things. She was trying to accommodate them, but seeing that Darla had arrived—and was waiting behind her—Colleen knew it was time for to move one. "Please, excuse me," she told them. "Miss Devon has arrived, and I'm sure that Mr. Miller can't be far behind." And now Colleen pressed beyond them, hurrying toward the doors.

"You did beautifully," Georgina quietly assured her.

"I had no idea you'd be such a hit with the press." Rory chuckled. "No complaints about that."

"Except that Darla looks like she wants to murder me," Colleen whispered back.

Georgina and Rory simply laughed, but Colleen felt reassured to have them flanking her on either side as they went inside the theater. They spent a few minutes exchanging greetings with studio people and some of the film crew, eventually going into the auditorium to find the seats reserved for them. Colleen's heart was still fluttering with excitement when the lights went down and the film projector began to run. Tonight had actually turned out to be more fun than she'd expected, sort of a nerve-racking fun. And as the movie began to roll, she could tell by the audience's reaction that it was well received. Aside from her usual self-criticism, Colleen was relieved to see that her performance was nothing to be ashamed of. It was, in fact, rather solid and believable. And, despite all of Darla's accusations that Colleen had been trying to steal the limelight or upstage her, Colleen felt confident she'd handled it right. By the time the house lights came on, Colleen felt sure this movie was going to be a hit.

Looking glamorous and confident and celebratory, Robert and Darla led the processional from the theater—their arms linked as if they were actually on speaking terms, which was a big fat lie. Outside, a number of reporters, including a couple of cameramen, were eagerly waiting. Clustered along the sidewalk, they pressed in to ask more questions but seemed to have more interest in Colleen than the main stars of the film. Robert and Darla actually stepped aside.

"Tonight's film is going to be released for the troops serving overseas," a reporter said directly to Colleen. "How would it feel to think your fiancé might see it?"

"That would be wonderful!" Colleen nodded happily. "That would mean Geoff had been released as a prisoner of war."

"Were you pleased with your performance?" the female reporter asked Colleen.

Colleen flashed her best Hollywood smile. "I think everyone in the film did an excellent job."

"What will you do next?" she asked Colleen. "Any new films lined up?"

"I, uh, I don't know for sure." She glanced at her agents.

"Maureen Mulligan will have lots of options," Rory assured all of them. "You haven't seen the last of this talented young lady."

"Any chance of a starring role for Maureen Mulligan?" a male reporter yelled out.

"Oh, I don't think I'm ready for that yet." Colleen smiled with gratitude.

"Miss Mulligan." An older reporter pressed to the front of the pack, his notepad ready. "Do you mind if I inquire about your brother?"

Colleen felt a small wave of sadness as one of the cameramen moved in closer. "What do you want to know?" she asked quietly.

"I just read that your only brother was killed at Pearl Harbor. Is that true?"

The crowd grew quiet as the reporters gathered in closer to hear Colleen's response. "Yes, yes...that's true." Her voice trembled slightly, and she wondered if she could handle this.

"Did your brother's death influence how you played your role in this film?" another reporter asked. "Since it was a war movie? Did you feel that gave you more authenticity?"

Colleen considered this, trying to form an intelligent answer. And then something unexplainable happened—it was almost as if Peter's hand settled on her shoulder, as if he wanted her to speak out. She squared her shoulders and looked directly at the reporters. "My older brother, Peter Mulligan, joined the navy a few months before the war began. He'd been following the news and felt certain war was coming. He enlisted because he wanted to do his part. Peter was aboard the USS *Arizona,* stationed in Pearl Harbor. He was aboard his ship that Sunday morning when the Japanese attacked. Just like thousands of others." She took in a breath. "Peter was my only brother. He gave his life for his country—and even though I miss him dearly, I couldn't be prouder of him."

Colleen felt shaky as she reached for Georgina's hand.

"I think that's enough questions for Miss Mulligan tonight. Thank you very much." Rory took Colleen by the arm, and then he and Georgina guided her past the reporters and cameramen, as well as past a stunned Darla and grinning Robert.

"Oh my." Colleen felt like a marionette whose strings had just been cut as she slid into the back of the limousine "That was harder than I expected. So many questions."

"It was only because the press adored you." Georgina squeezed her hand. "You were their darling tonight, dear. You couldn't have done better."

"I can't wait to read what they write about you," Rory added.

"And the news flashes they were getting," Georgina said. "What great publicity for Pinnacle."

"Speaking of Pinnacle, it's on to the party," Rory declared.

"Oh, yes...the party." Colleen felt uneasy.

"I heard that Pinnacle is pulling out all the stops tonight,"

Georgina told her. "Seafood being shipped in from all over—I don't know about you, but I'm ravenous."

"Uh-huh." Colleen's stomach felt like she'd swallowed a large rock.

"Aren't you looking forward to it?" Georgina asked.

"It's just that Darla..."

"Don't you worry about her," Rory said lightly.

"But I feel like she hates me."

"Just remember that Darla would only hate you because you're a threat." Georgina laughed. "And if you ask me, it's about time that prima donna felt threatened."

"Just the same." Rory waved a warning finger. "Should Darla offer you champagne, I suggest you politely decline."

"Meaning she'll lace it with arsenic?" Colleen feigned humor but at the same time realized she'd have to keep a safe distance from Darla tonight—and watch her back. It was funny how all the "Hollywood glitz and glamour" was never quite the way she used to dream it would be. And yet she didn't regret her career choice. It's just that it was different.

Eight

It was a slow Monday afternoon at the store with Mam tending Baby Peter up in Margaret's apartment, Jimmy out on deliveries, and Margaret feeling like her life couldn't possibly be more boring. She barely looked up when the bell on the door jangled.

"Good afternoon," a male voice called out.

Margaret looked up from where she was wiping the countertop by the cash register. "Good afternoon," she called back, trying to sound friendlier than she felt.

"Nice little market you have here." The gentleman smiled at her.

"Thank you." She forced a polite smile. "Can I help you find anything?" She felt certain this man hadn't been in the store before. As he glanced around, she did a quick inventory, taking in the well-tailored gray suit and neatly cut dark brown hair beneath a stylish felt hat. He reminded her of Cary Grant. For a relatively older man, probably in his mid- to late-thirties, he was quite good looking.

"I just need a few basics for my pantry." He picked up a carton of salt. "I just moved into the new apartment complex across the street. Not quite used to doing my own grocery shopping."

Margaret was curious—who normally shopped for him? But instead of asking, she picked up a basket and went over to join him.

"Well, salt is a good start. If you have a ration booklet, you might want a bit of sugar and—"

"Ration booklet right here." He patted his jacket pocket.

"Maybe you'd like some coffee? A loaf of bread? Butter? Oatmeal perhaps?"

He patted her on the shoulder. "You, my dear, are just what the doctor ordered." He took the basket from her, looping it over his arm. "How about if I carry this and you show me the way and help me fill it?"

And so Margaret led him through the store, picking out various items and dropping them into his basket. All the while, the appreciative gentleman praising her for her choices, until his basket was quite full. It was actually rather fun.

"Well, this should certainly be enough to keep you for a week or so," she finally told him. "And since it looks like a heavy load, we could have it delivered if you like."

"No, that's not necessary. As I said, I just live right across the street." He set the basket onto the counter. "If you pack this into a strong cardboard box, I think I can get it home just fine. And my apartment is only on the second floor, so I don't have to climb a lot of flights."

"That apartment building looks very nice," she said as she began ringing up his purchases. "Do you like it?"

"Yes. I was pleasantly surprised to find that it's much more spacious than my apartment back in New York."

"You're from New York?" She glanced up with interest.

"That's right." He nodded. "The corporation just transferred me to the West Coast. I wasn't sure I'd like it at first, but after less than a week in San Francisco, I'm discovering it's quite charming." His eyes twinkled. "And not just the landscape."

She felt her cheeks growing warm as she looked back down at the cash register. Was he flirting with her?

"And since we're neighbors, so to speak, I suppose I should introduce myself." He stuck out his hand. "I'm Howard Moore."

"I'm Margaret Mulligan—I mean Hammond." Margaret felt embarrassed as she shook his hand. "Mulligan is my maiden name. I've been married a little more than a year, but my husband has been overseas for most of that time. Sometimes I almost forget that I'm married." She grimaced at her words. "I don't mean that I forget I'm married," she hurried to correct herself. "I just forget that I'm Margaret Hammond sometimes."

He just chuckled. "I understand completely. I remember the early days of my marriage...it took awhile to adjust to being a husband." His smile seemed to fade.

"Has your wife made the adjustment to this move?" Margaret continued to ring up his groceries. "Does she like San Francisco?"

"I'm divorced," he said grimly.

"Oh, I'm sorry." Margaret wasn't sure if that was the right sentiment as she reached beneath the counter for a cardboard box.

"It was probably for the best," Howard told her. "My ex-wife never would've wanted to leave New York anyway. Although she'd already remarried by the time I got wind of my transfer."

"So that's why you aren't used to doing your own grocery shopping?" Margaret said absently as she loaded the box. "You haven't been single for long?"

"Just over a year. Although I did have a housekeeper back in New York. She took care of the shopping and cooking for me. But I'm not sure I want that kind of help here. I sort of like the feeling of being on my own." He smiled. "It's like a newfound freedom."

She smiled back. "I know just what you mean." And without really thinking she told Howard about how she'd renovated her apartment above the store. "I've been pretty happy up there. Oh, it's not luxurious by any means. But it does feel good to be independent and on my own." She set the loaf of bread on top of the other groceries. "And it's handy to my work." She told him the total of his purchases.

He grinned as he handed her a twenty-dollar bill along with his ration book. "Sounds like a smart plan to me."

She frowned slightly as she counted his change. "Although I must admit that I sometimes still miss my family. But at least I have Peter."

"Peter? Is that your husband?"

She laughed. "No, I thought I mentioned him already. Peter's my darling baby. He's just a little over six months old. He's often down here with me, but my mother is watching him upstairs. I felt they both needed a break."

He pocketed his change. "Well, it's been a real pleasure to meet you, Mrs. Hammond. I look forward to becoming a regular customer at Mulligan's Market. And I hope I get to meet young Peter soon." He tipped his hat. "Thank you for all your help today."

"You're very welcome, Mr. Moore." She was slightly surprised that she remembered his name...Howard Moore. "Have a good day."

Two days after the movie premiere—and with no movie contracts rolling in from the studios—Colleen decided it was time to go home. Besides the distraction it would provide, and the fact that she missed her family, she knew that they could use some help in the store. She would do her best to make herself useful...and if Hollywood called, well, she would go back.

The only one who knew Colleen was coming home was Molly, and the only reason she'd told her was because Colleen was driving, and she knew that her parents worried about her making such a long drive on her own. But the six-hour drive was surprisingly relaxing, giving her time to sort through her thoughts and consider her future.

Colleen had really expected that Geoff would've been released from the Japanese prison camp by now. Oh, she had no real reasons for thinking this way, except that it was so hard to imagine someone as energetic and independent as Geoff being confined for that long. In fact, she'd rather hoped he would've escaped. At least until she'd read that article about the horrible price the other inmates paid for an escapee's actions. Now she just hoped that none of Geoff's buddies would try to get away...and create problems for him.

Although she had no way to verify it, Colleen had a strong conviction that Geoff was still alive...and that he was going to make it out of there. Of course, this was just a feeling and sometimes, like if she were down, she would question that conviction. For all she knew, Geoff could be dead. It wasn't as if the Japanese were sending telegrams about the goings-on in their terrible POW camps.

Anyway, part of her reason for going home was to pay a visit to Geoff's family. She wanted to see if there was anything they could do—any of them—to help get Geoff safely home. Weren't negotiations sometimes made out of Washington DC? What if she used her clout as an upcoming actress in a major motion picture to get someone's attention? It seemed worth a try. But she really wanted to talk to Geoff's family about it first. She would feel horrible if she made an attempt that blew up in her face...and put Geoff into even more peril.

It was late afternoon when Colleen pulled up to her parents' house. It felt so strange to be here like this—as if she were a visitor— when this used to be her home and such a different sort of place. She parked in back, taking her time as she strolled through Molly's victory garden, admiring the young green plants sprouting through the dark brown soil. But before she made it to the steps by the back door, Molly burst out.

"Colleen!" she shrieked joyfully, leaping down the stairs and embracing her so tightly that Colleen's hat fell off. "I'm so happy to see you!"

"I'm happy to be here!"

"Dad's inside, but he still doesn't know you're coming. Neither does Mam, but she should be home in about an hour. Did you know that Mam drives the car now? And I'm the one who taught her."

"Will wonders never cease?" Colleen picked up her hat, dusting it off and giving Molly the once-over. "You look even more grown-up than you did in January." She frowned. "Are you taller?"

"Maybe." Molly grinned. "I'll get your other bags from the car. You go inside and surprise Dad. He's in his chair."

Colleen went through the kitchen, tiptoeing through the dining room and peeking around the corner to spot Dad in his chair with the newspaper across his lap. Although he wasn't sleeping, he looked tired. And pale. And unless she was imagining things, his complexion seemed slightly gray.

"Dad!" she said eagerly as she hurried to him.

"Well, I'll be!" Dad tossed his newspaper down, starting to stand.

"Don't get up." She leaned down to hug him, kissing him on the cheek.

"Where on earth did you come from?" he asked with wonder.

"Oh, I don't know." She tossed down her hat, pulling up the ottoman to sit across from him. "You and Mam used to say you found me under a cabbage leaf in the garden."

He chuckled.

"So how are you?" She reached for his hand, noticing that it felt frail and cool.

"Oh, good for nothing…as usual."

She peered closely at him. "When did you last go to the doctor, Dad?"

"Oh, doctors." He waved a hand. "They're for sick folks."

"They help people to stay well too," she pointed out.

"I don't need to—"

"Dad," she said firmly. "I've made up my mind. You and I are going to pay a visit to the doctor." Now she flashed her best Hollywood smile. "After all, don't you want to show me off? Your famous movie-star daughter?"

His lips curled into a smile. "Well, now that you mention it."

"So, we'll start with the doctor," she declared. "I don't want any argument from you. And after that…well, we'll see."

"You're going to be in Patrick's old room," Molly called as she carried in Colleen's luggage toward the stairs, "since it's not the nursery anymore."

"But there's no bed in there," Dad said.

"Yes, there is," Molly informed him. "I moved Colleen's old bed in there."

Dad frowned. "All by yourself?"

"It wasn't heavy, Dad. It's only a twin bed." She lifted one of Colleen's suitcases high. "Besides that, I'm strong."

"I do believe you've gotten taller." Colleen went over to stand next to her little sister. "Even in my heels, you look to be as tall as I am."

"Which means she's taller," Dad pointed out.

"That means you're the tallest Mulligan girl," Colleen told Molly.

"And since I'm so tall and strong, I'll take your bags upstairs for you." Molly winked.

"Thanks. I need to make a phone call." Colleen reached for the phone and the little black book of phone numbers, carrying them up the stairs with her.

"It's fortunate for you that I put in that long telephone cord," Dad called. "But you take care on the stairs."

"I think it's about time this house had an extension telephone," Colleen called back.

"Waste of good money," he muttered.

As Colleen dialed the doctor's office, she decided that even if an extension phone was a waste of money, she would waste her own in order to have one in her room. Just in case Hollywood called, which felt even less likely now that she was home again. After she got through to the doctor's office, convincing the receptionist that the need was urgent, she managed to get Dad an appointment for the next afternoon.

"Dad's going to the doctor?" Molly asked with wide eyes.

"He is." Colleen closed the little phone book with satisfaction.

"How did you do that?"

Colleen fluttered her eyelashes. "I just used my celebrity charm."

Molly laughed. "I'll bet you did." She hugged her again. "Now, if you'll excuse me, I want to get supper started before Mam gets home from the store."

"I'll be down to help in a little bit." As Colleen set the telephone down on the straight-backed chair next to the door, she vaguely wondered if anyone from the Knight Agency would be calling her anytime soon. Or ever again? What if this was it for her—what if after only one film, her acting career was over? She'd heard of that happening. Usually it was because an actor was a box-office flop. And that was understandable.

As Colleen hung up her suit jacket and kicked off her heels, she knew there was another reason a first-time actress's career was nipped in the bud. Occasionally someone in the industry—someone with more power—took an instant dislike to a newcomer. Usually it was a director who'd determined that an actor or actress was difficult or unreliable or unprofessional. But sometimes it was a fellow actor or actress—someone with more clout—someone like Darla Devon. And after the way Darla had publicly snubbed Colleen at the Pinnacle party last week, well, it seemed fairly likely that that was exactly what had happened to Colleen. And she decided as she went downstairs to help Molly, that maybe it was for the best.

Nine

Margaret tried to conceal how disgruntled she felt the next morning, but it wasn't easy. Especially since she seemed to get angrier with each passing hour. But shortly after their lunch breaks, Mam was no longer falling for Margaret's disguise.

"Why is your nose out of joint?" Mam finally asked during a lull in customers.

"What do you mean?" Margaret feigned nonchalance.

"You are clearly irked about something, Mary Margaret Mulligan." Mam's brow creased. "How is it I've managed to offend you?"

"It's not you, Mam," she sheepishly confessed.

"What then?" Mam demanded.

"It's Colleen."

"Colleen?" Mam blinked. "Why would you be angry at Colleen? She only just got here, and you haven't even seen her yet."

"That's just it." Margaret slammed a box of canned peaches down so hard that the counter shook. "Colleen sneaks into town, and she doesn't even tell me."

"She simply wanted to surprise us." Mam patted Margaret's shoulder. "And she'd have come in here today, but like I told you, she's taking your dad to the doctor this afternoon. Something we should all be very grateful for since no one else could get the stubborn old goat to go in for a checkup."

"Yes, yes." Margaret sighed. "I know. And I appreciate that."

"How about this," Mam suggested. "Why don't we encourage Colleen to come over and visit you this evening? That way she can see your new apartment, and you girls can have dinner together and catch up."

Margaret felt a rush of hope. "Do you think she'd want to do that?"

"Of course. She's your sister." Mam pointed to the playpen that Margaret had set up behind the counter. Peter was happily shaking a rattle. "Besides, Colleen will want to come see her darling godson."

"And you and Dad won't mind sharing her for one evening?"

"Not at all. In fact, I expect your dad will be worn out after his doctor appointment. And Molly has a night class tonight."

"I'm going to call Colleen right now," Margaret announced boldly. To Margaret's relief, Colleen not only agreed to come for the evening, she sounded truly glad about it. "And I'll order Chinese for dinner," Margaret told her. "That is, if you don't mind picking it up on your way over."

For the rest of the day, Margaret felt energized and encouraged. Tonight promised to be the most interesting evening she'd had in weeks...maybe months. She even sent Mam home from work early. "I can lock up fine on my own," she assured her. But the store got rather busy, and then just minutes before closing time, she heard the bell jingling again. To her surprise, Howard Moore walked in—surprising because he'd already been in this morning.

"Hello, Mrs. Hammond," he called out warmly.

"Good evening, Mr. Moore." She leaned the broom against the wall. "It's funny," she confessed as she went over to him, "whenever

I hear someone say 'Mrs. Hammond,' I expect to see my mother-in-law coming around the corner."

"Really?"

"That's because hardly anyone ever calls me that."

"Well, you are Mrs. Hammond." He picked up the afternoon paper. "Are you not?"

"Yes, but everyone who shops in our store calls me Margaret. And if you're going to be a regular customer, well, you should probably call me Margaret too." She headed back to the counter, preparing to ring up his newspaper and feeling a little disgruntled that he hadn't picked up a paper from the newsstand just down the street.

"I'll gladly call you Margaret, but only if you call me by my first name."

Margaret frowned, preparing to question his suggestion. After all, he was clearly her senior, and she addressed many of the older customers by their surnames. Instead, she turned around to check on Peter. She'd been trying to keep him awake all afternoon, in the hopes that he'd be tired enough to go to bed early so she and Colleen could chat uninterrupted.

"Hello, Prince Peter." Mr. Moore tipped his hat to the baby. "You're looking fine and dandy today."

"I'm afraid he's overdue for a nap," she confessed. "I'm trying to stretch him out a little."

Mr. Moore turned back to look at Margaret. "Well, just so you know, I do plan to be a regular customer, but I mean it—if I'm to call you Margaret, I insist you call me Howard."

"Fine." She reluctantly agreed. "Now, is there anything else I can help you with, uh, Howard? Because I was just getting ready to lock up for the night."

"I'm sorry." He checked his watch. "I didn't realize it was that late. But I was hungry for dinner and—"

"Oh, that's right." Margaret slapped her forehead. "I meant to order Chinese food for dinner by now."

"Chinese?" His eyes lit up as she reached for the phone. "Special occasion?"

"Yes." She started to dial. "My sister is here from Hollywood, and I promised her Chinese food tonight."

"A sister from Hollywood?" His brows arched with interest.

"Go ahead and gather up whatever you came in for," Margaret said as the phone rang, "while I make this call."

While Howard perused the canned food aisle, Margaret placed her order, making sure to get Colleen's favorite dishes. "There," she declared as she hung up. "Are you finding what you need?" She wanted to tell him to hurry but didn't want to sound rude.

"I suppose." He came over to the counter with several cans, setting them and the newspaper down with a frown. "I thought I'd try eating my dinner at home tonight, but hearing you ordering that Chinese food just now..." He grimly shook his head. "I'm not so sure that this canned soup is going to taste so good."

She chuckled as she rang up his items. "Well, how about if I write down the phone number for Lee's Restaurant? In case you change your mind."

"So you recommend Lee's?"

"Absolutely." She totaled his purchase then wrote down the phone number.

"So this sister from Hollywood..." He handed her some cash. "Is she married too?"

Margaret couldn't help but laugh. Poor Howard. He was

obviously lonely. "Colleen isn't married, but she's engaged." As she bagged his groceries, she quickly explained about Geoff's dilemma.

"That's rough." He pocketed his change and picked up the sack. "I hope everything turns out okay for him. And for your sister too."

"Oh, I'm sure it will. Colleen always lands on her feet." With the keys in her hand, she followed him. "She's the lucky one." She paused by the door, telling Howard how Colleen had recently been in a film that would soon release in San Francisco. "If you go see it, remember that Colleen goes by Maureen Mulligan."

"How interesting." His eyes twinkled with amusement. "I hope you girls have a good evening, Margaret."

"Thanks! I'm sure we will."

Howard held up his grocery bag with a hangdog expression. "And don't feel too badly for me, eating my canned soup, across the street, all by myself."

Margaret just laughed. "Bon appétit." She waved, then closed and locked the glass door, flipping the CLOSED sign over. As she gathered Peter, hurrying up to her apartment, she felt no genuine sympathy for Howard. He was probably used to eating anywhere he liked in this town. It might just do him good to be stuck at home with a can of soup for a change. After all, wasn't that what she did most of the time?

She'd already cleaned her apartment earlier, while Mam tended the store, and now she took a few minutes to change Peter's diaper and dress him in his little blue and white checked suit, complete with a tiny bowtie and brimmed cap. "You are so adorable," she said as she set him down in his crib. "Just don't fall asleep before Auntie Colleen arrives."

Now she went to her dressing table and attempted to re-pin her hair, which had gotten rather long during the past year. It was still thick and auburn but now a bit unruly. She considered changing into a prettier dress, but Peter was starting to fuss and she really wanted him at his best for Colleen's visit. She picked him up and, jostling him up and down, paced around her apartment, talking to him like she often did when she was feeling lonely. "There's your sweet daddy." She paused by Brian's army photo. Wearing his officer's uniform, he looked so dignified and handsome...so far away. "He promises to meet up with you before your first birthday," she said wistfully. "Hopefully he'll keep that promise."

"Hello up there?" Colleen called from downstairs. "Want me to lock the back door before I come up?"

"Yes," Margaret yelled down to her. "Thanks."

Soon Colleen was unloading the white food cartons on the kitchen table, and the two sisters, with Peter in between them, were happily hugging. "I'm so glad you could come," Margaret said as she stepped back to see Colleen better. "You look so glamorous." She shook her head over the stylish pink suit. "So Hollywood."

Colleen just laughed as she unpinned her hat. "And you look so lovely and motherly." She bent down to kiss Peter's cheek. "And you, my handsome nephew—you are definitely going to be a lady-killer." She smiled at Margaret. "You're both as pretty as a picture—a sight for sore eyes."

While Colleen set out their food, Margaret sat at the table, spooning rice cereal and applesauce into Peter's eager mouth. "How was Dad's doctor appointment?"

Colleen paused from dishing out fried rice. "Good and bad."

"Tell me the bad first." Margaret braced herself.

"Well, the doctor is fairly sure that the tuberculosis damaged Dad's heart."

"Oh..." Margaret sighed. "We'd been wondering about that."

"But if Dad keeps taking it easy, he should be okay. And the doctor insisted that Dad must have an oxygen tank at home. It will be delivered tomorrow. Apparently that could save his life, if he ever has an attack."

"It was good you took him in, Colleen. Otherwise we wouldn't have found that out. How did Dad feel about it?"

"He didn't even seem surprised." Colleen chuckled. "He seemed more interested in telling his doctor, and anyone else who would listen, about how I'm a movie star—and all about the new movie."

Margaret smiled. "Well, that must've been fun."

With Peter fed and sitting contentedly in his baby seat, Margaret and Colleen sat down to eat too. It was fun to catch up over the past several months. Of course, Colleen's news was much more exciting than Margaret's, but it was encouraging to hear that Colleen really did like Margaret's new apartment.

"It was so brave of you to move out like you did," Colleen said as they were finishing up their meal. "And to fix this place up—all by yourself. Molly told me how hard you worked on everything, Margaret. It's really impressive."

Peter was starting to fuss as they set their dirty plates in the dishpan. "I should get him ready for bed," she told Colleen. "He didn't have an afternoon nap and—"

"Oh, let me get him ready," Colleen begged.

"He's all yours." Margaret gladly handed him over. "His pajamas and everything you need are on the changing table. I'll fix him a bottle."

As Margaret got the bottle ready, she thought how great it was to have Colleen around like this. She hadn't even realized how much she'd missed her flibbertigibbet sister. But hearing her chattering away at Peter, laughing merrily, well, it made this place really feel like a home. Colleen insisted on giving him his bottle too, settling in the old rocker. Eventually, with Peter's tummy full, he drifted off to sleep. Margaret watched as Colleen gently laid him down in the crib, just like she'd been doing this all her life.

"I've got hot water for tea," Margaret whispered.

"And fortune cookies for dessert," Colleen told her.

"It's so fun having you here, Colleen," Margaret said as she poured hot water into the teapot. "Evenings can get kind of long after Peter goes to sleep."

"Speaking of evening." Colleen pointed to the window where the sun had just gone down. "Should we get those blackout curtains up?"

"Yes. Good thinking." Margaret set the teapot on her makeshift coffee table, then picked up the heavy drapes.

"I'll put up the ones in back," Colleen offered.

"Thanks." After the drapes were in place, Colleen turned on a table lamp, and they settled down in the living room area. "I can't wait until this war is over and we don't have to black out the windows anymore."

"I can't wait for this war to be over for a lot of reasons." Colleen kicked off her shoes, tucking her feet under her as she sipped her tea.

"Speaking of the war, any news about Geoff?"

Colleen glumly shook her head. "But I'm going to visit his parents on Sunday. I want to talk to them about putting some pressure on Washington DC."

"Pressure on Washington?" Margaret set down her teacup. "How do you expect to do that?"

"I've heard of movie stars who use their celebrity to get the attention of senators and congressmen." Colleen grinned. "I figure

I should give it a try too. The Japanese are completely ignoring the Geneva Conventions. It might not make any difference to go public with this, but you never know." Colleen told her about the press reviews she'd gotten after the movie premiere. "One of the writers wrote a nice piece about how Geoff was a prisoner of war—and how badly our servicemen are being treated in the Pacific."

"But can anyone really do anything about that?" Margaret felt doubtful.

"I honestly don't know, but I'm willing to do anything I can, including using my movie star status." She struck a pose that made them both laugh. "It might be impossible, but I want to try. And I need to get right to it. In case my career turns out to be a one-movie deal."

"Do you think that could really happen?"

It was like Margaret had uncorked her sister. Suddenly Colleen was telling her all about her cantankerous costar, Darla Devon, explaining how horrible Darla had been to work with and then how nasty and mean she'd been at a recent studio party.

"I think Darla may have ruined everything for me," Colleen finally said. "Honestly, I don't expect to get another film contract now."

"That's awful." Margaret grimly shook her head, but the truth was she felt greatly relieved. This might mean that Colleen would move back home for good.

"I don't want Mam and Dad to hear about this," Colleen said solemnly.

"Why not?"

"They'll be concerned about my finances. I've sort of been helping them—you know, to catch up with all Dad's medical bills. And I don't want to worry them."

"It's too bad you and Geoff weren't married...at least you'd have his navy stipend."

"I'm sad that we weren't married for a lot of reasons," Colleen said a bit sharply. "But that's not one of them."

"I'm sorry." Margaret waved an apologetic hand. "You know me, always being the practical one—worrying about the bottom line. It's from working at the store."

"I know, I know." Colleen sighed. "It's okay. And you're not the only one who's said that to me. In fact, I'll bet Geoff regrets that too. I hate to think of him—where he is—worrying about my welfare." Now she told Margaret how she'd been writing to Geoff. "Twice a week—can you believe it? He'll be so surprised to find such a stack of letters from me...I mean, when he's released."

"So what will you do, Colleen?" Margaret asked. "I mean if you're really finished with Hollywood? What's next for you?"

Colleen's brows drew together. "I don't know for sure. Maybe go back to work at the airplane factory. Or help out here at the store. I guess I could move back home...or find a place to—"

"You'd be more than welcome to move in with Peter and me," Margaret said eagerly.

"Thanks." Colleen glanced around the room. "I appreciate the offer, but it looks like you're pretty tight in here already."

"We could fit you in," Margaret insisted. "And I'd love to have the company." She grimaced. "The truth is, I've been pretty lonely."

"I know exactly how you feel," Colleen reassured her. "I was lonely in my apartment too. At first. But after a few months I got used to it. You will too."

Margaret wasn't so sure, but she simply nodded. Just the same, she knew that Colleen probably couldn't imagine how it would feel to work in the boring grocery store six days a week only to come up here, take care of a baby, and then spend the entire evening all alone. Colleen probably didn't fully appreciate the freedom she'd enjoyed down in Hollywood. She'd had an exciting job and interesting friends... She'd had a real life.

Ten

For the next few days, Colleen spent most of her time at the store. This allowed Mam to stay home and care for Dad, or at least make sure he wasn't overdoing it. After they closed the store each evening, Colleen usually spent an hour or two with Margaret and Peter, and she even spent the night on Saturday. While Margaret seemed to appreciate the company, she still seemed generally unhappy...or maybe discontent. But then, Colleen reminded herself, hadn't Margaret always been like that? And Sunday morning was no different.

"I still don't see why you won't go to Mass with us today," Margaret said in an irritated tone.

"I already told you, I'm going to see Geoff's parents today." Colleen bent down to straighten the seams on her stockings. Due to rationing and having attained a fairly nice tan while in Hollywood, Colleen didn't usually wear stockings. But she knew Geoff's mother was old-fashioned.

"But you could go see them afterward," Margaret insisted.

Colleen stood up and, smiling patiently at her sister, gauged her response. "Here's the truth," she said slowly. "While a lot of my old attitudes toward God and religion have changed—for the better—I am still not as committed to the church as you are, Margaret. Yes, I believe in God. Yes, I pray. But I haven't been to confession in ages, and the truth is that it makes me feel a bit hypocritical to go through the paces at Mass."

"Oh." Margaret's lower lip protruded slightly as she fastened the cap strap beneath Peter's chubby chin.

"But I'm happy to drop you two off." Colleen tickled a rounded baby cheek. "And then I'll be back to Mam and Dad's in time for supper, and I can give you a ride back here afterward."

"And spend the night again?" Margaret asked hopefully.

"Yeah, why not." Colleen was only doing this to pacify her sister, but maybe it was worth it. She set down her already packed overnight bag like it was proof.

"What about Easter Sunday?" Margaret asked as they were getting into Colleen's car. "Will you go to church then?"

Colleen knew her family would expect at least that much of her next week. "Sure," she agreed as she started the car. "That actually sounds nice."

After dropping off Margaret and Peter, Colleen took her time driving out to the Conrad farm. They were expecting her around noon, but it was such a lovely spring day, she decided to enjoy a leisurely drive through the lush green countryside. Plus, it gave her time to get her bearings. Although things had definitely gotten better, it was never particularly easy to visit Geoff's family. As usual, she'd dressed carefully. A classic navy blue suit, a conservative hat, white gloves...hopefully Ellen would approve. Colleen still had a hard time thinking of Geoff's mother as Ellen, but since she'd insisted Colleen call her by her first name, Colleen was determined to do so.

As Colleen parked in front of the big white house, she felt a fresh rush of nerves. The last time she'd been out here, Ellen had not concealed her displeasure regarding Colleen's new Hollywood career, but at least Geoff's grandparents had been enthusiastic and supportive. As she strolled up to the house, Colleen was relieved to realize that Ellen would be pleased that Colleen had no plans for another movie role.

The greetings exchanged between Colleen and Geoff's family seemed somewhat somber, and then they were all seated in the living room. "I suppose you've heard the news," Ellen said with a slightly grim expression.

"What news?" Colleen felt a wave of panic wash over her. "Is it Geoff? Has something happened? Is he—"

"We haven't heard anything specific regarding Geoff," Ellen told her.

"It was what we just heard on the radio," Geoff's grandma said.

"Have you been listening to the news the past few days?" Geoff's grandpa asked.

"Not exactly," Colleen admitted. "I've been pretty busy. Working at the store and staying at my sister's and—"

"So you didn't hear the president's address on the radio?" Geoff's grandma asked.

"Margaret usually keeps her radio tuned to music programs, probably because of the baby." The truth was that Margaret hated war news, but Colleen didn't want to go into that right now. "So, no, I didn't hear it."

"Well," Grandpa began slowly, "I'll try to catch you up. A few days ago, eighteen P-38 fighters, with the help of code breakers, managed to locate and shoot down General Yamamoto. It was quite a victory for the Allies. Yamamoto was a pretty big kingpin."

Colleen felt relieved. "But isn't that good news?"

"It should be good news," Ellen told her. "Except the Japanese have retaliated."

"That's right." Grandpa nodded grimly. "President Roosevelt announced that the Japanese have executed several airmen who participated in the Doolittle Raid."

"Airmen who were prisoners of war." Grandma sadly shook her head. "Poor boys."

"Oh." Colleen frowned, trying to remember the details of last year's Doolittle Raid. "Wasn't that attack done by the army air force? Not the navy?"

"That's true," Grandpa confirmed. "But now the Japanese have made a new announcement."

"We just heard it on the radio." Ellen twisted a handkerchief in her hand.

"Japan has officially announced that all captured Allied pilots will be given 'one-way tickets to hell.' Those were their exact words."

"You mean the Japanese will execute all the prisoners who are pilots?" Colleen covered her hand with her mouth, letting out a little gasp.

"That is what they are saying." Ellen dabbed her eyes with her handkerchief.

"It's just horrible," Grandma said with a choked sob.

"The Japanese have been fighting dirty right from the start," Grandpa declared. "But this just takes it all!"

"I hate this war!" Colleen exclaimed. "I just really, really hate it."

For a while, they all discussed what this meant, expressing their concerns for Geoff's welfare and their helplessness to do anything.

"We can pray," Grandma finally said.

"And we will," Ellen confirmed.

"Yes." Colleen nodded. "I pray for Geoff every day. But I plan to do more too."

"What more can you possibly do?" Ellen asked.

Now Colleen told them about the reporters at the movie premiere last week, including their interest in Geoff and her brother, and how they wrote articles about them. "You see, it's a war movie," she explained. "And it releases in theaters across the country starting next weekend. I'm not sure it will make any difference, but I plan to use what little celebrity I have to get some attention."

"But even if you get attention, what good would it do?" Ellen looked doubtful.

"I don't know, but it might make our country fight harder to get these men out of those prison camps," she declared.

"It's certainly worth a try," Grandpa said.

"That's right." Grandma nodded.

Colleen stood. "And time is precious right now. If you'll excuse me, I want to go back to the city and see if I can get someone to listen." She got her purse and gloves. "It's surprising the attention I get when someone hears that I'm a film star—and if I can use it to help Geoff, well, then I'll milk it for all its worth." She hugged each of them and, feeling like she was setting off on a mission, drove back to San Francisco.

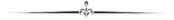

By Monday morning, Colleen's photo, as well as Geoff's, was on the front page the *San Francisco Chronicle*, along with a heart-tugging story that, according to the reporter she'd spoken exclusively with, was being picked up across the country—and around the world. Would it change anything? Or do Geoff any good? Only time would tell.

As a result of the news article, the store grew busier than ever. But when Margaret figured out that most of the traffic wanted glimpses or signatures from Colleen, she posted a big sign on the door that said: Store Patrons Only! Of course, that simply seemed to invite people in to make minimal purchases, which kept them busier than ever.

"Why don't we just lock up and call it a day?" Colleen suggested.

"It's two hours until closing time," Margaret pointed out.

"So?" Colleen was already removing her grocer's apron.

"We'll lose business." Margaret frowned.

"Just nickel and dime business." Colleen nodded to the noisy group of teenagers coming into the store. "Or else I could make myself scarce. That might help."

Margaret untied her apron. "Fine. If you're leaving, I am too."

Without further ado, Colleen began shooing customers out of the store. "Sorry, closing early today," she said cheerfully. "Come again."

"We'll be open all day tomorrow," Margaret called out.

"But I won't be here," Colleen sang out.

After Margaret locked the front door, she turned to Colleen. "You're not coming to work tomorrow?"

"I think you'll have a better day if I'm not here, Margaret. Mam can come in, and I'll sit at home with Dad. Let things cool off."

Margaret plucked Peter out of the crib. "So what do we do now?"

"Enjoy some time off." Colleen gave her a weary smile.

Margaret's brow creased as if this concept was completely foreign to her.

"Here." Colleen reached for the baby. "I'll take care of Peter, and you go out and have some fun."

"Fun?" Margaret looked dumbfounded.

"Remember fun?" Colleen teased. "Just go do something you don't normally get to do. Get ice cream. Or go shopping. Ride the cable car. Take a walk in the park. Whatever seems like fun to you, just go for it. I'm sure it will do you some good."

Margaret seemed to consider this. "Really?"

"Yes, really! Peter and I will be perfectly fine. I know his routines." She poked him in the tummy. "It's probably about time for a diaper change and then your afternoon bottle and a nap. I think Auntie Colleen can handle it."

"You're sure?"

"Of course, silly." Colleen waved her hand at Margaret's drab gray skirt and ratty blouse with a stain on the collar. "But first you have to change into something more festive."

"Festive?" Margaret looked doubtful.

Colleen frowned. "I hate to say it, Margaret, but you look like an old lady."

Margaret's brow creased. "Thank you very much."

"I've wanted to say something, but I hate to hurt your feelings. And I don't mean you look like an old lady—good grief, you're not even twenty-three yet. The problem is you dress like you're a granny. Even Mam looks more stylish than you."

"Well, all I do is work in the store and take care of the baby. How do you expect me to dress?"

Colleen considered this. "Like you care about your appearance." She pulled out a loose strand of Margaret's auburn hair. "And your hair is so thick and wavy and pretty, yet you pull it all back in a tight little granny bun."

Margaret shrugged. "It's easy to do."

"You want to know what I think?"

"Do I have a choice?"

Colleen smiled. "I think that when we go around looking like a worn-out old cleaning woman, we start to act like one, and then we begin to believe we are one."

Margaret rolled her eyes. "As if you would know. You always look like you stepped out of a fashion magazine."

Colleen waved a finger at her. "You forget how I looked when I believed that Geoff was dead."

Margaret's brows arched. "Oh, yes, that's right."

"Well, that's a bit how you look right now." She slipped an arm around Margaret's shoulders. "And we're going to do something about it."

In just one hour, Margaret felt like a new person. Staring at the Cheval mirror in disbelief, she almost didn't recognize herself. "Oh my." She touched her hair, which Colleen had combed smooth along the sides, artfully piling the curls on top. Very stylish. "Was that hard to do?"

"Not with your natural waves." Colleen handed her a tissue. "Now blot your lipstick."

Margaret blotted her lips then studied her image even more closely. Colleen had loaned her a stylish aqua-blue dress with black trim, and she was now pinning a small velveteen black hat on top of her curls. "I don't know what to say." Margaret sighed. "I feel like someone else. I don't even dress this nicely to go to Mass."

"Well, maybe you should." Colleen handed Margaret a pair of sleek black gloves. "You're ready to go."

"Go where?"

"Anywhere. Just get outside and hold your head high. And remember that you're a beautiful young woman." Colleen looked at her watch. "It's just a little past four. I don't want you to come back until six."

"And what happens then?" Margaret asked. "Will my carriage turn into a pumpkin and my dress back to rags?"

Colleen laughed. "No. It's just that dinner will be ready. I'm cooking tonight." She gave her a gentle push toward the door. "Have fun."

Margaret couldn't help but giggle as she went down the stairs and walked through the quiet store. She felt a tiny bit guilty, like a kid playing hooky from school, as she unlocked the front door and slipped outside, where the afternoon sun was still shining. Unsure of what to do, she looked up and down the street, finally deciding to start her two-hour excursion with a cup of coffee. That would give her a chance to create some sort of plan. It felt odd to be wearing her good black heels as she walked the half block to Dottie's Diner. But, like Colleen had instructed, she held her head high.

"Good afternoon."

Margaret turned to see that Howard Moore was walking alongside her. "Oh, hello," she said, suddenly feeling self-conscious.

"You look as if you're off to some special event," he said as he kept stride. "Do you mind if I walk along with you?"

"Not at all." She smiled nervously. "And the truth is I'm not going anywhere special. Just out for a cup of coffee." She giggled. "My sister Colleen insisted on fixing me up and sending me out like this while she takes care of the baby. I actually feel a bit silly."

"You look lovely," he told her. "As a matter of fact, I was just longing for a cup of coffee myself. Mind if I join you?" He paused by Dottie's Diner, opening the door for her with a flourish. "After you, madam."

Margaret felt a bit uneasy as she slid into the booth. What would people think to see her—a married woman—having coffee with a gentleman who wasn't her husband? She hadn't actually told Howard that he could join her, but then she hadn't told him he couldn't either. As he sat down across from her, she quelled her guilt by reminding herself that this gentleman was much older... perhaps as old as Dad. Wasn't this sort of like having coffee with her father? And yet it didn't quite feel like that.

"How about pie?" Howard pointed to the glass pastry display on the counter. "I can personally attest to their lemon meringue—it's heavenly."

"Pie?" Margaret realized that, thanks to the rush at the store, she had barely touched her lunch. And before she could protest or change her mind, Howard was ordering them both pie and coffee.

"I hope you don't think I'm presumptuous," he said apologetically. "But it's been awhile since I've taken a pretty young lady out for coffee. And the truth is I've been a little lonely since moving to San Francisco. I go to work and come home and then do the same thing all over again. I know I should get out socially, but it's been hard. I suppose my heart hasn't been in it. Or maybe I'm just getting old."

"I know just how you feel," she confessed. "In fact, that's why my sister forced me to dress up and go out. She's convinced that I'm turning into an old lady."

He shook his head. "You do not look like any old ladies that I've seen."

She felt her face flushing. "Well, thank you." And now she began telling him about the busy day at the store and how they closed early. "All because of the article about Colleen in the newspaper."

"You must mean the story about Maureen Mulligan and her fiancé? The one in the *Chronicle* today? That's your sister, right?"

"Yes. I think I mentioned that Maureen is her stage name."

"I read all about it this morning. I thought that was your sister. She's a very beautiful girl." He smiled. "But then, why should that surprise me? I suspect that all you Mulligan ladies are good looking. Didn't you mention that you have three sisters?"

"Yes, there are four of us." Margaret's cheeks warmed with each compliment. "But Colleen is definitely the glamorous one in the family. Although some people think that our little sister Molly is the prettiest one of the bunch. She just turned seventeen—and she actually looks a lot like Colleen. Then there's Bridget—she's the army nurse. And she's very pretty too, although she has little interest in things like hair or fashion. At least she never used to, but then she met this doctor and..." Margaret paused as the waitress returned with their coffee and pie.

"I'm not sure why I'm such a chatterbox today," she said quietly. "I'm sorry."

"Please don't apologize, Margaret. I love hearing about your family. You don't know how starved I am for normal, everyday conversation. Tell me more."

So she talked more about her sisters and her parents, even telling him about the many challenges they'd faced these past couple of years. "But the hardest by far was losing Peter. I still can't believe it sometimes."

"I'm so sorry," he said solemnly. "I actually wanted to enlist after Pearl Harbor."

"Why didn't you?"

"Well, I was still married at the time, and my wife was opposed to me enlisting. By the time we divorced, I was getting close to the age limit." He grimaced. "I just turned thirty-seven last winter."

"Thirty-seven?"

He smiled sheepishly. "I don't feel that old. Not usually. You see, I was so involved in my career...and I married late in life. And then my marriage lasted less than five years." He shook his head. "And no children. So to sit here and confess I'm that old, well, it's hard to believe."

"You don't seem that old. Not that thirty-seven is old. I mean, well, you're only fourteen years older than me." She smiled nervously. "It's not like you're my parents' age." And now, feeling even more uncomfortable, Margaret changed the subject, but as she continued to blather away at him, she felt like she'd stepped over some invisible line. And although she was enjoying his company and her unexpected freedom, she suspected that it was wrong.

Eleven

Molly was counting the days until graduation. Unwilling to admit that she might've bitten off too much, she was determined to make it through the next three weeks without a single complaint. At least to her family. She was grateful for her friendship with Mrs. Bartley—and her neighbor's willingness to listen with a sympathetic ear. Although Molly sometimes worried that she'd wear out her welcome with the old woman, Mrs. Bartley always seemed eager and happy to see her.

"I'd like to invite you to go to the cinema with us tomorrow night," Molly told Mrs. Bartley on a sunny afternoon in mid-May. The two of them were taking a break after about an hour of weeding the victory garden.

"I don't want to intrude on your family." Mrs. Bartley leaned her hoe against the wall. "Although I was planning on going, I don't need to—"

"Please come with us," Molly insisted. "You're like family. You can ride with my parents and me. Colleen and Margaret and the baby will go from the store. And we'll meet the Hammonds at the theater. Colleen has a whole row reserved. It'll be like a party."

Mrs. Bartley smiled. "Then I'd love to go."

"Colleen wants us all to dress up. She is expecting the local press to be there."

"How is her campaign going?" Mrs. Bartley sat down on the garden bench. "Has she heard any news from the powers that be? Or anything from Geoff?"

Molly glumly shook her head. "But that's not stopping her. And we've all been writing letters to our congressmen."

"As have I." Mrs. Bartley removed her gardening gloves. "And I told my bridge group to do the same...and to spread the word."

"I wrote an article about it in my school newspaper, encouraging students to write letters too." She frowned. "Not that anyone listens to me at that school."

"It's only because you've outgrown them." Mrs. Bartley sighed. "Now tell me, what do you hear from your good friend Patrick?"

Molly smiled. She'd confided a lot to Mrs. Bartley. Including her confusing and often changing feelings toward Patrick. Sometimes she thought of Patrick as a sweet older brother...but other times, well, she hoped he was something more. "I just got a letter from him." She sat down on the porch steps. "And even though it was brief, the tone was warm and friendly. Patrick seems to have finally accepted my plan to graduate early from high school."

"I'm sure that Patrick recognizes your maturity, Molly." She frowned. "And you should feel honored that he takes time to write as much as he does. From everything I've read lately, it has gotten quite involved on the Pacific front."

"I know what you mean. Our Australian allies have taken a beating lately." Molly cringed to think how close some of the battles could possibly be to Bridget, but she really didn't want to think about it. Too scary.

"When I read of the brutalities, well, I am very grateful that the

United States is so far from Japan." Mrs. Bartley grimly shook her head. "Otherwise, I'm sure we'd be suffering on the home front." She slowly pushed herself to her feet. "Well, my old bones are getting weary, Molly. And since I've got a big night to look forward to tomorrow, I think I will call it a day."

Colleen felt a tiny bit guilty for talking Margaret into hiring a baby-sitter for Peter on Saturday night. "It's not that I don't love my darling nephew," she told Margaret as she pulled on her white fur stole. "It's just that I felt certain you would enjoy yourself more if you weren't distracted with a baby. Besides..." She pointed to the black gown she'd loaned Margaret. "I don't want him spitting up on that."

"It's just that I've never left him before. Not with anyone besides family." Margaret frowned as she locked the back door.

"We've all known Sally McCormick and her parents for ages," Colleen reminded her. "Everyone says she's the best baby-sitter in town."

"I know, but what if something goes wrong while we're out?"

"Nothing will go wrong. And you left the number for the theater right by the phone." Colleen concealed her exasperation. They'd already had this conversation several times today. "This is good practice for you, Margaret. You can't always depend on family to watch Peter. Mam is busy with Dad. Molly is busy with everything. And, as you know, I'll be heading back to Hollywood next week."

Margaret let out a loud groan. "Don't remind me."

"Sorry." Colleen smiled inwardly. She'd been so thrilled to get the phone call from the Knight Agency yesterday evening—a movie contract with Pinnacle had finally been offered. Georgina had happily assured her that the delay had nothing to do with Colleen, but everything to do with the stars, Barry Coltaire and Laurel Wagner. Nothing could be nailed down until the famous dancing duo signed on. "But it's all come together beautifully," Georgina had gushed. "Leon is directing again. And Barry and Laurel both think you're absolutely adorable. They can't wait to work with you."

"I know you're over the moon about your new film," Margaret said sullenly as Colleen drove toward downtown. "And I'll try not to be a wet blanket, but I'm going to miss you."

"I know." Colleen patted her sister's hand. "I'll miss you and Baby Peter too. It's been so fun being together these past few weeks. I'm so glad we had all that time, Margaret."

For a while, neither of them spoke. Colleen knew that Margaret was feeling blue, but the truth was Colleen was hugely relieved to have a new project to look forward to. Besides bringing in some much-needed income, it would help to distract her from worrying about Geoff. Although his family still claimed that no news was good news, she still wasn't sure. So much so that, like Margaret, she had started to avoid reading the newspapers or listening to the radio. A bad habit that needed to be stopped.

"So this new role…" Margaret's tone was tentative. "Will it be bigger than your last film?" Colleen could tell that her sister was trying to be a good sport.

"That's what Georgina said, although I haven't seen the script yet. But with Barry and Laurel starring—well, I just know it'll be much better than the last picture. I can't tell you how relieved I am not to be stuck with Darla again."

"She sounds like such a nasty person."

"Only in person." Colleen chuckled. "She's so sweet on the screen that, as Rory Knight likes to say, sugar won't even melt in her mouth."

Margaret chuckled. "Well, I'm looking forward to seeing this movie tonight."

"So am I," Colleen declared. "Even more so than the premiere in Hollywood."

"Really?"

"Absolutely. For one thing, Darla won't be there. And my family will be. Besides that, I've invited the press, and I'm really hoping that they'll continue to push sympathetic stories about Geoff and the other prisoners."

Margaret sighed loudly. "You don't really think it'll make any difference, do you?"

Colleen gripped the steering wheel more tightly. "I don't know, but I hope so." She pulled up to a valet parking lot a few blocks from the theater. After instructing the young man, she and Margaret got into the backseat. "It's not exactly a limo," she whispered to Margaret as the man drove the short ways to the theater, "but better than hoofing it from the parking lot."

"It looks like your press is here," Margaret said as the car stopped in front of the theater.

"Here we go." Colleen emerged from the car as if it were a limousine and, with Margaret trailing her, waved to the press and was soon answering their questions and smiling for eager photographers. Amidst the photographers was her own little sister. Dressed in the sapphire blue gown that Colleen had given her last year, Molly had her own camera aimed and ready. Colleen struck a couple of good poses for Molly, and then, thanking them all for coming, she politely excused herself and her entourage to go into the theater.

Molly felt slightly star-struck—by her very own sister—when the film ended and the house lights came on. Everyone in the theater was clapping and cheering as the manager made his way to the front. "Wasn't that a wonderful film?" he said into the microphone that someone had set up. "As many of you know, our very own Maureen Mulligan from San Francisco played such a wonderful role in the movie. But perhaps you didn't know that we have the famous Miss Mulligan here with us tonight." He pointed at Colleen. "Would you mind coming up to say a few words?"

Colleen was already on her feet, gracefully making her way toward him to an even more enthusiastic applause.

"Isn't this exciting?" Molly whispered to Mrs. Bartley. The old woman simply nodded with wide-eyed interest as Colleen stepped up to the microphone, thanking the manager.

"And I want to personally thank each and every one of you for coming out to see this movie tonight," Colleen said graciously. "As you just saw, tonight's story was about patriotism, serving one's country, and sacrificing for the better good of the people. I can't even begin to describe what an honor it was to participate in such a fine film. As I told a reporter one time, it felt a bit like life imitating art—or art imitating life." And now she told them about Peter losing his life at Pearl Harbor. And about the Hammond brothers—one serving in the Pacific and the other on the European front. And finally, she told them about Geoff's imprisonment. "And as you probably know, the Japanese are in complete violation of the Geneva Conventions. They have no regard for humanitarian treatment of prisoners of war. For that reason, I have been pleading with our congressmen to do everything in their power to encourage the freedom and release of our prisoners." She held up her hands. "I know I'm just one woman, but I am determined to keep raising my voice in the hope that it will help our boys over there, either to receive more humane treatment or to be released. I pray that you will do the same. Because, as we all know, this war will be won both on the battlefield and on the home front. Thank you to everyone for doing your part." She grinned. "And, oh yeah, buy war bonds!"

The theater erupted into fresh and lively applause as Colleen returned to her seat. Soon they were all exiting the theater, and Molly could not have been more proud of her older sister. Even though Molly had no desire to become a film actress, she hoped that she would one day grow up to do something as powerful and beautiful as Colleen.

Colleen left for Hollywood the following Monday, and by Thursday afternoon Margaret felt lonelier than ever. She missed Colleen's help and companionship in the store and her involvement with the baby. But most of all she missed their little visits in the evenings—so much so that she almost wished Colleen had never come home at all. Her rationale was that it was hard to miss something you've never had.

Before her departure, Colleen made Margaret promise to have Sally baby-sit Peter once a week. "So you can get out and have some fun," Colleen had insisted, in her usual bossy fashion. And then she'd gone ahead and lined up Sally to baby-sit on Thursday evenings from six until eight. And she'd even pre-paid the teenager!

"Just call a girlfriend or Molly," Colleen had suggested to Margaret. "Or go to a movie. Or go dance your feet off at the USO."

But Margaret didn't really have a girlfriend she could call up like that. And Molly had a night class on Thursdays. And to go to a movie or the USO by herself? Forget it. But here it was Thursday and Sally was sitting at the kitchen table, spooning food into Peter. Margaret had even tried to talk Sally out of it, but the stubborn girl insisted that since she'd already paid her and was already here, Margaret should just go.

"I'll be in the neighborhood," Margaret said awkwardly as she picked up her purse. "Maybe at Dottie's Diner—in case you need to reach me."

"We'll be fine," Sally assured her.

"And I'd appreciate it if you didn't put him to bed too early. Stretch him out before his last bottle. He's been waking up too early for his three o'clock feeding."

"Okay." Sally nodded.

And so Margaret, still wearing her work clothes—which had improved somewhat thanks to Colleen's fashion help—exited the store feeling slightly lost. For a moment, she just stood there and, without any other particular plan, headed down toward Dottie's. A piece of lemon pie sounded rather nice, or perhaps she would splurge and order a hamburger. She glanced up at the apartment building across the street, nervously wondering if Howard might be up there, perhaps looking down on her right now. She hoped not. Hastening her pace, she quickly made her way into the diner and, sliding into a booth by the window, she picked up the menu.

She had just decided on the hamburger when she heard a tapping sound. She looked up to see Howard standing outside the diner, smiling down on her. He pointed to his chest and then to the seat across from her, mouthing the words "Can I join you?" Part of her knew she should say no, but the rest of her simply smiled and nodded. And suddenly he was taking off his hat and sliding into the booth.

"I'm so happy to see you," he said eagerly. "I've had to work late for every single night this past week, but I've wanted to come into the store and talk to you."

"Talk to me?" She laid down the menu.

"Yes. I saw the article in the paper on Sunday morning, the one about your sister's movie and how she and your family had all gone to opening night, and her challenge to everyone to do their part for the war effort. Very nice."

"Colleen really did a great job talking to the audience that night."

"So I went to see the movie myself on Sunday night."

"Oh, good." She nodded. "Did you like it?"

"Very much. That's why I wanted to stop in and chat with you, to tell you how much I liked it." He smiled sheepishly. "And, of course, I hoped I could meet your sister."

Margaret let out a deflated sigh. "Colleen's gone back to Hollywood." She told him about the new movie contract. "She was thrilled about it. But I have to confess, I was really sad to see her go. I miss her so much." Now she explained about Colleen's arrangement to have a weekly baby-sitter on Thursday nights. "So even though I had nothing to do, no one to see, I had to leave." She glanced down the street toward the store, almost as if she expected to see a fire engine tearing down the street toward it. "I told Sally she could call me here if she needed me." She shrugged. "I suppose that's silly."

"That's just being a good and responsible mother," he said gently.

The waitress came, and they both ordered hamburgers and coffee. "And lemon meringue pie for dessert," Howard added with a sly grin.

Margaret knew that, as a married woman, she should feel guilty for having dinner with a man who wasn't her husband, but she was having such a good time visiting with him that those feelings seemed to melt away. Besides, this wasn't about romance. They were simply two lonely people enjoying some much-needed companionship. What was wrong with that?

In fact, she decided as Howard was walking her back to the store, she would even write to Brian about it. She had nothing to hide. Thinking of Brian reminded her that he had barely written to her these past two months. Oh, he claimed it was because there was little time to write, but sometimes she wondered. She'd seen movies about servicemen getting involved with women in foreign countries. What if Brian had been caught up in something like that?

"Penny for your thoughts?" Howard said as they paused in front of the store.

Margaret glanced at the streetlamp that had just lit up on the corner. "My thoughts?" She wrinkled her nose. "Oh, I doubt that they're even worth a penny."

He chuckled. "Well, I enjoyed my evening tonight. Thank you."

"Thank you for paying for my dinner." She shook her head. "But you really didn't need to do that."

"I wanted to do that."

"Well, it wasn't a date," she reminded him.

"Yes, you made that clear. I know that you're a happily married woman with a child. But that doesn't mean we can't be friends, does it?"

She considered this. "No, I guess not."

He stuck out his hand. "Here's to friends."

She shook it. "To friends."

"Good night, Margaret." He tipped his hat.

"Good night." She turned away, sliding her key into the lock. But after she let herself into the store, locking the door behind her, she felt surprisingly shaky inside. What was she getting herself into? But hearing Peter crying upstairs jerked her back to the present and, running up the stairs, she burst into the apartment to see what was wrong.

"Is he okay?" she breathlessly asked Sally, who was just sitting down in the rocking chair with Peter. Dressed in his sleepers, Peter looked clean and well cared for, and the bottle quieted him right down.

"He's fine." Sally looked up with a calm expression. "Remember, you told me to stretch him out before bedtime? He just started voicing his hunger a few minutes ago. But he's perfectly fine."

Margaret nodded as she laid down her purse and sat down across from them. "Thanks for doing that. I'm impressed you could stretch him this long. It's nearly eight."

"Hopefully you'll get a longer night's sleep now." Sally handed Peter over to Margaret. "Did you have fun tonight?"

Margaret felt her cheeks flush to recall her evening spent with Howard. "Oh, I didn't really do much. Just got a bite to eat and walked around a bit, but it was fine." She looked down at Peter, watching him contentedly sucking on the bottle. She felt guilty as Sally gathered her things to leave. And although she hadn't lied just now, she felt deceitful...and confused...and knew she needed to go to confession.

Twelve

Molly felt sick as she read the headline of the Sunday newspaper. Without going back into the house, she sat down on the front step and continued to read the entire heartbreaking article. By the time she finished reading, she had tears streaking down her cheeks.

"Molly?" Mrs. Bartley called from down on the sidewalk. "Whatever is wrong, dear?"

Molly went down the steps. "Did you hear about this?" She held up the paper for Mrs. Bartley to read.

"Oh, my." Mrs. Bartley's eyes grew wide. "Is that really true? The Japanese sank a hospital ship?"

"Yes." Molly nodded grimly. "At first I was afraid it might involve Bridget—you know, because the *Centaur* was a hospital ship. Although Bridget hasn't written about serving aboard a ship, but then you never know, she's always getting moved around. Anyway, the *Centaur* was an Australian ship. It was transporting more than two hundred wounded servicemen. Our Australian allies."

Mrs. Bartley handed her a lace-trimmed handkerchief. "How tragic."

"And there were doctors and nurses onboard too. And the crew. It says more than three hundred aboard. With only around sixty survivors." Molly blotted her cheeks.

"Was the ship properly marked?"

"Yes." Molly angrily shook the newspaper. "It was clearly marked with a wide green stripe and red crosses all around—on every side. And the ship was sunk at night, but because it was a medical ship, supposedly protected by the Geneva Conventions, it had all its spotlights so that it could be easily seen from a distance and not mistaken as a military ship. But the Japanese submarine torpedoed it just the same." She handed back the hanky.

"Well, everyone knows that the Imperial Japanese military has no regard for the Geneva Conventions." Mrs. Bartley sadly shook her head. "I suppose we should not be surprised that they would sink an innocent hospital ship. As sad as it is, our enemies do not play by fair rules, Molly." Mrs. Bartley slipped an arm around her shoulders. "But we can be thankful that our dear Bridget was not aboard the ill-fated *Centaur.*"

Molly bit her lip. "Yes...except this makes me feel even more worried for Bridget. If the Japanese have no regard for a hospital ship, what will stop them from dropping bombs on clearly marked hospital units that are located on the ground?"

"I don't know." Mrs. Bartley sighed. "But I'm on my way to church right now...and I will say a special prayer for Bridget."

"Thank you. I need to get ready for Mass too." She grimaced. "Do you think it would be wrong to hide this newspaper until afterward? I know it will upset Mam...and probably Dad too."

Mrs. Bartley smiled sadly. "I don't think it would do any harm to save this bad news for later."

Colleen's campaign to put pressure on Washington to do something to help prisoners of war did gain some positive attention, but as far as she knew, nothing had really changed. However, as Geoff's grandfather had pointed out in a recent phone conversation, they still hadn't received any bad news about Geoff. "We can't give up hope," he'd told her. "And we all appreciate everything you've done to help, Colleen. Even Ellen has expressed some gratitude for your Hollywood connections."

Just two weeks into the new movie, Colleen was thoroughly enjoying the experience. Although this picture wasn't an upbeat musical like the last one, it was actually more fun. But that was probably due to Barry Coltaire and Laurel Wagner. The congenial couple had made more than a dozen films together, and it showed in how few takes it required to nail a scene. Everyone liked that. Even Leon, the director, seemed to be in much better spirits these days.

Consummate professionals, Barry and Laurel were not only easier to work with than Darla and Robert, they were helpful to Colleen. She really felt like she was learning a lot. Even at the end of a long day, she never felt worn out like she had on the previous movie. She felt like she could do this kind of work indefinitely. Although this film, since it wasn't a musical, would probably wrap up in about half the time. According to Leon, they would be finished by mid-July. Of course, this meant little time off, but for the most part, Colleen didn't mind. It gave her less opportunity to fret over Geoff. But today was the first Friday in June, and Colleen was feeling a bit blue.

"What's troubling you?" Stella asked as Colleen sank into the chair.

"Does it show?" Colleen smiled stiffly.

Stella nodded as she started pinning her hair into place.

"It's not anything big," Colleen confessed. "My little sister is graduating from high school tonight, and I just wish I could be there."

"Oh, that's too bad, doll. Even if we finished filming by six, which is doubtful, you probably wouldn't be able to fly up there in time."

"No. I already considered that. And then I'd have to be back here by seven o'clock tomorrow morning. I already told Molly that I'd be with her in spirit."

"Well, that Molly has a good head on her shoulders. I could tell by just the little time I spent with her. I'm sure she'll understand." She poked Colleen in the shoulder. "And I'll bet you sent her something nice."

"I got her a set of luggage with her monogram on it." Colleen chuckled. "When Molly visited me, she had some old pieces from our parents. I'm sure the big suitcase must've come over from Ireland with my dad."

"I bet she'll love your gift. And she can use it to come down and visit you."

"That's exactly what I told her," Colleen said. "An airplane ticket will be part of my gift."

"You're a good sister."

Colleen couldn't help but laugh. "It's funny to hear you say that. A couple years ago, no one ever thought I'd grow up to be a good sister."

"Were you the black sheep of the family?"

"How did you guess?"

"You'd be surprised at how many actresses have told me that very thing, Maureen. Not that I'll repeat any of their names. Over the years, I've learned to honor client privilege in my work."

Colleen chuckled. "Just like a lawyer."

"Except for the pay."

"Telegram for Colleen Mulligan," one of the assistants was calling out. "Is there a Colleen Mulligan—"

"That's me!" Colleen jumped from the chair, waving to the assistant. "I'm Colleen Maureen Mulligan." She suddenly reached for Stella's hand. "Oh, no—what if it's bad news."

"Easy does it," Stella told her as the assistant came over.

"Only my parents and Geoff's parents would know the address of this studio," Colleen told Stella. "Oh, I hope this isn't about Dad." She signed for the telegram with a trembling hand. "He's got a weak heart."

"Just take a nice deep breath," Stella said calmly.

But Colleen's hands were shaking so much that she couldn't get it open. She handed the telegram to Stella. "Please, can you?"

"Certainly." Stella used a fingernail file to carefully slit open the telegram. "Want me to read it to you?"

"Would you?" Colleen still clutched the older woman's arm, fearing for the worst. If it wasn't bad news about Dad, it might be that Geoff's family had received bad news from the War Department. They had promised to be in contact if they heard anything.

"Colleen," Stella began. "News on Geoff. His camp liberated. Geoff recovering in Honolulu. More to come later. Ellen."

"He's been freed!" Colleen yelled. "Geoff is coming home!"

Several of the cast and crew gathered around now, anxious to hear her good news. She read the telegram out loud for everyone to hear. And when she finished, they all let out a happy cheer.

"I can't believe it," she told Stella when she finally calmed down enough to sit back in the chair. "Geoff is coming home. Geoff is okay."

"Well, let's hope he's okay." Stella grimaced. "I mean, I don't want to rain on your parade, doll, but the boy's been in a Japanese prison camp for how long?"

"More than a year."

"Yes, that's my point. He might not be in such good health. You'd better be prepared for that."

"That's true. But he's alive," Colleen declared. "He's alive—and he's coming home."

"Yes. He's alive and coming home. You're right. We should be celebrating that."

As Stella worked on her hair, Colleen wondered just what sort of shape Geoff would be in. She knew that the prison camps were brutal. Besides malnutrition and diseases, it was possible that Geoff had been tortured. She'd heard of men coming home with missing appendages or even limbs as a result of Japanese guards' cruel treatment. Well, she decided, even if Geoff came home severely changed, she would still love him just as much. And just like she'd promised in the stack of letters that she hoped he'd be reading soon, she would still want to marry him. And that was that.

Molly could hardly believe it—she would graduate from high school tonight! She'd passed all her college classes and her high school equivalency tests, the hard work was over, and she would finally be free. But as she walked to her locker for the last time, she felt a tiny wave of sadness. What if she had been wrong to hurry things along by graduating a year early? What if she'd regret stepping out into the grown-up world?

Before she turned down the hallway where her locker was located, she heard a couple of guys in a heated argument, but when she strained her ears to hear what was the matter, she had to just roll her eyes. They were practically coming to blows over which baseball team was better. Really? In a world where young men were dying overseas, these guys wanted to argue over the Yankees and the Dodgers?

As she came to her locker, the usual bunch of girls were clustered together—the ones who liked to give her the mean looks or snicker behind her back. The same clique that her former best friend Dottie had been recruited into...at about the same time that Molly had been cast aside. Today they actually seemed to be waiting for her and, judging by their expressions, it wasn't to congratulate her for her upcoming graduation.

"There she is," Barb Phillips said snidely. "Well, I hope she knows we won't miss her around here next year." Barb was the leader of these girls. Molly had known her since grade school, but they'd never been friends.

As usual, Molly ignored them as she opened her locker. Fortunately, there wasn't much in here to take home today, but she hurried to shove what was left into her book bag. The sooner she got out of here, the happier she would be. She was just about to leave when Barb came over, blocking her way.

"You think you're better than everyone, don't you, Molly?" Barb narrowed her eyes. "Just because your sister is famous and because you—"

"That's enough," Dottie said sharply. "Leave her alone."

Barb looked slightly shocked. "Well, well... Dottie Harris, I thought you'd learned that Molly is bad news. I can't believe you're—"

"You're just jealous of Molly," Dottie declared. "And I'm sick of it, Barb. And I'm sick of you."

Barb's eyes narrowed. "Wait until I tell Bill about—"

"Go ahead and tell Bill whatever you like," Dottie shot back at her. "I broke up with him today. For all I care, you can have him."

She glared at Barb. "You'd like that, wouldn't you? Especially since you don't even have a boyfriend." Dottie linked arms with Molly. "As for Molly, she *is* better than you. Better than all of you! I'm sorry I lost track of that." She turned to Molly. "Come on, let's go."

Molly was too stunned to talk, but she allowed Dottie to lead her toward the front door. "I'm sorry," Dottie said quietly. "For everything. I know I've been the worst friend ever to you. I can't believe I sacrificed our friendship for a stupid boy. But what I said is true—I did break up with Bill today. I'm just sorry I didn't break up with him months ago." She looked hopefully at Molly. "I hope you'll forgive me."

Molly blinked back tears as she nodded. "Of course I forgive you, Dottie."

"I really am sorry," Dottie said again. "Really, really sorry."

"It's okay," Molly assured her as they went outside.

"I can't believe you're graduating," Dottie said sadly. "I sure wish you weren't."

"It's taken a lot of work, but I'm really glad I did it."

"You know what I wish, Molly? I wish I was graduating with you." Dottie sighed. "I can't believe I have to put up with all that for a whole 'nother year."

"Just pick some better friends next fall." Molly knew that was easier said than done.

"There won't be any friends as good as you," Dottie declared.

"Thanks for saying so." Molly paused to hug Dottie. "And we'll still be friends. It's just that I'll be going to college and working at the store."

As they walked toward home, they got caught up on a lot of things and, although Molly appreciated that Dottie wanted to restore their friendship, she could see that they'd grown apart since last fall.

Dottie talked a lot about her relationship with Bill, making Molly suspect that it wasn't really over. In fact, Dottie seemed confused about a lot of things. By the time Molly got home, she was relieved to say good-bye.

"Thanks for standing up for me today," Molly told her. "And if those girls have any sense, I'll bet that they respect you for it."

Dottie shrugged. "Not if Barb has anything to say about it. And, believe me, she will."

"I'm guessing there will always be some Barbs in this world," Molly told her. "But you have to learn to move past them, Dottie. Just keep going forward and choose what's best for you. Eventually it'll work out."

"You grew up faster than the rest of us," Dottie said with a somber expression. "I've sometimes thought it was because of losing Peter. I think it made you older somehow."

"How's your brother?" Molly asked. "Is Warren doing okay?"

"So far so good." Dottie sighed. "But you never know."

Molly hugged her again. "Well, I'll keep him in my prayers."

"Congratulations on graduating tonight."

"Thanks!" Molly smiled and waved, hurrying into the house.

"Molly Irene!" Dad exclaimed as soon as she got in the door. "We just got some news."

"What is it?" She hurried over to where Dad was standing next to the telephone table with an odd expression. "Is it anything bad?"

"No, no. It's good. Very good." Dad sat down in his chair with a happy smile. "Colleen just called. She got a telegram today. Geoff has been liberated from the Japanese prison camp. He's in Honolulu right now. Can you believe it?"

Molly dumped her book bag to the floor then bent down to hug Dad. "That's the most wonderful news, Dad. The very best news!"

"I've not heard such joy in Colleen's voice for more than a year." Dad sighed.

"When will Geoff come home?"

"Colleen doesn't know, but she promised to keep us informed."

"This is the best graduation present ever!" Molly began dancing around the living room, singing loudly, while Dad laughed. It was truly a happy day.

Thirteen

fter graduation, Dad insisted that Molly enjoy a full week of complete freedom with no responsibilities whatsoever. After sleeping in and lazing around on Monday, she got up early on Tuesday, putting all her energy into weeding the victory garden. The next morning she met Prudence for coffee, listening to her complain about her boring summer job washing dishes at a busy restaurant. "But it'll help with my college tuition," Prudence finally admitted. "If I don't throw in the towel first."

"You need something to get your mind off of your work." Molly told her about how writing to her friends in the military had helped her get through what was actually a rather stressful year. "There's something about writing a cheerful letter that puts you in a cheerful state of mind."

"I don't have anyone to write to...anymore."

Molly suddenly remembered that Prudence had lost a brother in this war too. "Well, I have more than enough people to write to." Molly quickly told her about the boy she'd met at the USO. "Tommy was so lonely and frightened, about to deport. He grew up in an orphanage, so he doesn't have any—" She grabbed Prudence by the arm. "That's it!"

"What's it?"

"You can start writing to Tommy."

"Why me?"

"Because you're my friend. And Tommy doesn't have anyone. And if you start sending him letters, I won't need to write so many. Oh, please, Prudence, say you will."

Prudence reluctantly agreed. "I guess I could give it a try."

She grinned. "Who knows? You might discover you like him. He's awfully sweet. Anyway, you can get to know him through letters to find out. And you can send him a photo and—"

"A photo of me?" Prudence looked horrified. "That'll scare him off for sure."

Molly studied her friend, trying to see her the way Colleen might. "What if we fixed you up some?" she offered. "Then I could take your picture, and you could send it to Tommy." By the end of the day, Prudence—looking like a whole new girl—was posing for Molly's camera and promising to do her best to become Tommy's new pen pal.

But by Thursday morning, Molly felt antsy. "I can't think of anything else to do with my spare time," she told her parents at breakfast. "And I'm afraid I'm about to get really bored." She smiled hopefully at Mam. It hadn't escaped Molly's notice that her mother seemed haggard and weary lately. "So if you don't mind, I'd like to go in to the store for you today."

"But you promised Dad you'd—"

"I want to go to the store," Molly protested. "Besides, I haven't spent time with my nephew for quite a while. Plus Margaret and I need to catch up." She held up the V-mail letter she'd received from Bridget yesterday. "And I can share this with her. Margaret will be so excited to hear Bridget's news."

"What about writing to Bridget?" Dad asked Molly. "Have you told her Colleen's news yet?"

"Yes." Molly nodded firmly. "I wrote about that to both her and Patrick a few days ago."

"Well..." Mam held up her hands. "If you really want to work at the store, I won't stop you." She turned to Dad. "To be honest, I wouldn't mind spending the day at home."

"Great." Molly eagerly stood. "And I won't take the car." She grabbed her purse. "It's such a nice day, I'll just walk." As she walked toward the store, Molly felt surprisingly light and happy. And for sure, she had several things to be happy about. For starters, she was done with high school and night classes. Besides that, Colleen's Geoff would soon be home. Or at least in San Diego. According to Colleen, the navy planned to transport him to the naval hospital there, which would be convenient for Colleen. But the frosting on Molly's happy cake was that Bridget was coming home for leave. Not until mid-July, but that was only a little over a month away. What a joyous reunion they all would have!

"Molly!" Margaret exclaimed as Molly came in through the back door. "What're you doing here?"

Molly explained as she tucked her purse in the closet. "I'm not used to sitting around so much," she confessed. "And Mam seems tired."

"I know." Margaret was about to set Peter down into the playpen.

"Wait a minute." Molly went over to extract the baby from her arms. "I need some nephew time here."

"You're more than welcome to him," Margaret said. "But I'll warn you, he's teething. And he can get a little grumpy."

"You won't be grumpy with Auntie Molly, will you?" She cooed at him, making him smile. "Oh, yeah!" Molly nodded toward her skirt pocket. "There's a letter there, Margaret. From Bridget."

Margaret extracted the V-mail, eagerly reading it then letting out a happy shriek that made Peter jump. "She's coming home!" Margaret exclaimed. "Our long-lost Bridget is coming home."

"Only for two weeks," Molly reminded her. "But we'll make the most of it. And I talked to Colleen last night. She said that Geoff is being transported to San Diego right now. He might be there as soon as this weekend. She's so excited."

"I wonder what kind of shape he'll be in." Margaret carefully refolded the letter, sliding it back into Molly's pocket. "After more than a year in prison camp."

Molly nodded somberly. "Colleen sounded a little worried too. Apparently he'll need to be hospitalized for a while."

Margaret checked her watch then jingled her keys. "Well, I'm thrilled you're here, Molly, and I'd love to catch up with you, but it's opening time and I haven't even done the till yet."

Molly took the keys. "You get the till, and Peter and I will get the door."

It was fun working with Margaret and, because the store was fairly busy, the time passed quickly. Much more quickly than it had been passing at home the past few days. And, before she knew it, Margaret announced it was closing time. Together they took care of the usual chores, and then Molly scooped up Peter. "Now we can catch up," she said as she headed for the stairs.

"Oh?" Margaret looked surprised. "You're not going home?"

"No," Molly said happily. "I get to stick around and visit with you now. It's been so long since we've had time together. I thought I might even spend the night. We can fix something for dinner and—"

"But this is my night out."

Molly frowned. "Your night out?"

Margaret looked uneasy. "Oh, it's something Colleen set up for me when she was here. She hired Sally McCormick to come watch Peter for me. Just one night a week. So, you see, Thursday is my night out."

"That's great. You and I can go do something together. We could get some dinner and go to the USO or take—"

"I don't think so." Margaret pursed her lips.

"Oh, do you have other plans?" Molly waited with curiosity. Margaret had always been more of a homebody. She worked at the store then spent evenings at home. She'd never been one to do much with friends. In fact, she used to give Colleen a bad time for being such a gadabout.

"Well, I, uh, I sort of do have other plans." Margaret grimaced. "I hope you don't mind."

"No, of course not." Molly considered this. Why was Margaret acting so strangely?

"So, I, uh, I probably should get ready." Margaret reached for Peter. "Sorry."

"That's okay." Molly smiled. "Maybe I can spend another night here—I mean, if you're not too busy."

Margaret let out a laugh. "I'm never too busy. Well, except for Thursdays."

"So maybe tomorrow then?" Molly suggested.

"Yes. Tomorrow is perfect."

As Margaret walked Molly to the front door, she chattered in what seemed a nervous sort of way. "See you tomorrow?" she asked as she prepared to lock the door behind Molly.

"Sure." Molly nodded. "Mam doesn't know it yet, but she's the one who'll be taking a forced vacation now." She waved to Margaret and

Peter and then turned to walk away. But something about this night out business felt wrong. It wasn't that Molly didn't think Margaret needed a free evening. But why was she acting so odd about it? Unless Molly was imagining things, her older sister was feeling guilty about something. And, naturally, that made Molly suspicious.

Molly walked a short distance before she suddenly remembered her conversation with Mam this afternoon. She had told her mother that she planned to stick around and have dinner with Margaret tonight. So knowing Mam and Dad weren't expecting her, Molly decided to pop into Dottie's Diner and get a bite. And, probably because there was an investigative reporter inside of her, Molly took a table by the window—with a clear view of the store. She had no idea what she expected to see, but she was determined to watch.

It was nearly six when Molly spotted Sally knocking on the front door of the store and, after a bit, the door opened and Sally went inside. Well, so far that matched what Margaret had told her. But where was Margaret going off to—and so mysteriously? Would Molly be willing to follow her? And if she was, could she be discreet enough not to be noticed? And, really, wasn't this all pretty silly?

Feeling embarrassed for being such a nosy busybody, Molly paid her check and was about to leave when she noticed a man loitering outside of the store. Dressed in a dark suit and hat, he checked his watch then glanced up at the upstairs front window with an expectant look. Molly couldn't really get a look at his face, but even from a distance, she could tell that he was an attractive man. But what was he doing there?

Molly stayed just inside the door, curiously staring out the window. Margaret emerged from the store. Dressed in a pink-and-white striped dress and looking surprisingly pretty, Margaret smiled at the man and, just like that, the two of them walked away together.

Molly was too stunned to even think straight. What on earth was going on? Why was Margaret going out with a strange man? Who was he? And what about Brian? Molly felt sick inside.

"Do you need something else?" the waitress asked her.

"No, no thank you." Molly forced a smile. "Just thinking."

"Have a good evening."

"Thanks," Molly muttered as she watched the image of her sister and the strange man growing smaller. They were headed for town and, although Molly wanted to know more, something inside her told her not to follow them. Instead, she turned toward home with a dejected heart, attempting to make sense of what she'd just witnessed.

Colleen felt certain that it wasn't because of her that the movie production suddenly took two days off. And it was simply a coincidence that she was getting this unexpected free weekend shortly after she heard the news that Geoff was scheduled to arrive in San Diego on Friday. Really, she didn't have that much clout. Just the same, she was over the moon with gratitude.

"You give that boy a hug for me," Stella told Colleen as they were packing up to leave.

"Oh, I will," Colleen promised as she gathered her things. "I'll run home, throw a few things in a bag, and drive directly there. I think I can make it by eight."

"And you've got someone to stay with down there?" Stella asked in a motherly way.

"No, but I can get a hotel."

"Oh, doll, don't be so sure about that." Stella grimly shook her head. "My sister Lil lives in San Diego, and she claims that, ever since the war started, there's hardly any vacancies anywhere. She even rents out her spare room to a sailor's wife."

"Oh?" Colleen frowned.

"But she might be able to put you up on her couch," Stella offered hesitantly. "Although I'll warn you she's got three teenage boys, and they can raise an awful ruckus. I stayed there a few days last year, and I wouldn't exactly call it restful."

"I guess I could wait and drive down there tomorrow and—" Colleen paused as Laurel came over to join them.

"Nice work today." Laurel patted Colleen on the back. "Your last scene looked just about perfect."

"Thanks." Colleen attempted a smile.

"But I thought you'd be halfway to your young man by now," Laurel teased. "What're you waiting for, darling?"

"Stella was just telling me how hard it is to find lodging in San Diego." Colleen frowned. "I might need to wait and drive down tomorrow morning and return later that night."

"You mean you don't have any place to stay down there?" Laurel asked.

Colleen just shook her head.

"Then you'll have to use my little beach house."

"Really?"

"You bet. Now, it's not fancy, but it's comfy." Laurel pulled a notepad from her bag and quickly wrote something down. "The key is under the flowerpot by the front door. The one with a little palm plant in it." She handed her the note. "Here's the address."

"Really?" Colleen felt close to tears. "I don't know what to say."

"Just say you're on your way, darling." Laurel hugged her. "Your young man is waiting."

Colleen felt like she was floating as she drove to her apartment.

Was it possible she was really going to see Geoff tonight? Or perhaps it would be too late for visiting hours by the time she arrived... but at least she could leave him a note telling him that she'd be in first thing tomorrow morning. She carelessly tossed clothes into a suitcase and was back in her car just a few minutes after six, driving due south toward San Diego.

As she drove along the beautiful Pacific coastline, Colleen tried to imagine what this reunion would be like. So far, she knew nothing regarding Geoff's condition. In fact, she'd yet to even speak to him. During her break earlier today, shortly after she got the telegram informing her of his transport to San Diego, she'd called Geoff's family. Although Ellen was thrilled to hear that Geoff would soon be stateside, she still hadn't heard anything specific about her son. "I hope he's all right," she'd said nervously. "Give him our love, and tell him that we'll take the train down there as soon as we can. Maybe by Monday if all goes well." Colleen promised to do that, as well as to be in touch as soon as she knew more.

A multitude of questions jostled around in Colleen's head as she drove. The biggest one—would he be okay? She tried not to dwell on the disturbing stories she'd heard about returning servicemen—sad tales of missing limbs, lost eyesight, disfiguring burns, paralysis, devastating diseases... it was all very troubling. On a lesser scale, but equally worrisome—what if Geoff came home severely changed? What if he was no longer the same happy, carefree spirit that she'd fallen in love with? And, really, how could she expect him to be unchanged? After all, she was changed, and she hadn't even been to war.

Aside from being jaded or depressed or apathetic—all understandable reactions to a cruel imprisonment—he could be psychologically damaged. He could be suffering from shellshock or battle fatigue. She'd heard of bad cases where veterans had to be institutionalized for long periods of time. What would she do then?

As much as she hated to admit it, even if only to herself, she was extremely worried about one particular possibility. A very selfish one too. What if Geoff had fallen out of love with her? How would she handle *that?* After all this time of worrying and waiting...and the months of deeply grieving. Throughout everything, Geoff had seemed such a huge part of her life that it was difficult to imagine how she would feel if he was done with her. Or if he'd outgrown her. Oh, she knew that she was a flibbertigibbet. At least she always had been...she'd been trying to change. But what if Geoff had grown up and realized that she wasn't right for him after all?

Colleen knew he'd never had the chance to receive some of her earlier letters—messages that could've easily been misread. But it's possible that he had suspected as much about her. What if he'd woken up one morning with the realization that their relationship had no future? Or what if he'd fallen for some smart and pretty navy nurse? Or what if—

"Stop looking for trouble before it's here," she scolded herself aloud. Good grief, she was starting to act just like Margaret. To distract herself, Colleen switched on the radio, tuning it to *The Burns and Allen Show*. Grateful for their familiar voices and their slapstick humor, she felt relieved to laugh out loud...and to temporarily forget her worries. Because, like George kept telling Gracie, "What's the big deal?"

Fourteen

By midday Friday, Margaret realized something was wrong with Molly. Usually chatty and cheerful, Molly had not been herself all morning. Oh, she was working hard enough, and in typical Molly-style, she didn't complain. Not even when grumpy old Mrs. Jones came in and attempted to torture them by whining about the produce selection, which looked just the same as always. Later on, when Margaret questioned Molly, inquiring about her health and even checking her forehead for signs of fever, Molly simply brushed her off. But by the end of the day, Margaret was determined to get to the bottom of it.

"What's wrong with you?" Margaret demanded after she locked the front door.

"Nothing." Molly continued sweeping, keeping her eyes down.

"Are you mad at me for not spending time with you last night?"

"No." With a blank expression, Molly shook her head. "Not at all."

"Oh, good." Margaret felt a bit of relief as she plucked Baby Peter out of the playpen. At least this wasn't about her. "So are you going to stick around for dinner tonight? I thought we could make some Irish stew together. You're still spending the night, right?"

"I don't know..." Molly pursed her lips.

"Do you have plans?" Margaret used the teething bib to wipe

some drool from Baby Peter's chin. "A big date perhaps?" She smiled slyly.

"No, I don't have a big date," Molly said curtly. "Not even a little date." Her brows drew together. "But speaking of dates, Margaret. What about you?"

"Huh?" Margaret was caught off guard. "What about me?"

"I saw you leaving the store last night, Margaret. I couldn't help but notice you were with an attractive man. And, well, it looked like you were going out on a date."

A wave of panic wash over Margaret. "What?" she said weakly, trying to think of a response. "You must've seen someone else... someone who looked like me. Or else you're just imagining things."

Molly locked eyes with her. "I'm not imagining things. You were dressed up, Margaret, in that pink-and-white striped dress that you made a couple years ago, before the war, and it looked as if you'd shortened it. You had on a straw hat that used to be Colleen's, and you were wearing your white platform sandals and—"

"You were spying on me? My own sister is a—"

"I wasn't spying," Molly exclaimed. "I was having dinner at Dottie's Diner, and I just happened to see—"

"And so you jump to the conclusion that I was going on a date?" Margaret demanded. "You honestly think that I would—"

"I said that it *looked* as if you were on a date. I wasn't trying to draw any conclusions, Margaret. I simply felt confused, and it's been bothering me ever since. That's why I'm speaking to you about it now."

"Did you tell Mam and Dad?"

"No, of course, not. I don't see how that would—"

"What about Colleen?" Margaret felt anger rising. "You're always talking to her. Did you tell her that you—"

"No, Margaret. I didn't tell anyone."

The baby was starting to fuss. "Well, I can't stand here and discuss this right now—Peter is probably hungry for his supper." Margaret started for the stairs, trying to think of a plan, of some way to sweep all of Molly's suspicions beneath a great big rug.

"Do you still want me to stay?" Molly asked quietly from behind her.

"I don't know," Margaret retorted as she stomped up the stairs. Then, pausing at the top, she turned to look down at her youngest sister. "I'm not sure that I like your insinuations about me, Molly Irene. They're not very sisterly."

"Oh, Margaret." Molly sounded exasperated as she traipsed up the stairs. "I didn't want to turn this into a fight. I simply wanted to find out what's going on."

As they stood face-to-face in the apartment, Baby Peter's fussing grew louder. Welcoming a distraction, Margaret walked him over to the kitchen area. She really didn't know what to say or do. And she felt mortified. This was not a scenario that she'd ever imagined could happen—to have Molly calling her out like this.

"Here." Molly reached for the baby. "I'll take him while you get his food ready."

Relieved for a chance to think and gather her thoughts, Margaret busied herself heating the tea kettle, getting out a box of baby cereal, and opening a can of applesauce. As she slowly measured and poured, she knew she needed to make a decision. Should she tell Molly the truth? Or attempt to put forth a believable lie?

"I forgot to bring up the milk," she told Molly. "Would you mind running down for some?"

Molly handed over the baby then scurried off. And now Margaret sank into a kitchen chair, bouncing Peter on her knee and willing herself to calm down—and come up with a plan. She had already fabricated several explanations about Howard. Just in case. One was that he was a salesman, trying to convince her to carry his line of goods in the store. That actually happened occasionally. Or she could say he was an insurance man, which wasn't completely untrue since he was an insurance executive. But she would say they'd met to discuss the store's policy...perhaps to increase the coverage—and he'd insisted they do it over coffee or dinner. She'd cooked up these stories whenever she got worried about being seen by someone she knew. Although she'd never expected it to be a family member. That would be trickier.

"Here's the milk." Molly opened the quart bottle and placed it on the table. Then she pulled out the other kitchen chair and sat across from Margaret.

Margaret quietly thanked her as she poured some milk onto Peter's cereal and applesauce. "Here you go, big boy." She spooned the first bite into his eager little mouth.

"Look, Margaret," Molly spoke slowly, "I did not tell you about seeing you last night just to make you angry. I told you because I care about you. I want to know what's going on."

Margaret put her entire focus on Baby Peter, aiming the spoon for his O-shaped mouth.

"I've been thinking about it a lot, trying to figure it out," Molly continued. "And I realize that you are probably very lonely, Margaret. You and Brian never got to have very much time together. And he's been gone for a year and a half. Actually more than that, if you count all the years he spent at college. I mean, in some ways, it's as if he's been a ghost in your life. I'm sure that's been hard."

Margaret looked up in surprise. "That's actually true."

"But he is your husband, Margaret. And he's Peter's father. And even though—"

"I know that. Do you think I don't know that?" Margaret glared at her little sister. "I'm not stupid."

"I know you know that." Molly sounded impatient. "That's not why I'm telling you this. I'm just reminding you that you made a commitment. And I know that you love Brian. You've always loved him. But now he's gone, off serving his country and you—"

"I know what you're saying." Margaret took in a sharp breath. "But you are all wrong, Molly. You have no idea what you're talking about. If you'd just let me explain."

"That's what I want," Molly said eagerly. "For you to explain."

"Well, let me finish feeding Peter in peace and get him ready for bed," Margaret said quietly. "Then I'll explain."

"Fine." Molly stood. "I'll start making the stew while you take care of him."

Margaret took her time caring for her baby, even giving him a quick pre-bedtime bath. Meanwhile, Molly worked on the stew. Neither of them spoke. But during this quiet time, Margaret persuaded herself that her best plan was to convince Molly that Howard was an insurance man. Especially since that *was* true. But it wouldn't do any good for Molly to think that Margaret was dating or romantically involved with Howard. Because the truth was, Margaret was not. Sure, she'd appreciated his companionship. And she couldn't help but like the fact that he openly admired her and enjoyed spending time with her. But she didn't have any interest in pursuing anything more than that with him.

Finally, with the stew simmering on the hotplate and Peter smelling sweet and wearing his flannel pajamas, Molly and Margaret sat down in the living room area. Margaret cleared her throat, getting ready to make her freshly rehearsed speech. "The man you saw me with is Howard Moore," she began carefully. "He lives in the neighborhood and is a regular customer at the store. We've chatted from time to time. Mr. Moore works for Metro Insurance Company." Margaret sighed, glad that so far everything she'd said was true. "Anyway, Mr. Moore simply wanted to talk to me about changing the store's policy. I didn't want to be distracted from customers, so he asked to meet after closing hours. And since Colleen had already arranged for Sally to come, I offered to meet with him then."

Molly looked unconvinced. "But why were you being so mysterious about it yesterday? Why didn't you just tell me you planned to meet with an insurance salesman?"

Margaret shrugged. "I don't know. I suppose I felt a little uncomfortable about it. I didn't want you to take it the wrong way."

Molly still seemed uncertain. "But when I brought it up today, well, you acted so strangely, you made me believe that my suspicions could be right."

Margaret considered this. "Well, imagine how I feel. My baby sister comes in here practically accusing me of going out with another man when I'm a married woman and a mother." She sniffed indignantly. "How was I supposed to react?"

Molly's brow creased. "I really didn't mean to make an accusation, Margaret. I just wanted to know the truth."

"The truth is I was already uncomfortable about the situation. You know, there I was, stepping out with a man who's not my husband. I mean, it was perfectly innocent and all, but, well, it felt strange to me. So out of character, you know? I suppose that's why I acted like that, Molly. I'm sorry."

Molly looked relieved now. "I'm the one who should be sorry,

Margaret. I should've known there was a logical explanation for it. Thanks for telling me."

Margaret smiled. "That stew smells good. How long do you think until it's ready?"

Molly glanced at her watch. "Twenty minutes."

Margaret stood, handing Peter to Molly. "Here, you hold him while I fix his bottle. I can tell he's getting sleepy. Might as well put him down a little early. That way we can have a nice, quiet supper."

As Margaret prepared Peter's bottle, she felt torn in two. Part of her was relieved to have regained Molly's trust...but the other half—and it was a heavy one—was overwhelmed with guilt. What kind of person was she becoming? Margaret had always been the straight stick. School chums used to call her Goody Two-Shoes. She was the girl who played strictly by the rules and judged those who did not. What would people think if they knew what she was really like—if they knew that she, a married woman, had been secretly enjoying the company of an older divorced man? She used to believe that Colleen was the black sheep of the family...but now she wondered.

It took Colleen a few seconds to remember where she was the next morning, but the sound of waves reminded her. Laurel's beach house...San Diego. It had been too late to see Geoff last night, but the hospital's night receptionist had promised to have Colleen's note delivered to Geoff at breakfast time, informing Colleen that visiting hours would begin again at nine.

Colleen went straight to the window, eager to see the ocean by the light of day. Big and blue and beautiful—it felt like a good omen. Like this day was going to be much better than her dark imaginings last night. At least she hoped so. Exploring the beach house, which was much bigger and better than Laurel had described, Colleen felt like she could happily live here. Especially if Geoff was with her. The open floor plan probably made the space seem larger than it was, but it also gave one a view of the ocean from almost every room.

She would've been content to remain in this sweet place, taking a leisurely stroll down the beach, but she was so anxious to see Geoff that, even though it was barely past seven, she started getting ready—taking almost as much care as if she were about to have a screen test. She wanted to look perfect for him. Since it was a warm, sunny day, she decided to wear her white and blue sundress, along with her wide-brimmed white hat and short white gloves. Very cheerful and attractive.

Colleen took her time driving over to the naval hospital, driving around a bit until it was almost nine. Then, unable to wait any longer, she parked and made her way to the wing that the receptionist had told her about. She was surprised at how large and busy this hospital seemed. But she was glad that wounded sailors had such a good facility to recuperate in. It was just a few minutes past nine when she was standing outside of the door that supposedly led to Geoff's hospital room. But the door was closed and, suddenly, Colleen felt a rush of nerves. Even more so than when she was getting ready for a big scene in a movie. This was real life. Whatever she found behind that door, whatever happened once she went in...it was more than a take. No second chances to do it again.

She took a deep breath then knocked lightly on the door, but not hearing anything, she cracked it open. "Geoff?" she said quietly. What if he was sleeping? Or what if he was all bandaged up and in pain? What if he didn't even recognize her?

"Colleen?" a hoarse voice answered. "Is that you? Come in."

"Geoff," she said warmly as she entered the room, preparing

herself for whatever she was about to find. And there in the bed, looking very much like himself, was Geoff Conrad. "Oh, Geoff!" she cried out as she hurried to him, tears streaming down her cheeks. "I'm so glad to see you." And suddenly they were embracing—both of them sobbing—and Colleen felt certain that nothing between them had changed. Well, except that he was so skinny, it was like hugging a skeleton.

"Colleen," he whispered. "I can't believe I'm holding you in my arms. You know how many times I dreamed of this?"

"I can't believe it either," she said in a husky voice. "I can't believe you're really safe, really home." She pulled back to look into his eyes, placing her hands on both sides of his thin face. "It's so good to see you." She leaned down to kiss him tenderly. Finally, standing up straight again, she reached for a handkerchief.

"You're a sight for sore eyes, Colleen Mulligan." He grinned at her. "Honest to goodness, you're even more beautiful than I remember." He pointed to a nearby chair. "Sit down, honey. Tell me what you've been up to for the last year and a half."

As she pulled the chair near his bed, she could feel his hungry eyes on her—and it felt good. Like nothing had really changed. He still loved her just as much as ever. Maybe even more.

"Did you get my letters?" she asked as she sat down. "I wrote at least two a week to you—I mean, after we found out you were alive."

"You thought I was dead?" His brow furrowed.

She quickly relayed the story to him. "I was a complete mess for months," she confessed. "I went to work at the factory, then came home. That was all. The whole time, I felt dead inside. The truth is, I didn't want to live without you."

He reached for her hand. "Oh, sweetheart, I'm so sorry."

"But here you are," she said brightly. "Alive and well. Except you are so thin, Geoff. You look half starved."

He nodded. "That pretty much describes it."

"So it's true what we heard about those awful Japanese prisoner of war camps?"

"I'm sure you didn't even hear the half of it. All I want to say for now is that it was unimaginable torture. Hell on earth," he said grimly. "Fortunately, there was one humane guard. Without him, well, I probably wouldn't even be here."

"How did you manage to get out of the prison? I never heard any details."

He sighed. "The island we were held captive on was being liberated by American troops. Just in time too. Our guards were getting ready to execute a bunch of us."

"Oh, dear." She held more tightly to his hand.

"The one good guard I mentioned, Makoto, he knew that the island had been invaded. He helped us to escape."

"Really?" Colleen was surprised. "What happened to him?"

"He's imprisoned in one of our camps now, but the Americans know that he's a good guy, so he'll be treated well. The other guards... well, from what I heard, they didn't fare so well."

"Well, thank God for Maka... Whatever his name was."

"Makoto. Yes, thank God for him." He sighed. "I assured Makoto that he could look forward to much better food in our prison camps. Americans don't starve their POWs."

She frowned. "You're terribly thin, Geoff."

He grew somber. "Believe me, I know. I can't even eat solid foods yet." He pointed to the IV tube in his emaciated upper arm. "Besides that, I get a bowl of clear broth and some fruit juice every few hours. But the nurse promises that will change in a week or so. I keep imagining a big fat New York steak, mashed potatoes and gravy, and a huge hunk of apple pie à la mode." He smacked his lips. "But that would probably kill me right now. The doc says my stomach is about the size of a shriveled apple. We've got to get it stretched out."

"Sounds like a wise doctor."

"Enough about me." His brows knit together. "I want to hear about you, honey. You say you sent me some letters? Where did you send them to?"

She explained about sending them care of his supervising officer. "Your family was writing to you too. There's probably a big pile waiting for you."

"The navy probably forwarded them to...well, somewhere." He shrugged. "They'll show up someday."

"Anyway, I told you all about what I've been doing this past year." She attempted a smile. "But since you never got them, well, you obviously have no idea what I've been up to." She gave an uneasy laugh.

His brows arched. "You've been up to something?" He looked at her left hand. "Just as long as you didn't marry someone else..." He pointed to her engagement ring. "I assume that means you're still mine."

"Of course I'm yours." She touched his cheek. "I've been waiting patiently for you. Well, not always patiently." She sighed. "But as to what I've been up to... Goodness, I don't even know where to begin."

"Last I recall, you'd just started to work at the airplane factory. I thought that was just swell, Colleen. My gal builds 'em—and I fly 'em, I'd brag to my buddies. What could be better? So, tell me, how's that going? I bet you're a real Rosie the Riveter by now."

She grimaced. He obviously hadn't gotten her letters. "I haven't been at the airplane factory for a while now." She began telling him about how she'd made the promotional film. "It was well over a year ago, about women on the home front. Not anything as wonderful as *Mrs. Miniver*, but—"

"Mrs. who?" His brow creased.

"Oh, that was a fabulous movie that came out last summer," she explained. "Greer Garson and Walter Pidgeon play an older couple in England, doing their part for the war effort. The sort of film that you never forget. It was released to the armed forces afterward. Of course, you would've been in the prison camp...." She grimaced.

"Not many films shown there," he said in an ironic tone.

"Anyway, our little movie was partly filmed in the airplane factory, but some footage was shot at home with my sisters and mother and me."

"So you were in a real movie about the home front?"

"Just a short one—and a very small part. Molly actually had a bigger role in it than I did." She cringed to remember how horrified she'd been to see herself on the big screen, without makeup and wearing an old house dress.

He ran his fingers through his short-cropped hair with a hard-to-read expression. "Interesting."

Colleen felt uneasy now. What would Geoff think about being engaged to an actual movie actress? What if he didn't like the idea of his girl up there on the silver screen for the whole world to gape at? How could she gently break it to him? Fortunately, a nurse was just coming in with a food tray. So instead of disclosing this somewhat startling news, she made pleasant small talk while Geoff slowly consumed his chicken broth and apple juice.

Fifteen

After finishing his liquid lunch, Geoff seemed to be fading, and Colleen insisted that he should rest. "The nurse warned me not to wear you out." She stood. "I'll take a little walk, get a bite to eat, and then come back." As she reached for her purse, he protested. But as she leaned down to kiss him, his eyelids looked heavy. She knew he'd be snoozing before she exited the building.

Grateful for this little break, Colleen knew it was time to come up with a plan—a gentle way to inform Geoff of her new career path. But by the time she'd had a light lunch and a short walk, she was no closer to an easy explanation. Perhaps it was best to just get it over with—like ripping off a bandage—fast and final.

Geoff was wide awake when she returned to his room. "My angel is back," he said happily.

She leaned down to kiss him again then, slowly removing her gloves, sat down in the chair. "So..." she began. "Do you still want to hear about what I've been up to this past year?"

"Yes, of course. Tell me everything." He leaned back into his pillows with a contented expression.

"Well, after the promotional film released, the strangest thing happened. I was called by a Hollywood agent and invited to make a screen test." She smiled nervously.

"A screen test?" His blue eyes grew wide. "For a real motion picture?"

"Yes. Someone had seen me in the home front promotional film and thought I'd be perfect for a Pinnacle movie."

"Pinnacle Productions?" He sat up straight. "You're kidding?"

"Not at all." She twisted her handkerchief. "I'd been in deep grief over you, Geoff, for what felt like years, although it was probably about six months. But it felt like I was in a deep, dark black hole, so it was rather shocking when the Knight Agency called—"

"I've heard of the Knight Agency." He stared at her in wonder. "That's a big deal, Colleen."

"I know. Well, one thing led to another. I met with Rory and Georgina Knight, and they liked me. So I did my screen test and then auditioned for Pinnacle—and, unbelievably, I was chosen for the role. In a film with Darla Devon and Robert Miller."

"Are you serious?" He looked incredulous.

"Absolutely."

"Darla Devon and Robert Miller are big stars, Colleen. That's amazing. What sort of role is it?"

"A supportive ingénue role. I played a teen girl."

He grinned. "You could pass for that."

"Yes, complete with pigtails when needed." She felt hopeful now. Geoff seemed to be onboard with all this.

"So you've already started filming?"

"Started and finished. We wrapped in February."

"Well, I'm just flabbergasted. My girl is a movie star." His eyes seemed larger than possible in his overly thin face.

"Not a big star, but it's been so amazing, and already I've learned so much. It hasn't been much like I used to imagine. Mostly it's a lot of hard work. But I really enjoy it. Although Darla Devon is... well, she's something else, Geoff."

"Is she one of those actresses who is great on the screen but not so nice up close?"

She nodded. "Anyway, the movie released to the public in April and it did okay."

"I can't believe it. Your first movie has already been in theaters!"

"It's scheduled to release to the armed forces this month."

"Maybe I'll get a chance to see it here in the hospital. I've heard they show films to the patients sometimes. Imagine me bragging that the gorgeous blonde on the screen is engaged to this skinny bag of bones." He winked.

"You won't be skinny for long, Geoff." She pointed to the glass of pineapple juice that the nurse had just brought in. "Why don't you drink that?"

He held it up like a toast. "Here's to my movie-star girl."

"And now I'm making my second movie. This one is with Laurel Wagner and Barry Coltaire and—"

"I love their movies!" He sat down his glass with a clink. "Laurel Wagner is a real dream girl."

Colleen pretended to be worried.

"Not as dreamy or beautiful as you, darling."

"Well, she's a real dream to work with. And so is Barry. So much better than Darla and Robert. I feel so fortunate, and I'm learning even more on this film. And Laurel is so kind and generous. She's even letting me use her beach house while I'm here in San Diego." She told him a little about the charming little house with ocean views.

"But back to your movie making," he said. "Is this something you plan to continue doing?"

"Well, I'm not really sure. I mean, it all depends." She nervously twisted her gloves between her fingers. "I've yet to land a starring role. I might never get one. Some actors never do. But both these movies were good solid secondary parts." She told him more about the storylines of the two films and how they differed and what she liked about both of them.

"I'm still just so stunned by all this." He leaned back into his pillows, letting out a long sigh. "You're living in Hollywood, making motion pictures... I hardly know what to say, Colleen."

"So do you mind? I mean, being engaged to a film star? Not a big star, mind you, but—"

"Are you kidding?" He grinned. "I think it's great. I'm proud of you, Colleen. I can't wait to brag about you to my buddies. A movie-star wife—what could be better?"

"Wife?" She felt her brows arch.

"Well, we are engaged." He looked slightly worried now. "You haven't changed your mind about marrying me, have you?"

She smiled reassuringly. "Not at all. I just wondered when. When do you plan to make me your wife, darling?"

He chuckled. "Well, not until I get out of here. According to the doc, they won't release me until I've gained about thirty pounds."

"Then you better keep stretching that stomach," she told him. "Just imagine how much fun you'll have eating once you're on solid foods. You'll be able to eat anything you like. I'll be jealous since I have to watch my weight."

He frowned. "I don't see why. It seems to me that you've lost weight. I don't remember you being this thin before."

"I did lose weight when I was pining for you. I had no appetite. Ironically, that helped me to get into the movies. Most people don't realize that the screen adds pounds. That's because it's two-dimensional. So it was helpful that I was thinner. And my studio likes its actresses on the slender side." She wrinkled her nose. "That means lots of green salads these days. And not many New York steaks."

He squeezed her hand. "Well, I think you'd look great with a few more pounds on you, honey."

She smiled. "Thanks. Same back at you."

"So tell me more about this movie you're working on now," he urged. "I want to hear everything, Colleen."

"So do I," she told him. "Let's take turns." And so they continued, talking and talking—just like they used to do, like nothing had really changed. Although, she could tell he was weak, so as he wore down she tried to do most of the talking, sometimes insisting that he take a break to rest or take some nourishment. And finally it was evening and visiting time was over.

"You'll be back tomorrow?" he asked hopefully.

"For sure," she promised. "I have to drive back to Hollywood tomorrow night. We're supposed to report back to the studio early Monday morning."

He looked disappointed.

"But I'll come down here every chance I get, Geoff. And I'll call you long distance every evening after work. If that's okay with the hospital."

"I'll find out." He frowned. "When will you be done with this movie?"

"We're supposed to wrap the second week of July."

"That's only a month away. I bet I'll be out of here by then." He brightened. "How about we set a wedding date?"

"Really?"

"Yes. We could plan it for after your film is finished and I'm released from the hospital. How about late July?"

"Are you sure you'll be well enough by then?"

MELODY CARLSON

"I'll do everything the doctor orders to get myself healthy again," he assured her. "Just wait and you'll see. I'll be fat and sassy by the end of July."

She laughed. "Not too fat."

"And I don't want you too thin," he warned. "No one likes a skinny bride."

"Let me talk to the studio and check a calendar to find out if late July really works. And there are our families to consider too. Which reminds me, your mom and grandparents send their love. They plan to take a train down here, I think by Monday. So even though I'll be back at work, you'll have someone to keep you company—and make sure you're eating and minding the doctor's orders." She leaned down to kiss him.

"You're the best medicine, Colleen." Geoff eagerly kissed her. "Seeing you today makes me feel like I'm well on my way...on the road to recovery."

"Sleep well, sweetheart." She ran her fingers through his sandy brown hair then kissed him again. "I'll see you in the morning."

As Colleen left the hospital, she hoped that Geoff wasn't pushing himself too hard in the hopes of a wedding. Especially since late July was only about six weeks away. Which made her wonder how she'd manage it herself. Although, she'd never wanted a fancy wedding. That had always been Margaret's dream. Colleen would happily marry Geoff at City Hall. A lot of film stars did that, and it had always seemed sort of glamorous in an understated way. But would she be ready for that in six weeks?

As she drove back to Laurel's beach house, she wondered if she'd been foolish to agree to his plan. And yet he seemed so cheered up by the possibility, how could she say no? Anyway, time would tell. If it was meant to be, Geoff would be well and they would get married. Mostly she was thankful that Geoff was still Geoff, and that he still loved her and she loved him. Even in his emaciated form, a shadow of what he'd once been, she still loved him just as much as always. Maybe even more.

Sunday morning passed much like the previous day—Colleen and Geoff catching up and visiting while he had the strength and energy to talk. Although the head nurse took Colleen aside again, sternly warning that it wasn't good for Geoff to overdo it. So whenever Colleen saw him tiring, she'd encourage him to close his eyes and have a little rest. And she encouraged him to finish off every liquid nourishment set before him, reminding him that this was the first part of his recovery.

The late afternoon was broken up by a telephone call. When Colleen realized it was Geoff's mother, she offered to leave the room, but he just waved at her to remain there.

"Honestly, I'm doing just fine," he assured his mother for at least the third time. "Colleen has been with me all weekend, and already I feel so much better. Colleen told me that you sent your love and that you might be coming down here soon."

Colleen occupied herself with a *Life* magazine while Geoff visited with his mother and then his grandmother and grandfather. He even told them about his hope for a late July wedding. Colleen had no idea what was being said on the other end, but as the call wore on she could tell Geoff was growing weary. She wanted to suggest he end the conversation but didn't feel it was her place to interfere with his family.

Finally, he said good-bye. As he handed her the receiver to hang up for him, he let out a long sigh. "Well, that mother of mine...she sounds just the same as ever."

"What do you mean?"

"Oh, you know, Mom's the absolute expert on everything—and not the least bit shy about sharing her opinions."

Colleen couldn't help but giggle.

"But I know she loves me." Geoff smiled. "And, like I told her, I am looking forward to seeing her. And my grandparents too. They will be here on Tuesday."

"That's great, Geoff."

His smile faded. "Yeah...I guess so."

"What's wrong, honey?" She laid the magazine aside.

"Oh, nothing. At least I hope it's nothing." He looked intently at her. "Mom sounds pretty worried about you."

"About me?"

"She's got it into her head that an actress will not make a good wife." He rolled his eyes toward the ceiling. "Don't ask me what she bases this on or where she gets her information. It's not like she ever goes to see a film, and I'm certain she's never picked up a movie-star magazine. Although Grandma does. Maybe Mom has sneaked some of them from her." He chuckled. "Anyway, she seems to think she knows all about it."

"I'm aware that your mother doesn't approve of my acting career," Colleen confessed. "I've tried to win her over, but it seems futile."

Geoff reached for her hand. "Fortunately, you are not marrying my mother, Colleen."

"Maybe not. But I will become part of your family...just like you'll be part of mine."

"Speaking of family, you haven't told me much about yours," he said quickly. "I want to hear all about them. Did Bridget make it into the ANC like she'd been hoping to do?"

So for the rest of the afternoon, Colleen filled him in on the comings and goings of her family during the past year. She even told him about helping Margaret when her baby was born. "It was pretty frightening, but it turned out okay. And Baby Peter is a doll."

"Well, I am impressed." Geoff squeezed her hand again. "And maybe someday Margaret will have the opportunity to repay you. I mean, when the time comes."

"What time?"

"Oh, you know. When you're having our baby, Colleen." He grinned. "Hopefully in the not so distant future. Who knows…maybe even a year from now."

Colleen felt a rush of panic mixed with embarrassment. "Oh, I hope it's not that soon, Geoff. Honestly, I didn't plan to have children right away. Not for the first few years of our marriage."

"What?" Geoff looked surprised. "Why not?"

"Oh, I don't know." Colleen knew that wasn't totally honest. A big part of the reason was that she didn't want to derail her Hollywood career before it got fully off the ground, but that wasn't all. "Margaret had her baby before her first anniversary and…well, it hasn't been easy for her. I honestly think she regrets it at times. Oh, she loves Peter. But I suspect there are times when she wishes they'd waited. And, really, I don't want to have children until I feel I can welcome them with both arms."

"Oh?" He looked dismayed.

"But this isn't something we need to figure out today," she said lightly. "You need to concentrate on getting well, Geoff. And I need to get my movie wrapped and plan for our wedding." She leaned down to kiss him good-bye. "And now I must head back up to Los

Angeles. It's more than a two-hour drive, and I'd like to get there before dark."

Try as she might, Colleen found it difficult to think about anything for the next two hours except the fact that Geoff seemed intent on having children in the not too distant future. Even knowing that her parents would side with Geoff on this did nothing to persuade Colleen. And it was quite disturbing to be in opposition with her fiancé. It was the first time they'd ever really disagreed on anything. And this was no small thing either.

As she got closer to Los Angeles, Colleen wondered if it was selfish on her part to procrastinate on having a family—especially when Geoff felt so differently. But in all honestly, it wasn't only about her acting career...it was simply because she knew she wasn't ready for motherhood yet. Hopefully she could convince Geoff.

Sixteen

M olly was committed to working full-time in the grocery store, at least for the summer and longer if needed. Her hope was to allow Mam time to be home with Dad, but Mam wasn't having it. For that matter, Dad wasn't very happy about it either.

"I like being at the store," Mam protested on Sunday evening, shortly after Molly had made her announcement. "There's not so much to do around the house anymore, what with all you kids grown-up." She glanced at Dad. "And he doesn't need me nearly as much as you girls seem to think."

"That's right," Dad agreed. "I'd enjoy some peace and quiet. Maybe I'd get some if your mam was working at the store again."

"How about if you just work part time?" Molly suggested. "Maybe in the mornings since that seems to be the busiest time."

"Yes," Mam agreed. "Then I could be home in the afternoon to fix supper and do some housekeeping."

"And it wouldn't have to be every day," Molly said. "Maybe just on the busy ones."

They had just agreed on this plan when the telephone loudly jangled. "Seems a bit late for callers," Dad said in an irate tone. "Some friend of yours, Molly?"

Molly didn't think so but hopped up to answer it anyway. To her pleased surprise, it was Colleen.

"Sorry to call so late," Colleen said. "I hope Mam and Dad haven't already gone to bed."

"No, they're still up." She grinned at her parents. "It's Colleen!"

"Well, I just got back to Beverly Hills and had to call."

"How was Geoff?" Molly asked eagerly, waiting as Colleen filled her in on his condition. "And was he glad to see you?"

"Very glad. So much so that he wants to get married in late July."

"How exciting!"

"Yes, but I'm not so sure about it. After all, it's only about six weeks away and I have to—"

"But that's when Bridget has her leave!" Molly exclaimed. "Wouldn't it be fabulous to get married while she was here? Oh, she would love it, Colleen."

"I hadn't even thought of that. But, yes, it's a good idea."

Molly went over to the calendar hanging by the kitchen. "What day are you thinking of?"

"Geoff just said late July."

"How about the thirty-first? That's the last Saturday. And Bridget will still be here then."

"I would love for Bridget to be at my wedding..."

"Then do it!"

"Okay. Tell Mam and Dad that's the date," Colleen declared. "But I don't want to be married in the church, Molly."

"Where then?"

"I'm not sure. But I'm not eager to tell Mam and Dad. I know they'll throw a fit."

"Want me to break the news?"

"Oh, Molly, I would be forever in your debt. Do you think you can soften them up for me?"

"I'll do my best." Molly could see that her parents were trying to listen in, but probably without much success. "This will give me some practice in diplomacy."

"I'll bet. So, anyway, I want a small, intimate wedding. Just immediate family. I'd thought about having the ceremony at City Hall, but I'm not sure how many they can accommodate."

"Want me to find out for you?"

"Could you?"

"I'd love to." Now Molly got an idea. "What about the Fairmont Hotel, Colleen? Isn't that where Geoff proposed to you?"

"Oh, Molly, that'd be perfect. Geoff and I could get married at City Hall then have a reception at the hotel. I'd love that."

"Want me to check on it for you? For the thirty-first?"

"Oh, please, do. Try to get some estimates if you can."

"It might be expensive." Molly glanced nervously at Mam and Dad, both of them still staring with wide-eyed interest.

"I think I can afford it. The movie will wrap by then and, according to my agency, I could have another offer at that point."

"My rich movie-star sister," Molly teased.

"Well, that is overstating it. But I did want to ask you something, Molly."

"Yes? Something else for the wedding? I'd love to help in any way I can."

"That's not what I meant, although I'd really appreciate anything you can do to help with the wedding. But I've been meaning to ask you about your plans for next fall. You'd mentioned wanting to continue your education, Molly. I want to help you with tuition at the state college."

"Really?"

"Yes. So while you're checking on the Fairmont, find out what your tuition would be. And then let's talk."

"Oh, Colleen, you are the best!"

"Well, if anyone deserves to go to college, it's you, Molly. I told Geoff about how hard you worked to graduate high school a whole year early, and he was very impressed. So much so that he agreed we should do what we can to help you go to college. You know he went to San Francisco State College too."

They chatted awhile longer, but Molly could tell that her parents' patience was wearing thin. "I think Mam and Dad are eager to hear your news," she quietly told Colleen.

"And I have to be at the studio quite early tomorrow," Colleen said. "I should probably get my beauty sleep."

They agreed to talk again in a few days, then Molly hung up and turned to grin at her parents. "Colleen and Geoff want to get married on July thirty-first," she announced happily.

"That's wonderful," Mam said. "But such short notice. I hope Old Saint Mary's is available on that day. I better call Father McMurphey first thing tomorrow—"

"They'd like to have their wedding at City Hall and their reception at the Fairmont Hotel." Molly braced herself.

"A wedding at City Hall?" Dad looked scandalized.

"It's better than eloping to Las Vegas," Molly said solemnly. "Don't you think City Hall and the Fairmont would be nicer? It won't be a big affair. Colleen said they only want immediate family."

"But Colleen grew up going to Old Saint Mary's." Mam looked close to tears.

"Yes, but the Fairmont is where Colleen and Geoff got engaged." Molly let out a blissful sigh. "I think it sounds so romantic. And much better than just getting married at City Hall and then leaving for their honeymoon. This way we can celebrate with them."

"But it's not the same as a church wedding." Dad grimly shook his head.

"Well, you're both aware that Geoff's not Catholic," Molly said cautiously. "And yet you both agreed to the engagement last year."

"But I thought he would convert," Dad said.

"Yes," Mam agreed. "I'd hoped so too."

"He hasn't had a lot of time to do that," Molly pointed out. "What with being locked up in a Japanese prison camp this past year and a half."

"That's true...." Mam's face softened a bit. "I forgot to ask, how is he?"

"Colleen said he's skin and bones and won't even be released from the hospital until he gains thirty pounds."

"Poor boy."

"And he really wants to get married," Molly continued. "He's the one who pushed for the July date. After all he's been through, wouldn't it be nice if it worked out—without a lot of controversy? You don't want them to elope...or just go by themselves to City Hall then take off. And don't forget, Bridget will be here then. Wouldn't it be great to have everyone together for a fun reception at the Fairmont?"

They talked a while longer, and the whole time Molly gently but firmly persuaded her parents to let Colleen and Geoff plan their own wedding, until she felt like they were finally onboard—or else simply worn out. So to change the subject, Molly told them about Colleen's kind offer to pay for her college tuition. And to her relief, that seemed to seal the deal for her parents.

"What a generous thing to do," Mam exclaimed.

"Our little flibbertigibbet has grown up into a fine young woman," Dad said proudly. "And if she truly wants to repeat her marriage vows in a hotel, I do not intend to stand in her way."

"Nor do I." Mam let out a resigned sigh. "Although Colleen would make such a beautiful bride in a big church wedding... I can just imagine it."

"She will be a beautiful bride no matter where she is married." Molly hugged them both then, trying not to act too victorious over the slightly awkward conversation, she excused herself. "I need to write letters to Bridget and Patrick—to tell them all the latest news and the wedding date." Of course, she would write to Colleen as well, but no need to rub it in.

Although Margaret was glad to hear about Colleen's news the following day, her happiness for her sister was tinged with envy. "Her wedding will probably be grand and beautiful," she said glumly to Molly as they freshened up the produce section during a slump in morning customers. "She can certainly afford it."

"Not at all," Molly assured her. "They want a small wedding. Just immediate family."

"You're kidding. I figured Colleen would pull out all the stops for her big day. After all, she's a rich movie star now." Margaret peeled a wilted leaf off of a head of lettuce, tossing it into the chicken feed bucket that Mrs. Lewis's son picked up every evening. "And, from what I've heard, Geoff's family is quite well off too. Those two could probably have a fabulous wedding."

"Maybe, but Colleen doesn't want it to be big." Molly set an overly soft tomato in the basket that would go home with her later, full of vegetables for Mam to put into soup or stew. This war had taught all of them not to let anything go to waste. And, according to her elderly neighbor, the victory-garden tomatoes wouldn't produce for a few more weeks yet.

"Why not?" Margaret picked up another head of lettuce.

"I don't know. But she wants to get married at City Hall and then they'll—"

"What?" Margaret wiped her hands on the front of her apron. "Why not at Old Saint Mary's?"

"You know that Geoff's not Catholic."

"I thought he was going to convert."

"Well, I don't know about that, Margaret. But after all, it's their wedding. And here's the really good part. Colleen wants me to check out the Fairmont Hotel for their reception. Won't that be glamorous? In fact, if you don't mind, I'll run over there on my lunch break today to talk to the manager and—"

"The Fairmont?" Margaret blinked. "That will be scandalously expensive."

"Like you said, they can probably afford it. But isn't it exciting? And just think, Bridget will be on leave and at home by then. Won't she have fun?"

"It just seems so extravagant. But, of course, Colleen will want her big day to be showy. I wonder what she'll wear—probably something terribly expensive and Hollywood glamorous. Do you think she'll call the press to—"

"I don't think so." Molly picked up the home basket just as the bell on the front door jangled. "I'll go put this away," she said quietly.

Now Margaret felt even worse. Molly probably thought her snide and jealous and childish. And maybe she was all those things—and more. But it wasn't because she didn't love Colleen. Sometimes it just felt unfair. Everything good always seemed to land smack dab in the middle of Colleen's pretty lap. Meanwhile, Margaret's carefully laid plans usually went totally awry. It just wasn't fair.

But Peter was just waking from his morning nap and starting to fuss. So Margaret set her unsisterly thoughts aside and the chicken-feed bucket behind the counter then called out to Molly.

"I'm going to feed the little prince now. When I get done, you can go on over to the Fairmont if you like."

"Great," Molly called back.

As Margaret carried Peter into her apartment, she felt embarrassed to see that it looked pretty shabby up here. She had no real excuse for the unmade bed or piles of clothes and clutter scattered about the small space. She and Baby Peter had spent the whole afternoon in this space after church yesterday, but Margaret had felt no incentive to tidy things up. It wasn't as if she were entertaining...or had a husband to please. It was just her and the baby. And he certainly didn't care.

As she prepared Baby Peter's bottle, she thought about her friendship with Howard Moore. And, really, it was only that. Just a friendship. And yet she so looked forward to her Thursday evenings with him...as well as the random times when he popped unexpectedly into the store for a newspaper or groceries. She knew it was silly...and bordering alongside wrong, and yet she couldn't seem to nix it.

In fact, it seemed that the more she saw of Howard, the easier it became for her to imagine what life would be like if she were married to this older man. In some ways, these imaginings weren't all that different than the ones she used to entertain about Brian. They would share a lovely home together, sit down for meals, go for walks or to the theater or out for dinner and dancing.... But instead of seeing Brian's face in these pleasant little daydreams, she saw Howard's.

And, of course, that filled her with even more guilt. And the guilt made her feel even more unhappy. And that probably made her say those snide comments, like she'd just done with Molly, which made her even more miserable.

As she gave Peter his bottle, she knew that one of her favorite remedies for feeling miserable was to think about Howard. She hadn't seen him since Friday, when he'd strolled into the store just before closing time, like he often did. But she always enjoyed those few minutes, simply exchanging pleasantries with him before she locked up. As a result of looking forward to those moments, she'd been taking more care with her appearance, which was one reason her apartment was strewn with clothes right now. Margaret would dig through her makeshift closet, trying to come up with an attractive ensemble, hoping to earn a compliment from him.

Yes, it was childish and foolish—but worst of all, she knew it was wrong. Just the same, she couldn't seem to stop herself. And today would be no different. She was already looking forward to closing time in the hopes that Howard would pop in for some insignificant purchase. With no one else in the store, he would smile at her, offer her some sweet compliments, and they would happily chat until she knew it was time to lock the doors. Sometimes she would briefly imagine what it would be like to invite him upstairs to continue the conversation.

The mere idea of that filled her with terrible dread. So much so that she wondered...had she been letting the apartment remain this messy simply as a deterrent? She looked around the unkempt space and sighed. If this is what it took to keep her on the straight and narrow, so be it.

Seventeen

For the next month, whenever she got the chance, Colleen went to San Diego. Whether by car, bus, train, or even plane, she made the trip every time she got a day off. Unfortunately, the movie's demands didn't afford her much downtime. But between her trips south, she and Geoff talked on the phone. And in some ways, that was almost nicer—it gave them the opportunity to get reacquainted without the distraction of being face-to-face. The other upside of being apart was that each time she went to visit Geoff, he seemed remarkably better.

Today was no different. "Oh, Geoff," she said happily as he met her in front of the naval hospital. "You're dressed!" She smiled at his handsome officer's uniform. "You look so good!"

"Not as good as you." He swooped her into a hug.

"And I can tell you're putting more meat on your bones," she said after they exchanged a few kisses.

"Ready for some good news?" He linked her arm in his.

"Always."

"I'm getting out of here." He led her down the sidewalk away from his wing of the hospital.

"Right now?" She blinked in surprise.

"Well, not today. But this week. The doctor promised."

"So you made your weight goal?"

"Nearly." He grinned. "But I feel great."

She happily squeezed his arm. "I'm so glad!"

"The plan is to release me on Monday," he explained. "Of course, I'll still be on medical leave, but at least the doctor's allowing me to go home. I've already arranged a flight to San Francisco, and my mother will pick me up. Naturally, they're all excited about my homecoming."

"Naturally." She smiled. "They'll probably wait on you hand and foot."

"Probably." He cleared his throat as he paused by a wooden bench. "Colleen?"

She could tell by his tone that he was uncomfortable about something. "What is it?" she asked with concern.

"Let's sit."

They both sat down, and she turned to study him more closely. Although he looked handsome and healthy, she suddenly felt worried. She knew the doctors had been going over him with a fine-tooth comb, testing all of his vital organs to ensure that the prison's deprivations hadn't caused any permanent damage. "Are you okay, Geoff? Did you hear back on your medical tests yet?"

"Yes, yes," he reassured her. "It all came out just fine. My doctor thinks I must be made of some pretty sturdy stuff."

"Oh, good." She reached for his hand. "You had me worried there."

"Sorry, honey." His brow creased.

"But something's wrong, Geoff. What is it?" Colleen felt another rush of nerves. Had he changed his mind about getting married? They'd been going over all their wedding details on her visits and, thanks to Molly's help, it all seemed to be falling neatly into place. The hotel was reserved for the thirty-first, and Molly had made deposits on a cake and flowers. Meanwhile, Colleen had already picked not one, but two wedding outfits—a handsome suit for City Hall and a gorgeous white gown for the hotel.

"Yes...we need to talk." His expression became so somber that she grew more uneasy.

"Please, tell me what's troubling you," she pleaded.

"It's my mother."

"Oh...?"

"I don't even know how to tell you this, Colleen, but she's so doggoned determined."

"You mean about us?" Colleen suspected that his mother was putting her foot down regarding their marriage. Ellen did not approve of Colleen's acting career. She never had. Surely she would do everything in her power to put the kibosh on this.

Geoff simply nodded.

Colleen felt sick inside. Was Geoff going to cave to Ellen? Would he turn his back on Colleen in order to please his mother? She didn't know what to say.

"I know you've got all our wedding plans all made," he said gently. "And Molly has been such a trooper to help you with everything. I feel like a bum saying this, especially with such short notice...with the wedding date only two weeks away." He looked so miserable that she actually felt sorry for him.

"But you want to cancel it," she said quietly. "You don't want to marry me because your mother has—"

"Wait a minute!" He held up both hands. "No, no! You don't understand, Colleen. That's not it all. I do want to marry you, darling. Nothing will change that. Come hell or high water, we are going to be married. I promise! And, just for the record, I don't care if we get married in City Hall or Reno or Jake's Chowder House."

She felt reassured but confused. "What is it then?"

"My mother—and it sounds like my grandparents too—are all very opposed to a City Hall wedding." He grimaced. "There, I said it."

"Oh?" She looked into his troubled blue eyes. "What if we had the ceremony at the hotel? Would that make them feel better?"

He grimly shook his head. "My mother believes we should make our vows before God." He rubbed his chin. "And here's the truth, Colleen. I think I agree with her. You see, when I was in the prison camp, I got into a habit of praying. I guess that's not uncommon when a fellow gets in a tough spot. Anyway, I decided that if God got me out of there alive—and there were many times when that seemed impossible—but if he got me out, I made a commitment to live my life differently. You know?"

She couldn't help but smile. "Believe it or not, I had a similar experience, Geoff. I'd never been one for praying. Not like the rest of my family. I hung up my rosary as a teenager. But when I heard you were being held prisoner, I learned how to pray again. It became my only hope. And while I didn't exactly make a commitment to live my life differently, I do think I began to do that."

He looked relieved. "So maybe you can understand why I agreed with my mother. I would like for us to make our marriage vows before God."

"But my church is Catholic...and you are not."

He grimaced. "I know."

"And I wouldn't ever ask you to convert," she confessed. "Because the truth is I have not been a very devout Catholic for the past few years. I would feel like a hypocrite to force you to accept something that I'm still not sure about. I mean, I do believe in God and I believe in prayer...but I'm still figuring a lot of things out."

"That's how I feel too." He held both of her hands in his hands.

"But your family wants us to get married in a church?"

"Right. And this is where my grandmother stepped in. Without even consulting with me or anyone, she went ahead and reserved our church for the thirty-first of July. Now, I realize that this might not be acceptable to you. And I told them that you have the final say, Colleen. Wherever you want to get married is where we will get married. But I promised my family I would present their case."

"I'm not opposed to getting married in your family's church," she said slowly.

"You're not?" He leaned over to kiss her. "You're as understanding as you are beautiful, darling. Thank you!" He kissed her again.

"Would we still have the reception at the Fairmont?"

"We will, darling, if that's what you want. But I have to tell you the rest. Only because I promised. But it is your choice. Understand?"

"Understand." She smiled.

"My dear mother has offered to host our wedding reception at the farm." He chuckled. "I thought maybe she'd lost her mind. But it turns out she's been talking with a friend, and they've gotten all these grand ideas about putting a marquee in the backyard with string quartet and, well, all sorts of things."

"You mean she will handle everything for us?" Colleen wasn't sure how to feel. On one hand, she knew it was the bride's responsibility to plan and pay for a wedding. On the other hand, if Ellen really wanted to do this...well, why not?

"She will plan and handle everything, Colleen. All we have to do is show up."

Colleen grinned. "Count me in."

He swept her into a standing hug, swinging her around like a rag doll. "You're the best, Colleen. A guy couldn't ask for a better girl."

As he set her down, she smoothed her rumpled blouse and skirt then laughed. "You really are getting back into shape, Geoff. You don't even sound winded."

He mockingly flexed his biceps for her. "I've been doing my exercises and eating my spinach. Just like the doctor ordered."

"Good for you."

"Let's go back inside," he said. "I promised to call my mother as soon as I got your answer. She is going to be over the moon, Colleen." He glanced at her. "You're sure you're really okay with this? Not disappointed?"

She shrugged. "Well, I did like the idea of being at the Fairmont."

"I know." He held a finger high. "We'll spend the night there after the wedding. Two if you like. How does that suit you?"

She smiled. "That sounds nice."

"After that, I have something even better lined up." He winked as he opened the door for her. "But it's a surprise."

Before long, they were back in his hospital room and he was calling his mother on the phone. First he told her the good news and then, after talking a bit, he held the receiver out to Colleen. "She wants to talk to you."

"Oh, Colleen," Ellen gushed. "Thank you for allowing us to do this. I know you had other plans, but it was very generous of you to let us handle everything."

"It's very generous of you to want to do this," Colleen said. "I know it'll be a lot of work for you."

"There's definitely a lot to get done—and not much time to do it—but I believe we can put together a very nice wedding. I do hope your family doesn't mind. Although with all those daughters, they should have plenty of weddings to plan for." She laughed. "Whereas we will only have this one."

Colleen considered this. "Well, it was my sister and I that were doing most of the planning for the wedding anyway. And we were trying to keep everything fairly simple and straightforward." She explained about Molly's help so far.

"Why don't you put Molly in touch with me?" Ellen said.

Colleen promised to do so. "My movie will wrap in a week, and I planned to go home to stay with my family until the wedding." She explained about Bridget's leave.

"Oh, that's wonderful. Will your sisters be your bridesmaids?"

"I hadn't really considered this. I mean before...when we were going to marry in City Hall, well, it didn't seem practical."

"Well, I'm sure your sisters would love to stand up with you, Colleen. It would make for a lovely ceremony."

"I'll talk to them about it."

They chatted for a while longer, but Colleen felt slightly overwhelmed by the time she hung up the phone. She hoped that Ellen wouldn't get too carried away with the wedding—and part of her regretted giving in so easily. Still, she reminded herself, it was only one day. Hopefully it wouldn't end up being a mistake to entrust Ellen with all these details.

She turned around to see Geoff sitting in a chair by the window with a rather grim expression. Was he questioning their change in plans too? "What's troubling you?" She went over to stand beside him, placing a hand on his shoulder.

He pointed to the front page of a newspaper in his lap. "Just this."

She could see it was an article about the war. "Bad news?"

"Not at all. A bunch of B-24 Liberators bombed Wake Island a few days ago. Flew in from Midway and took the Japs by surprise. The mission was a huge success. That's good news."

"Then why so glum, chum?" She sat on the arm of the chair, smoothing his hair, which had grown out nicely since being shorn after his rescue. "Are you worn out from our little walk and all this wedding business?"

He smiled, but his eyes still looked troubled. "No, I'm not tired at all." He looked out the window to where a navy training plane was streaking by. "I'm just starting to miss it."

"Miss what?"

"Being up there." He continued to stare out the window. "I miss the action, Colleen. Being up there in my plane, doing my part to knock out the enemy. I really miss it."

"Oh." She grimaced to think of Geoff back out there in the thick of the fight again. "But I thought you were done."

"Done?" He turned to look at her. "Seriously?"

"Well, you don't plan to go back, do you?"

"Of course I plan to go back."

Colleen felt slightly sick inside. "After all you've been through, you really want to go back?"

"Sure. Why wouldn't I?" He frowned.

"It's just that I thought—I thought you'd already done your part, Geoff. I sort of assumed you were finished with that now. You barely survived that prison camp."

"But I did survive." He slowly shook his head. "I'm not done yet, Colleen, not by any means."

"But are you even well enough to go back." She gave his arm a squeeze. "You still seem underweight, Geoff."

"Of course I can't return to active service for a while. First of all, we've got the wedding..." He clasped her hand. "And the honeymoon. Plus, my commanding officer has already informed me he won't take me back until the doc officially signs off on me—and according to the doc, that probably won't happen for about six more weeks."

"Six more weeks?" She tried to keep the disappointment out of her voice, but that did not sound like much time.

"Let's not think about that now." His face brightened. "Tell me about your conversation with my mom. Did you girls get it all worked out?"

Suddenly her concerns about letting Ellen plan their wedding seemed diminished...in comparison to Geoff's startling news. She couldn't imagine how she would feel six weeks from now, newly married and telling him good-bye...knowing that he was headed straight back into the chaotic mess that had nearly killed him before. More than ever, she hated this war.

Eighteen

Molly was somewhat disappointed to hear that Geoff's mother had taken over the wedding plans. At least initially. But after a conversation with Mrs. Conrad on Monday, followed by a visit to the farm and the family church on Wednesday, Molly felt much better. The farm looked so pretty, surrounded by lovely shade trees and lush green fields and with colorful flowers blooming everywhere. It was a delightful location for a wedding reception.

And the Episcopal Church building, although not as historic as Old Saint Mary's, was strikingly beautiful with its stone walls, high arches, and gorgeous stained glass windows. And the priest, who seemed quite nice, reassured Molly that an Episcopal wedding was not greatly different than a Catholic wedding. Molly wasn't so sure about this but conveyed this message to Colleen on Wednesday night.

Colleen seemed relatively unconcerned. Probably because she was so focused on the final week of her film project. "I did find someone to make the bridesmaid gowns though. She's a young costume designer who was hungry for work. She promised to have them done in time. I'm just hoping Bridget's measurements haven't changed—but we can always get Mrs. Hammond and Mam to help with alterations if needed."

"What will the gowns look like?"

"The fabric is a lovely grade of satin in an iridescent blue. They'll have softly draped necklines and cap sleeves. The bodice is loosely fitted but there's a generous flowing hemline that will be lovely for dancing. It's a simple yet elegant design. I think they'll look perfect with my bridal gown, which wasn't designed to be one, but I love it."

"It all sounds beautiful."

"And I have a question for you, Molly."

"What's that?"

"Would you be my maid of honor?"

Molly was stunned. "But I'm the youngest one and—"

"I've always felt close to you, Molly. We shared a room all those years. You have always been a good friend to me. I'd like you to be my maid of honor."

"Well, I would be honored." Molly was almost too stunned to speak.

"Thank you. I'll be home early next week, and I'll try to take over all the wedding plans from there."

The only problem now was Mam and Dad. Colleen had begged Molly to keep the change in wedding plans under wraps for the time being. Colleen would break the news to them when she got home. Molly knew their parents would throw a full-blown Irish fit when they heard that Colleen planned to be married in a church...but not a Catholic one. Molly planned to be gone when Colleen made her announcement.

Although Molly tried not to think about Colleen's dilemma while she worked at the store on Thursday, it was probably still troubling her. But she hoped and prayed her parents would get over Colleen and Geoff's decision in time to enjoy the wedding.

"You seem a little somber today," Margaret said later in the afternoon. "Is everything okay?"

Molly looked up from where she was unloading a case of canned corn. "Oh, sorry. I guess I'm a little preoccupied."

"With what?" Margaret reached for a can, setting it on the shelf.

"Colleen's wedding plans." Molly glanced around the store to see that it appeared to be vacant of customers.

"But I thought you had it all worked out. Is there a problem with the Fairmont?"

Molly pursed her lips. So far she hadn't confided in Margaret about the change of plans. Not because Colleen had asked her not to, but because Mam had been working at the store all week. Today was the first day she'd remained at home. "Can I tell you something, Margaret, in complete confidence?"

Margaret looked surprised but very interested. "Of course. You can trust me with anything, Molly. What is it?"

So Molly quickly told Margaret about the last-minute change of wedding plans, about Geoff's family and the farm and the church. "Colleen will tell Mam and Dad when she gets home next week. Until then, we need to keep a lid on it."

"Oh, my." Margaret's brows shot up. "Mam and Dad will be so upset."

"I know. I'm praying they'll get over it quickly. And Colleen wanted to ask you in person to be in her wedding, but she's so busy with her film right now. I hope you don't mind."

"Of course I'd want to be in her wedding."

Now Molly told Margaret about the bridesmaid dresses and a few of the other details that Geoff's mother had shared.

"Did Colleen say who would be her maid or matron of honor?"

Molly nodded. "I couldn't have been more surprised too. She asked me, Margaret. Can you imagine?"

Margaret frowned. "That seems a little odd. I mean, you're pretty young."

"I thought so too, at first. But like Colleen said, she and I shared a bedroom all those years. And we've gotten even closer in the past couple of years." She smiled. "I feel very honored."

The bell on the door jingled and several customers came in, bringing their conversation to a close. But as Margaret went to assist them, Molly noticed a stiffness in her sister's voice. Was she hurt that Colleen hadn't asked her to be the matron of honor? Bridget had been her maid of honor, so it wasn't as if Colleen was beholden to Margaret.

As the workday came to an end, as silly as it seemed, Molly suspected that Margaret's nose was out of joint. When it was closing time, Molly confronted her.

"Oh, that's ridiculous." Margaret turned away, going up front to lock the door.

"Really? You don't mind?" Molly trailed her with the broom.

"Oh, well, certainly I was surprised by it. You're rather young for such an honor, Molly. Some might think you'd be better off as a junior bridesmaid."

Molly tried not to take offense at what felt like an intentional jab. "Well, it's Colleen's wedding. Hers and Geoff's, anyway. I'm just happy to be part of it." She put her focus on sweeping now, hurrying to complete her end of the day tasks so that she could leave.

"I can do that." Margaret reached for the broom.

"That's okay." Molly continued to sweep.

"Really," Margaret insisted. "I'll clean up. You go on home, Molly.

You probably have lots to do—you know, to help with Colleen's wedding. By the way, have you started planning a bridal shower yet?"

Molly stopped sweeping. "I hadn't even thought of that."

"Well, you'd better get busy. No time to waste." Margaret took the broom. "I'll finish up in here."

Molly stared at Margaret. "Oh, that's right. It's Thursday. Your night off. Do you have big plans?"

"Oh, no...not really. I mean, I hadn't really given it any thought."

"That's great. Why don't you and I go out for dinner, and you can help me plan a bridal shower for—"

"Oh, I can't do that, Molly." Margaret leaned the broom against the counter.

"Why not?" Molly frowned at her.

Margaret smiled in a slightly sly way as she untied her grocer's apron. "Because you are the maid of honor, Molly Irene. It should be up to you to plan her bridal shower. Good luck."

Molly didn't only feel dismissed by her sister, but put down as well. Why was Margaret being so mean? Was this all about Colleen's wedding? Or something more? But Peter was starting to fuss now, and Molly could tell that Margaret was eager for her to leave.

"Well, have a good evening." Molly went to get her purse, getting out her store key. "I'll go out the back and lock up behind me." Without another word, Molly hurried out, but as she locked the backdoor, she felt upset. She wasn't sure if she was hurt or mad or maybe both. But as she went around to the front of the store, she realized that she was something else too—she was suspicious. Margaret had been acting strangely for weeks now. And even more so on Thursdays.

Molly hurried across the street and into Dottie's Diner. She took a table by the window, but back in a corner where she could be more discrete—and where she had a direct view of the store's front door. After she ordered a light supper, she took out her reporter's notepad from her purse and began to jot down names of people that she planned to invite to Colleen's bridal shower, but the whole while she kept one eye on the store, watching as Sally arrived and was let in. Moments later Margaret emerged from the store, looking fresh and pretty in a pale-yellow summer dress that Molly had never seen before. And then, like clockwork, the insurance salesman appeared. And off they went, smiling and chatting like old friends...or something more.

By the time the waitress brought over her bowl of split pea soup, Molly had completely lost her appetite. She played with it a bit then laid some money on the table and left. She didn't know what to do... she wanted to talk with someone...but who? If Colleen weren't so busy, Molly would call her. Or if Peter were alive and at home, she would definitely go to him. Or even Bridget. But she did not think she could go to Mam and Dad with this. With Dad's bad health and Mam's preponderance to worrying, she didn't think they needed this burden. As she walked past the Hammonds' house, she considered going to Mrs. Hammond. She was like an aunt. But then realizing she was also Margaret's mother-in-law, she knew that was no good.

As she slowly walked home, she tried to think. What should she do? What should she do? Perhaps it was none of her business and she should do nothing. And yet, she knew that it *was* her business. Margaret was her sister. Peter was her nephew. More than anything, Molly wished she could talk to Patrick about it. After all, he was Brian's brother and Peter's uncle. Like her, he would be concerned, and Patrick would know what to do. He always had good advice, good ideas, and a lot of common sense. But Patrick was halfway around the world right now. And, judging by his last letter, he had his hands full. As an officer, he had many men to oversee. His primary goal was for them to do their best and make it home alive.

Molly completely respected that, but she also felt concerned. She might've been reading between the lines, but Patrick had seemed a little wearier than usual in his last letter, probably in need of some leave time. As always, he'd ended on a cheery note, telling her to share his warm regards with Colleen and Geoff and saying that he wished he could be there for their wedding. She'd written back the next day, saying how she wished he could be there too.

More than that, she wished he could be here right now.

Finally, as she got closer to home, Molly knew that the only thing she could do at the moment was to pray. Thanks to her many life lessons these past couple of years—Peter's death, Dad's illness, having loved ones scattered all around in dangerous places—she'd learned that sometimes prayer was all she had. And so that was what she did—she handed the whole dilemma over to God, silently saying amen as her own house came in sight.

"Hello, Molly." Mrs. Bartley waved from her front porch. She smiled down from her wicker rocking chair. "Lovely evening, isn't it?"

"Hello!" Molly eagerly called out and, without even thinking, she hurried up the steps. "I need to talk to someone," she said urgently. "Do you have time?"

"About all I have nowadays is time." Mrs. Bartley motioned to the other rocker. "Have a seat and tell me about what's troubling you."

Without even bothering to edit or censure herself, Molly poured out the whole scandalous story. It sounded even worse when she put it into words, yet she knew she needed to get it out. And she knew she could trust Mrs. Bartley. "Oh, my," she said finally. "I hope I haven't shocked you too much."

Mrs. Bartley smiled sadly. "Don't worry. You haven't. Not in the least."

"Really?"

Mrs. Bartley slowly shook her head.

"Well, I feel shocked by this," Molly confessed. "Of all my sisters, Margaret was always the most proper and correct. She was the most pious, often chastening the rest of us, making us mind our manners and act respectable. I just never expected something like this from someone like her."

"The ones riding the high horse have the biggest falls."

"But I don't want Margaret to fall," Molly declared. "She's got Baby Peter to consider. And what about Brian, off serving in the war? I just don't understand how she can be so selfish."

"Do you want to know the truth, Molly?"

She blinked. "Well, yes...of course." Did Mrs. Bartley know something about Margaret that Molly didn't?

Mrs. Bartley picked up her glass of lemonade. "Go into the house and get yourself some lemonade. Give me a moment to think about this."

Feeling slightly confused but extremely curious, Molly hurried inside, filled a glass, and then hurried back out, waiting expectantly for her elderly neighbor to continue.

"I'll tell you why Margaret's story doesn't shock me. It's simply because something similar happened to me—long ago, when I was a young woman." Her smile looked faint and faraway...and sad. "What some thought a rather attractive young woman."

"Really?" Molly tried to hide her surprise. "I mean, I'm sure you were a beautiful young woman, Mrs. Bartley. But the rest of what you said...that something similar happened to you."

"I don't think I ever told you about my husband being in the military."

Molly frowned. "I know your son Henry was killed in the previous World War, but I thought your husband was too old."

"That's true. But my husband, Henry senior, was in the Spanish-American War. Back in 1898. We'd only been married a couple of years at the time. We were still living in Charleston. Henry junior was just a baby when his daddy signed up to go fight down in Cuba." Mrs. Bartley grimly shook her head. "I never told anyone this, but I was furious about his decision to go. I was selfishly indignant and felt he'd abandoned my baby and me." She took a slow sip of her lemonade then continued.

"Well, an old beau lived down the street. Samuel Arlington. He'd wanted to marry me before Henry came along, but I'd refused him. When Samuel learned that my husband was gone to war, well, he began to pay more attention to me. But, to be perfectly honest, that was my fault. You see, it was springtime going into summer—a nice time for walks in the park. So I'd dress all up, Henry junior and me, and then I'd stroll with the baby carriage—right past Samuel's house. Before long, Samuel was accompanying me on these walks. I told myself that it was innocent enough, but it didn't take long for me to realize that Samuel's intentions were not completely honorable."

Molly didn't know what to say, so she simply sipped her lemonade and waited.

"Well, the truth is I only wanted Samuel's companionship, Molly. I was lonely and still a little miffed at my husband for going off to the war. I suppose I was acting like a spoiled child. But like I told you, I was young...and I was selfish. As a result, I wound up hurting everyone. At least that's how it seemed. Although I'd done nothing truly scandalous, the gossipers started to murmur. When I discovered what was being said, I bid Samuel adieu and stayed in my house, hoping the gossip would die down before my husband came home. But it was a short war—in less than five months Henry senior returned. Of course, the rumor mill was still going strong." She took a slow sip.

"It put quite a rift in our marriage, and my reputation was permanently ruined." She sighed. "That's why we left our families behind to move to San Francisco. My Henry eventually forgave me, but our relationship was damaged by my silliness. And I still regret it. To this day I am sorry."

"Oh..." Molly's tongue was tied.

"Now, I doubt that my story offers much encouragement to you, Molly. But it is the truth. The sad and unvarnished truth. And I felt it was good for you to know."

"Thank you for telling me." Molly set down her glass then smiled at Mrs. Bartley. "I'm honored you would trust me with your story."

"I felt you were old enough, and wise enough, to hear it." Mrs. Bartley smiled. "Thank you for listening."

"So, tell me, what do you think I should do about Margaret?"

Mrs. Bartley's brow creased as if deep in thought. "Do you think Margaret would listen to me?"

Molly considered this. "She might. Especially if I put some pressure on her. And I could easily do that, simply by telling her that I know what's going on, that I know what she's been up to."

"Sort of like blackmail?" Mrs. Bartley chuckled.

"If that's what it takes to get her attention, I don't really care."

"Then why don't you send her my way, Molly? And we will see if a word to the wise truly is sufficient."

Molly agreed to this plan, but before she went to bed that night, she prayed that Margaret would accept the invitation to listen to Mrs. Bartley...and that she would be wise enough to put a stop to whatever was going on—before it was too late. If it wasn't already too late. Molly prayed that it wasn't.

Nineteen

Colleen had mixed feelings when the movie wrapped in mid-July. On one hand, she was hugely relieved because she had so much to do before the wedding. But on the other hand, it was difficult to part ways with Laurel and Barry. They'd come to feel like family to her. Parting really was such sweet sorrow. She was close to tears as she said good-bye.

"This isn't good-bye," Laurel told her as they stood in the shade outside of the studio. It wasn't even noon yet, but their final scene had gone so well that the director had called it a wrap then called it a day. "I plan to ask that you be cast in our next film. I think they're scheduled to start shooting in October. Isn't that right, Barry?"

He nodded. "I just read through the script last night, and I think you're right, Laurel. Maureen would be perfect as your niece. I'll request her too."

"Thank you," Colleen said gratefully. "That would be wonderful."

Laurel lit a cigarette, taking in a slow drag. "I'll be looking for that wedding invitation you promised."

"I already gave both your names and addresses to my fiancé's mother," Colleen assured them. "She's taking care of all that."

"And don't forget my offer of my San Diego house for your

honeymoon," Laurel reminded her. "I'll be shooting in Rio for most of the summer. Someone might as well use it."

"I told Geoff about it. And he said we can talk more about it when I get home." Colleen smiled. "I'd love to stay there. I think it's a perfect spot for a honeymoon."

"And maybe you can convince him that you kids should buy it from me before I list it for sale in the fall." Laurel winked. "It'd save me some trouble if you do."

"I'd have to get an awfully nice movie contract in order to afford it," Colleen told her.

"You never know." Laurel ground out her cigarette.

"That's right." Barry grinned. "You could be on the cusp of a breakthrough."

They all hugged then turned to go their separate ways. Colleen hurried toward the studio parking lot where her car was waiting, already loaded with her packed bags. Her plan was to drive straight to San Francisco and, with an earlier-than-expected start, make it home before dinnertime. But it had been such a long week, with long days...she felt dog-tired. And the classical music program that her radio was tuned to was not helping to keep her awake. So she changed it to a station playing the noontime news. Naturally, the hottest topics were war related.

Colleen was slightly surprised to learn American and British troops had invaded Sicily last week. She'd been so busy with the film that she'd lost track of the news. It sounded as if the troops were in the thick of battle right now. And, according to the broadcast, the fighting was brutal and casualties were quickly adding up on all sides.

Colleen felt relieved that Geoff wasn't involved in active duty yet. He was safe and sound at his family's farm. Continuing to recover, he was resting and eating and getting lots of fresh air. But even as she felt relieved for Geoff, she felt a wave of concern for her brother-in-law. It was highly possible that Margaret's husband could be involved in those battles. Hadn't Brian been over in that part of the world? Poor Margaret, was she terribly worried about him? Or was she still playing the ostrich with her head in the sand?

Well, in some ways, Colleen didn't blame her. What good did it do to hear about all the sordid details of war?

As she tuned the radio back to the music program, Colleen decided that ignorance really was blissful at times. There was no denying that the world was a crazy mess, but Colleen and Geoff were about to have a beautiful wedding, and then they'd go on a lovely honeymoon. What happened after Geoff's medical leave was over... Well, they had no control over that. But if they couldn't take a break from the world's madness for the next few weeks, when could they?

She thought about Laurel's offer of the San Diego house. It had been so incredibly generous, and Colleen not only loved that sweet little house but knew it would save Geoff and her some money too. However, Geoff had sounded slightly hesitant about it yesterday when they'd talked on the phone. Apparently, he'd put together a different plan. But they would discuss all this tomorrow. Colleen had promised to spend Sunday on the farm with Geoff and his family.

Ellen had been hopeful that Colleen would attend church with them in the morning, but Colleen hadn't made a commitment yet. She wasn't sure that was such a good idea. Especially since she hadn't told her parents about the change in wedding plans yet. She wanted to just get it over with and tell them tonight. But it would probably add insult to injury if she took off to go to Geoff's church tomorrow.

She was not looking forward to informing her parents about her change in plans. But when she'd warned Molly that she'd break the news tonight, her wise little sister had decided to spend the night with Margaret and Peter—and Colleen knew she needed to just get it over with. The sooner she told her parents the news, the better. It would give them more time to recover before the wedding.

As Colleen drove north, she rehearsed various speeches that she might use for her parents. Although some of it actually sounded pretty good to her ears, she knew how her parents would hear it. All they would grasp would be that she'd chosen to say her wedding vows at an Episcopal church. They would think that she'd turned her back on Old Saint Mary's. No matter how carefully she said it, they would take her choice personally. And they would probably assume that it was her first step toward completely abandoning the faith of her childhood. If only she could make them see—this was her wedding. Hers and Geoff's.

Molly's reason for spending Saturday night with Margaret was twofold. Certainly, she did not want to be in the house when Colleen told Mam and Dad about the new wedding location. But perhaps even more than that, she wanted to use this opportunity to convince Margaret to go talk to Mrs. Bartley. However, she decided to wait until they'd had supper and Peter was soundly asleep. She felt that if the baby was sleeping, Margaret would have to keep her voice down—so as not to wake him. Then to sweeten the atmosphere even more, Molly insisted on washing up the dishes while Margaret put her feet up and listened to a music program on the radio.

Finally, it was time. Molly went into the living area, sat down, and took in a deep breath. "I need to talk to you about something," she said in a quiet yet serious tone.

"Is something wrong?" Margaret looked up from the women's magazine she was flipping through.

Molly nodded. "Yes."

Margaret laid aside the magazine, giving Molly her full attention. "What is it?"

"I know about you and Mr. Moore."

Margaret looked slightly alarmed then covered it with a smile. "Of course you do. I told you he's selling me insurance for the store."

"That's not the truth, Margaret." Molly locked eyes with her. "You know it's not."

Margaret glanced away.

"I'm not telling you this so that you can deny it," Molly continued. "And I don't want you to make up some big story again. I'm not buying it, Margaret."

Margaret looked back up with narrowed eyes. "So what?" she said in a surprisingly callous tone. "I'm friends with Howard Moore. What of it?"

"What of it?" Molly didn't try to hide her shock. "You're married, Margaret. You have a baby. Your husband is right now risking his life overseas."

"Yes, I'm well aware of all that, Molly. What is your point?"

"My point is that it's wrong for you to be carrying on with Mr. Moore."

"Carrying on?" Margaret made a disgusted look. "What exactly do you mean by that?"

"I mean you're getting yourself all gussied up, and you're walking around town with him, Margaret. For anyone to see. And it looks bad. If you don't care for your own sake, you should at least care for Brian and Peter's sake."

"I'm not doing anything wrong," Margaret said stubbornly.

"You honestly don't think it's wrong?" Molly stared at her. "In your heart of hearts, you don't feel a little bit guilty, Margaret?"

Margaret shrugged then looked away.

"Fine." Molly stood up, starting to nervously pace back and forth. "If you don't think what you're doing is wrong, you won't mind when I tell Mam and Dad about it. And while I'm at it, I guess I'll tell Mr. and Mrs. Hammond too."

Margaret stood too, coming over to face Molly. "Why would you do that to me, Molly? Do you hate me that much?"

"I love you, Margaret. But I hate to see you throwing your life away like this."

"But I told you, I haven't done anything wrong. Howie and I simply take walks, share a meal, visit a little. That's all there is to it."

"So you wouldn't mind if Dad and Mam or your in-laws knew?"

Margaret planted her fists on her hips. "I know you're the baby of the family, Molly, but I never took you for a tattletale."

"Here's my deal, Margaret. I will keep quiet about this if you do something."

"Is this blackmail?"

"Call it whatever you like, but if you want me to keep my mouth closed, you have to go talk to Mrs. Bartley."

"Mrs. Bartley?" Margaret blinked. "Why on earth would I go talk to that old lady?"

"Because she's a wise old woman, and she understands what you've gotten yourself into."

"You told her about me?"

"I had to tell someone, Margaret. As it turned out, Mrs. Bartley was the perfect person to tell." Molly looked at her watch to see that it was nearly eight o'clock and enough time had passed for Colleen to have told Mam and Dad her news. "I'll give you twenty-four hours to talk to Mrs. Bartley. If you don't talk to her, I'm telling Mam and Dad." Molly went to get her purse. "And I've changed my mind about spending the night. I'm going home."

"But you won't tell them, will you?" Margaret asked in a slightly desperate tone.

"Not for twenty-four hours. But only if you talk to Mrs. Bartley." Molly headed for the door. "I'll see you in church."

As Molly let herself out of the store, locking the door behind her, she felt a tiny bit guilty for being so hard on Margaret. And yet, she knew that was what Margaret needed. Someone to call her out on her senselessness. Hopefully it would work.

Molly took her time walking home, getting there just as the sky was getting dusky. To her relief, Colleen's car was parked in back, and when Molly touched the car's hood, it was cold. Colleen had been there awhile. As Molly tiptoed through the back porch, listening for the sounds of raised voices, she noticed that no one had closed the blackout curtains. As she hurried to cover the kitchen window, the only sound she heard was the radio softly playing in the living room. But when she saw Dad sitting dejectedly in his chair, just staring into space, she felt worried.

"Hello, Dad," she said softly.

He looked up in surprise. "Oh, Molly. I thought you were staying over at Margaret's."

"Well, I was going to..." She hurried about to put up the blackout curtains. "But I changed my mind."

"Seems that a women's prerogative has taken over this household. Plenty of mind changing going on round here."

Molly sat down on the ottoman by his chair. "So Colleen told you?"

He nodded grimly.

"I know it must be a shock," she said gently, "but I understand why they're doing it, Dad."

"How's that?" He looked doubtful.

"Both Colleen and Geoff have had a pretty rough year. I'm sure you must agree to that."

He gave a halfhearted nod.

"And Colleen told me that before all that happened, neither one of them were very good at praying...and perhaps didn't fully believe in God. But Colleen and Geoff have changed, Dad. And now they both want to make their wedding vows before God. So wouldn't you agree that a church is the perfect place to do that?"

"Certainly." His brow furrowed. "What's wrong with Old Saint Mary's?"

"You know Geoff isn't Catholic, Dad. And there's not enough time for him to convert." Molly reached for his hand, clasping it between her hands. "You're a godly man. I know that you are—and I love that you are. So why wouldn't you be glad that Colleen and Geoff want a church wedding? Isn't that better than just signing a marriage license at City Hall?"

He thoughtfully rubbed his chin. "Hearing you put it like that... well, it does shed a different sort of light on things."

"I actually feel that Colleen and Geoff are trying to be respectful to their families by doing it like this. Don't you think so?"

He seemed to consider this. "You could be right."

She squeezed his hand. "If it's any comfort to you, I still dream of getting married in Old Saint Mary's...someday."

His eyes lit up. "To a good Catholic boy?"

"I hope so." She smiled.

"Good girl." He let out a weary sigh. "Well, I'm all tuckered out, Molly. Your mam already turned in. Guess I will follow her lead."

Molly helped him to his feet then linked her arm in his. "I look forward to the day that you'll walk me down the aisle at Old Saint Mary's," she told him. "And I know that Colleen feels the same way... even though it's not Old Saint Mary's. The important thing is that her family will be there for her big day. Don't you think?"

"Family is family." He paused by the bedroom door.

"Family is family." She kissed him on the cheek and said good night.

As Dad went into the bedroom, Molly quietly crept up the shadowy stairs. Eager to see Colleen, she hoped she hadn't already gone to bed. Molly jumped in surprise to find her sister on the landing. Without saying a word, Colleen hugged Molly—long and hard. "Thank you."

"You were listening?" Molly whispered, leading Colleen into her bedroom and quietly closing the door.

"Every word." Colleen's eyes were red and puffy. "You were great. I couldn't have said it better." She sniffed. "I obviously didn't."

"So they didn't take it so well?"

"That's an understatement. Mam went to bed with a headache. Probably from all the yelling. I was worried that Dad was going to have a heart attack, so I called it quits too."

Molly grimaced. "He seemed tired, but his coloring was okay."

"Hearing him just now...well, it gave me hope that he might get over this." Colleen sank down on Molly's bed with a tired sigh. "He's so stubborn."

"Well, you must've worn him down." Molly sat on the chair across from her.

"Maybe, but I still really appreciate what you said. You're a good sister."

"I'm glad someone thinks so."

"What do you mean?" Colleen's brow creased. "Hey, weren't you supposed to spend the night at Margaret's? What happened?"

Molly felt close to tears now. "Oh, Colleen—I'm so worried."

"What is it?" Colleen sat up in alarm. "Is it the baby? Is he sick? Is something wrong with—"

"No, it's not the baby. Not really. But it involves him." Molly bit her lip. "I'm not sure I should say any—"

"Of course you should. What is going on? Tell me, Molly."

"Well, I promised Margaret I wouldn't tell Mam or Dad. Or the Hammonds. But I didn't promise not to tell you."

"Tell me what?" she demanded. "Is this about Brian? I heard bad news on the radio just this afternoon. Has Margaret been—"

"No, no, it's nothing like that." Molly took in a deep breath. "I'll tell you, Colleen, if you promise not to interrupt. Just let me get it out."

"Go for it."

Molly quickly poured out the story, clear up to the part where Molly blackmailed Margaret to talk to Mrs. Bartley and gave her twenty-four hours to do so.

"Are you kidding?" Colleen's eyes grew wide. "Our perfect sister is seeing a man?"

"She keeps insisting they've done nothing wrong—and if she means, well, you know, being unfaithful to Brian...then I do believe her. But it still seems wrong for her to be going around with Howard Moore."

"I'll say it's wrong. And I don't care what Margaret says. She knows better than to do this." Colleen frowned. "Do you think she'll really talk to Mrs. Bartley?"

Molly shrugged. "You said Dad's stubborn, but Margaret is being a mule."

"Do you really believe Mrs. Bartley can straighten her out?"

Molly quickly relayed what Mrs. Bartley told her.

Colleen's brows shot up. "Oh, my. Who knew?"

"I think it's so kind of her to offer to talk to Margaret. It wasn't easy for her to tell me about it. And you must promise not to repeat it."

"Do you think I should talk to Margaret?"

"It couldn't hurt."

"I know stories about actresses who've messed up their lives and marriages by doing that sort of thing. Sure, they might call it innocent flirting, but it's not as innocent as people like to think. Believe me, someone always gets hurt."

"That's what Mrs. Bartley said. She still feels badly for it—all these years later."

"And Margaret will too, if she doesn't nip this in the bud."

Molly hoped that Margaret's involvement with Mr. Moore was still in the bud.

"Anyway, I'll talk to her. Whether or not she talks to Mrs. Bartley, I will give her a piece of my mind." Colleen stood up and stretched. "Now, if you'll excuse me, I am so exhausted, I feel like I could sleep for a week. But I need to get up early. I promised Geoff I'd spend the day at the farm tomorrow. Don't tell Mam and Dad, but I'm going to church with him in the morning."

"It's a really pretty church," Molly told her. "And their priest—at least, I think he's called a priest—anyway, he seemed really nice."

Colleen hugged Molly. "Thanks again for talking to Dad."

"I think he'll be okay...in time."

"You know when you promised that you'd get married in Old Saint Mary's?" Colleen paused by the door. "Well, I could just imagine you as a beautiful bride—and do you know who I envisioned as your handsome groom?"

Molly frowned.

"Patrick Hammond." Colleen patted Molly on the cheek.

"Oh, Colleen!" Molly pretended to be irked.

Colleen just giggled then, saying good night, hurried out. But as soon as she was gone, Molly sat down to write Patrick a letter. Tempted to tell him about Margaret's situation, she stopped herself. Patrick was Margaret's brother-in-law. He didn't need to know about any of that. Instead, Molly wrote to him about Colleen and Geoff's changed wedding plans and how Mam and Dad were still getting used to the idea. Of course, she wrote about other things too, finally telling him—like she always did—that she missed him dearly and prayed for him daily. She really wanted to sign it *Love, Molly* but felt that was going too far.

Twenty

Colleen felt thoroughly happy as she drove back to San Francisco on Sunday evening. The day with Geoff and his family could not have gone better. To her surprise and relief, Ellen never once expressed her disapproval over Colleen's acting career. Of course, she didn't inquire about it either. But that was better than getting into a disagreement. Colleen guessed it was simply because Ellen was so caught up in the wedding plans. According to Geoff, his mother could hardly believe her good luck—that her future daughter-in-law was so willing to hand over the wedding reins.

Colleen couldn't help but chuckle since she'd never wanted to waste a lot of time and money on a big wedding in the first place. Why not let Ellen knock herself out if that's what she wanted? And Colleen had to admit that, so far, everything Ellen had told her and showed her seemed just fine. And their house and yard looked absolutely lovely—the perfect location for a reception.

The best part of the day was when Geoff took her on his own tour, showing Colleen all his favorite boyhood places—finally ending up in the hay loft where they'd enjoyed some good old-fashioned, country-style kissing. Now that was fun! But as she drove through the city, she remembered her promise to Molly—that she would speak to Margaret. Although she wasn't looking forward to this conversation, she did like the idea of getting it over with. Either Margaret would listen...or she wouldn't. But Colleen would at least try.

After Margaret got over the surprise of seeing Colleen at the back door, and after Colleen got to get a sweet little peek at her slumbering nephew, they settled down in the living area to chat. Colleen filled Margaret in on the wedding plans, glossing over their parents' reactions. "And the church is pretty," she said. "Not as grand as Old Saint Mary's, but just fine. And, like I keep telling everyone, the wedding is just one day. Sure, I want it to be nice, but what matters most is what comes afterward." She narrowed her eyes slightly. "Speaking of that, I was a little surprised to hear that you've been spending time with a man, Margaret. Is it true you've got a boyfriend?"

"That is a lie." Margaret's eyes flashed in anger. "Did Molly tell you that?"

"She told me you've been stepping out with a man on Thursday nights, which actually makes me feel slightly guilty since I'm the one who set up your baby-sitter. But trust me, dear sister, that is not what I had in mind."

"Molly had no right to—"

"Molly is sick with worry about you, Margaret. She's seen you with him. You get yourself all dressed up then go out with this man—Howard Moore, I think she said was his name—and that you claim he's an insurance salesman. But if you think anyone would buy that, you're not nearly as smart as I thought you were."

"He is only a friend and—"

"He is a man, Margaret. You're going out with him. Call him anything you like, but if anyone sees you together, they will assume the worst. You can't possibly be that naïve. Good grief, for all you know, someone besides Molly may have seen you already. What if this gets back to the Hammonds? Can you imagine how they would feel? Or Mam and Dad? Worst of all, what if Brian got wind of it?"

"How would that happen?"

"Are you kidding?" Colleen scowled. "Have you forgotten about some of the busybodies that shop in this store? What if someone like Velma Jones or her mother saw you with Howard?"

"I've been very careful."

"Careful?" Colleen shook her head. "How did Molly see you?"

"Molly should mind her own business."

Colleen stood up, getting her purse. "I can't believe you would say that, Mary Margaret."

"Don't go off in a huff." Margaret stood too.

"Well, I can see it's pointless trying to talk sense to you. Did you even go see Mrs. Bartley like Molly asked?"

"I went there after church. She told me her story."

"And it meant nothing to you?"

Margaret's chin quivered slightly. "You don't know what it's like for me, Colleen. Living alone and—"

"I do know what it's like. Remember I stayed here with you? I saw how it was for you. That's why I set up the baby-sitter so you could get out. But not like that. And speaking of lonely, I know what that's like. Remember that I live alone? Sure, I don't have a baby, but I've been plenty lonely.

"But you go to the Canteen and dance with—"

"Yes, after a long day's work, I sometimes go to the Canteen and dance with lonely servicemen until my feet want to fall off. But that is it. I don't go walking around town with them or let them take me out for a meal. Even when I wasn't sure if Geoff was dead or alive or ever coming back, I never took up with a fellow. And it's not that I haven't had my offers." She laughed. "Believe me, I have. But throughout it all, for that whole uncertain time, I was faithful to him."

"I've been faithful to Brian."

"Have you?" Colleen put her face just inches from Margaret's. "What do you think Brian would say if he could see you and Howard Moore strutting around town together? Sharing a meal—and whatever else it is you do? Would Brian call that faithful?"

Now Margaret was starting to cry. But Colleen was tired and fed up—and not particularly sympathetic. "You're a wife and a mother, Margaret. It was your choice. In fact, as I recall, you pushed hard for it. So if that means you have to be lonely for a while, well, so be it."

"Are you leaving?" Margaret asked in a weepy voice.

"Yes. I'm exhausted. I'm going home, and I plan to sleep for a few days." Colleen turned to lock eyes with Margaret. "Why don't you think about what I just said? If you come to your senses, we can talk again."

"Meaning you won't talk to me otherwise?"

Colleen shrugged. "I don't know. The truth is, I don't have much respect for you at the moment, Margaret. But like I said, I'm very tired. Maybe I'll feel differently tomorrow." Then without saying another word, Colleen left.

Molly went to work at the store as usual, but she could tell that Margaret was mad at her. Molly tried to gloss over the rift with small talk, but Margaret's responses were short and sharp. As a result they barely spoke. So much so that by midday Wednesday, Mam became suspicious. "It certainly has been quiet around here," she mentioned as she gathered her things to go home.

"Just been keeping busy," Margaret said as she scurried to the backroom.

"Don't have much to say," Molly added as she straightened a stack of baking soda boxes.

"Well, I guess I should appreciate the peace and quiet." Mam chuckled. "What with Bridget coming tomorrow, we'll be almost a full house. I expect it will get noisy at home."

"Oh, I can't wait to see her!" Molly exclaimed. "I wish you'd let me go to pick her up at the—"

"Dad and I get the privilege this time," Mam told her. "And Margaret needs your help here."

Molly wanted to point out that it might be nice if Margaret acted like she needed her help, but she bit her tongue instead. No sense in worrying Mam. Still, as the day came to a close, Molly was fed up with Margaret. And so she decided that, before she left the store, she would speak her mind and, as soon as Margaret locked the front door, she began.

"You are obviously perturbed at me, Margaret. To be honest, I'm not feeling particularly loving toward you right now. I know you talked to Mrs. Bartley, although she wasn't convinced that you heeded her warning. And I know that Colleen spoke to you, but again, it doesn't sound as if you listened. For all we know, you plan to go out with Howard Moore again tomorrow and—"

"That is where you are wrong," Margaret snapped. "I will not go out with him. I already told him as much."

Molly blinked. "Oh."

"But I still resent your intrusion into my life, Molly. I feel you stepped over a line and—"

"Fine." Molly pulled off her grocer's apron. "I am officially giving you my resignation, Margaret. I refuse to work for a sister who resents me like you do." Molly grabbed her purse and headed through the backroom.

"You can't do that," Margaret called out. "Mam and Dad will—"

"Mam and Dad will what?" Molly demanded. "I can find another job. And I'll assure them that I will keep helping out at home. Maybe I'll find something more profitable than here. And certainly more enjoyable than working for a boss as unpleasant as you have been."

"But what will you tell them," Margaret asked with wide eyes, "about why you've quit?"

"Just the truth." And without saying another word, Molly hurried toward the backdoor. Let Margaret think whatever she liked. Molly didn't really care.

"Wait!" Margaret cried out.

Molly paused with her hand on the doorknob.

"I'm sorry, Molly." Margaret had tears in her eyes. "I don't know why I've turned into such a horrible person, but I am sorry."

Molly's heart softened.

"I'm just so confused—about everything. But what I said about Howard is true. I told him I can't see him anymore." Margaret was crying hard now. "And that's not easy, Molly. I don't expect you to understand. But I've been very lonely. And my friendship with Howard helped to keep me going. I looked forward to it and—"

"If you're that lonely, why don't you just move back home?" Molly suggested. "Mam and Dad have plenty of room."

Margaret wiped her eyes with her handkerchief. "I don't know."

"Just come home for a while," Molly suggested eagerly. "Think how much fun it would be for you to be home while Bridget is here, Margaret. And with all the wedding preparations going on. Wouldn't you like to be part of that? And we can all help you with the baby. Imagine how much Bridget will love getting to spend time with him. Oh, please, Margaret, say that you'll move back home—at least while Bridget is here."

"Do you think they would mind?" Margaret looked hopeful.

"Why would anyone mind?"

"Well, someone would have to share a room. I mean, Peter and I can stay in my old room, but—"

"I don't mind sharing."

"I'd like to come home," Margaret said meekly.

"Then do," Molly insisted. "At least for a while. It'll be like old times. It'll be fun!"

Margaret hugged Molly. "I'm sorry I was so mean to you. I don't know why I was. Except that I've just been so unhappy inside. Thank you for not giving up on me, Molly."

"How about if I go home and get the car? I'll tell everyone about our plan. In the meantime, you can pack up what you think you and Peter will need, you know, just for the night. And I'll come back and pick you up."

Bridget tried to act the same, but she felt like a different person as Mam drove them toward home. And it was different seeing Mam behind the wheel—and a little unnerving when she nearly ran down a pedestrian. Even more so when Dad yelled at her to, "Watch out!"

Bridget tried to be pleasant, answering her parents' many questions, but it felt strange to be back in a city—unsettling and overwhelming. So many cars and people moving about. So many streets and buildings all around. It all felt so vastly different from the jungle where she'd been living in a small tent with two other nurses, doing pretty much the same thing every day. Caring for wounded soldiers, administering medications, assisting in surgery—again and again, over and over...day after day. Certainly there was always an element of excitement beneath it all, not knowing how close the enemy might be or if their medical unit might be bombed. But mostly it was just a lot of extremely hard and never-ending work.

"Margaret and the baby have moved back home," Mam was telling her. "The girls thought it would be fun to have the whole family together while you're home."

"I'll warn you, it can get noisy," Dad said a bit grimly.

"And how is your health?" Bridget turned around to ask him. "Molly wrote to me about your heart trouble. Are you taking it easy, Dad?"

"All I do is take it easy," he grumbled.

"That's not true," Mam countered. "You're always trying to do something that you shouldn't. Yesterday I caught him pulling weeds in Molly's victory garden."

"I just wanted some fresh air," he argued.

"I'm sure fresh air would be good for you, Dad. But probably not pulling weeds. Why not just take a little walk?"

"Here we are," Mam announced as she pulled into the alley behind the house. "Margaret and Molly are still at the store. The baby too. But Colleen is home."

"My movie-star sister?" Bridget mused.

"I'll get your bag," Dad offered as they got out.

"No thanks." Bridget beat him to the trunk.

As they walked through the back, Bridget stopped to admire the garden. "Oh, it's marvelous," she told them. "We try to grow things in the jungle, but it's a constant battle with the bugs and birds. Although our banana tree is nice."

"A banana tree." Mam shook her head. "How interesting."

Colleen met Bridget in the kitchen, encompassing her in a big hug. "Oh, Bridget, I'm so glad to see you." She held her back at arm's length. "Is it my imagination or have you gotten even prettier?"

Bridget shrugged. "Thanks, but it's probably your imagination."

"No, it's not. And you've lost weight too. You used to be much more round." Colleen gave Bridget a little turn. "It looks good on you though."

"Thanks."

"But I'll have to take in your bridesmaid dress." Colleen led Bridget through the house. "You're going to be in your old room," she said as they went upstairs. "Margaret and the baby are in Peter's old room, and I'm bunking with Molly."

"I don't mind sharing," Bridget said. "I'm used to it."

"That's exactly why we all decided that you should have your own room. We want to make sure you have a really good rest during your leave."

"Thanks." Bridget sighed. "I am a little tired."

"Why don't you get yourself settled?" Colleen suggested. "Take a nap if you want. Or a bath if you—"

"A bath!" Bridget unbuttoned her jacket. "I can't even imagine how nice that would be."

"Then go for it," Colleen urged. "Molly and Margaret won't be home for a couple of hours, so this might be the best time to have the bathroom all to yourself." She held up a finger. "And I'll grab some goodies for you. I've got the nicest shampoo and scented soaps. You'll love them."

Bridget thanked her, and before long she was luxuriating in a hot tub of rose scented bubbles. Oh, she still felt different...but it was good to be home!

Twenty-One

Molly loved having a full house again. Sure it was loud and busy, and the waits for the bathroom were longer, but it was all worth it. "Tell us another story," Molly begged Bridget as they gathered in the living room after supper on Saturday.

"Haven't you heard enough yet?" Bridget bounced Baby Peter on her knee.

"No." Colleen paused from her sewing. She was taking in Bridget's bridesmaid gown. "We want to hear more about all those spiders and snakes and creepy things."

Bridget laughed. "But maybe I want to forget them for the time being."

"Yes," Mam agreed. "I'd like to forget them too."

Margaret shuddered. "I still can't believe the spiders are as big as your hand, Bridget. I was worried I'd have nightmares after you told us about that."

"And they're hairy too," Bridget reminded her.

"Tell us about something that was fun," Colleen urged Bridget.

"Fun?" Bridget's brow creased. "Did I tell you about being in the submarine?"

"You were in a real submarine?" Molly asked. "I have a suspicion that Patrick might be serving on a submarine."

"Really?" Dad's brows arched with interest. "What makes you think that, Molly?"

"Some things in his letters seem to hint at it. But, of course, he never says anything very specific."

"We're constantly reminded to be extremely careful about giving out information in letters," Bridget said. "That's why I can never say exactly where I'm stationed."

"So tell us about the submarine," Molly pressed. "I've heard of hospital ships, but is it a hospital submarine?"

"No, it was a Gato-class navy submarine. Very sleek and modern and big. I think the admiral said it was more than three hundred feet long," she directed to Dad.

"I heard those subs can run close to three million dollars," he said.

"Well, it was a handsome boat," she told them. "And everything in it and on it was spick-and-span."

"I wish you could bring home photographs," Molly said wistfully.

"I don't think that would've been allowed. Anyway, the sub was in for some minor repairs. I guess I can tell you now, since we're not stationed there anymore, but our medical unit was on an island called Efate. The officers invited several of us to come for dinner." She smiled. "It's not unusual for nurses to get invited out—both by army and navy officers."

"Especially the pretty nurses like you," Colleen teased.

Bridget rolled her eyes. "Anyway, we hardly ever turn down navy invitations since they have the best food. Plus, we were pretty excited about seeing the submarine. As usual, we wore our uniforms. The army recently came out with these wrap-around seersucker dresses for nurses. They're not terribly fashionable, but they wash well and are cooler in the tropics. But as it turned out, we should've worn our trousers—like we often do while we're working."

"Why would you wear trousers to a dinner party?" Margaret asked.

"Because you have to go down a ladder to enter the submarine." Bridget laughed. "Those skirts turned out to be a bit risqué. You should've heard the whistles we got before the admiral silenced his crew."

They all laughed.

"So how was the submarine food?" Molly asked.

"It was pretty good. Although their menu is understandably limited, due to space and storage issues. So it didn't quite match up to what we've had on some of the aircraft carriers. Hands down, the carriers have the best food. Probably because their galleys are so much bigger and better equipped. Plus they have lots of room to stock up on food when in port. We nurses never reject an invitation to dine on an aircraft carrier. Not that we get many since we're usually stationed inland. Although they will sometimes send vehicles to pick us up."

"What kind of food do you normally eat?" Dad asked. "When you're not living high on the hog with the sailors?"

"It depends. If we're on the move, we get by on K-rations."

"What is a K-ration?" Margaret asked.

"It's packaged for use in battle. Very basic. Hardtack, some form of canned protein, sometimes a chocolate bar and—" She laughed. "Cigarettes. But to be honest, it's about the worst sort of food imaginable. But when it's all we have, I remind myself that it's the same thing our troops are eating when they're on the battlefield. Some of them have K-rations for weeks on end. We usually only suffer through them for a few days, when we're on the move or cut off from supply shipments. Most of the time, when our unit is stationed, we eat at the mess hall. The food is very basic and the quality depends on the cook. Sometimes they'll enhance the menu with local produce. Occasionally, if we lose a cook, we might rely on C-rations for a while. They're a step up from K-rations. More cans of food, more variety." She smiled at Mam. "But nothing is as good as your cooking."

"You haven't said a word about your doctor friend," Margaret said abruptly. "What is going on with—"

"Oh, don't pester Bridget about that," Mam told Margaret. "She doesn't need to tell us about him unless she wants to."

Bridget's smile looked stiff. "There's nothing to tell."

"Is he still working at the same hospital as you?" Margaret pressed on.

"He was...when I left. But I heard we might get transferred. For all I know, my unit could be sent to a completely different location by the time I go back in August."

"Wouldn't Dr. Cliff be transferred too?" Margaret asked.

"I really couldn't say." Bridget's tone had grown crisp.

"Okay, Lieutenant Mulligan." Colleen stood, shaking out the bridesmaid dress so that the shiny, iridescent fabric glimmered in the light. She held it up to Bridget. "Time for you to try this on and see if it fits."

"It's so beautiful." Bridget fingered the fabric.

"What color is that?" Dad asked. "First it looks blue, then purple, then silver, then green."

"It's called iridescent," Colleen told him. "But mostly it's blue."

"Reminds me of the ocean," Mam told her.

"Go try it on," Colleen told Bridget. "You can give Mam and Dad a sneak preview."

"What kind of flowers will your bridesmaids carry?" Mam asked.

"Geoff's mom and grandma are overseeing all the wedding

flowers," Colleen explained. "You should see their flower garden, Mam. It's gorgeous."

"Do you mean to say they'll be making all the arrangements and bouquets for the whole wedding—just the two of them?" Mam asked.

"They have some ladies from their church helping," Colleen told her.

"But what if you don't like what they do?" Margaret asked with concern.

"I gave Ellen a scrap of fabric from the bridesmaid dresses and asked her to make sure the flowers look nice with it. I told her that I'd like mostly blue and purple and pink colored flowers."

"That sounds pretty," Mam said quietly.

"And I asked for white roses for my bouquet," Colleen continued.

"I still feel a little odd about the groom's mother handling everything for the wedding." Mam's tone was sad.

"Just remember that Ellen has no daughters," Colleen reminded her. "You've got four, Mam. No need to be selfish. And remember you've already done one wedding—with two more to go. This is your chance to simply relax and enjoy my wedding without having to lift a finger."

"I suppose so." Mam still looked uncertain.

Molly went over to put an arm around Mam's shoulders. "Don't forget that you have something to help me with," she said quietly as Bridget came down the stairs wearing the beautiful bridesmaid gown. While Colleen went over to check her alterations, Molly whispered in Mam's ear. "We're going to make Colleen's surprise bridal shower the best one ever."

Now Mam actually smiled. "That we will," she said quietly.

And that was just what they did a few days later. With Mrs. Hammond's help, they held a perfectly delightful bridal shower that caught Colleen completely off guard. With ingenuity, donated sugar rations, and lots of helping hands, it was an event that Molly knew the ladies in attendance would be talking about for months to come. She took lots of photos, and after it was over with, she and Bridget remained behind to clean up.

"Do you think Colleen really liked it?" Molly asked Bridget as they were packing up the borrowed china.

Bridget laughed. "Well, I'm not sure what she'll do with all that kitchen stuff. Everyone knows that Colleen doesn't cook."

"Oh, but she'll learn to cook." Mrs. Hammond put the crystal punch bowl into a box. "Her husband will expect it."

"Don't be so sure of that." Bridget winked at Molly.

"Anyway, she won't need to cook for a while," Molly said. "Geoff will be overseas, and Colleen will be making her next movie."

"Well, whether Colleen ever puts the kitchen things to use of not, it was a delightful evening," Mrs. Hammond declared. "You girls did a marvelous job putting it all together so nicely."

"That was Molly's doing," Bridget told her. "She organized everything."

"But everyone helped," Molly reminded her as she closed up the box of china she'd borrowed from Mrs. Bartley.

"Well done, Molly." Mrs. Hammond beamed at them. "I've been just bursting with good news all night long, but the trouble is I'm not supposed to tell anyone."

"A secret?" Bridget teased. "Do you want us to worm it out of you?"

"Oh, I don't know." Mrs. Hammond giggled like a young girl. "But if I can trust you girls not to tell anyone, I might be inclined to share it. It's awfully hard keeping it all to myself. I haven't even told Mr. Hammond."

Molly chuckled. "Well, now you've aroused our curiosity."

"Will you both promise to keep it quiet?"

"Yes, ma'am." Bridget saluted her.

"Loose lips sink ships," Molly said.

"Well, I just got a letter from Brian today. It seems that he and Patrick have been in communication. They've been trying to coordinate their leave time so that they can see each other."

"That would be so nice for them." Molly knew that Patrick had been worried about his brother...and missing him.

"But why such a big secret?" Bridget placed the last piece of a silver tea set into a box.

"Because the boys hope to meet up at Colleen's wedding!"

"Mrs. Hammond," Molly exclaimed, "that would be wonderful!"

"Yes, it would. But we don't know for sure that it will happen, so Brian asked me not to tell anyone." She smiled nervously. "So now I must swear you both to secrecy. I especially don't want to get Margaret's hopes up and then have her be disappointed."

"Mum's the word," Molly promised.

"You can trust me," Bridget said. "The army's trained me about confidentiality."

"I just hope that it all works out," Mrs. Hammond said. "I miss my boys so much." She looked hopefully at Bridget. "And I don't think it's any coincidence that Patrick wants to be here while you're here, dear." She touched Bridget's cheek. "And you're looking so pretty too."

"That's Colleen's doing." Bridget patted her new hairstyle. "She insisted on working me over yesterday."

"Well, I've never seen you looking so pretty." Mrs. Hammond turned to Molly. "Don't you think so too?"

"I've always thought Bridget was beautiful," Molly said. "But I agree she's even more so now."

"Well, it just seems providential," Mrs. Hammond said. "I'm praying that both my boys make it."

"I'll be praying too." Molly picked up a carton of dishes. As she carried it out to the car, she felt uneasy. Oh, she knew that Mrs. Hammond was a little behind the times, thinking that Bridget and Patrick might truly be interested in a relationship...and yet, how could anyone know for sure? Besides, Mrs. Hammond was right that Bridget was looking better than ever these days. And, based on what Bridget was saying—or not saying—about Dr. Cliff, it was hard to know exactly how she felt. At one time she'd been over the moon about this particular doctor, but she hadn't even mentioned him once during her leave. Maybe it was over. And perhaps that shouldn't matter. More than anything else, Molly hoped and prayed the Hammond brothers would make it here in time for the wedding!

Twenty-Two

Margaret had mixed feelings as she spooned applesauce into Peter's mouth on the morning of Colleen's wedding day. Certainly she was happy for her sister and for how neatly everything seemed to be falling into place for her big day. But at the same time she felt the old, familiar nag of jealousy. She hated feeling like this...and yet Margaret had been the one to dream of a big summer wedding. Instead, she'd settled for a rushed winter ceremony and a brief honeymoon. It didn't help that even though Colleen was about to have a fabulous and beautiful wedding, she didn't seem to care.

Perhaps more troubling than her envy was accepting that everything would change following the celebration. Margaret had enjoyed being surrounded by family. She didn't want it to end. But by the end of the day, Colleen and Geoff would leave for their honeymoon, and in a few more days Bridget would head back to her medical unit in the Pacific. And Margaret and the baby would return to the lonely little apartment above the store. She would've prolonged her stay, except that Mam and Dad had both hinted about the need for some peace and quiet.

Margaret used the spoon to clean Peter's chin. As much as she hated to admit it, her biggest worry was that, in her loneliness, she might turn to Howard for company and comfort. What then?

"Why are you looking so glum?" Molly asked as she came into the kitchen.

"Oh, I was thinking about how everything is about to change," Margaret confessed. "I don't want Colleen and Bridget to leave. I want everything to stay just how it is."

Molly patted her on the back. "Well, that's not going to happen. But before everything changes, you might want to enjoy what's right here, right now. Colleen's invited us all to join her upstairs."

"What for?"

"She wants us to have manicures and pedicures." Molly giggled. "She's got all the stuff ready. And besides that, I thought we should help her pack for her honeymoon."

"Why on earth would Colleen need our help to pack a suitcase?"

"Because it'll be fun! You should see what she's got up there, Margaret. Her friends down in Hollywood gave her a trousseau shower before her movie wrapped."

"A trousseau shower?"

"That's what she called it. Anyway, she's got all these beautiful things to pack, and I just thought you might want to—"

"I'm coming." Margaret eagerly scooped up Peter and, carrying his dish and spoon, hurried up the stairs to Molly's room. "We're here," she said as she and the baby flopped down on the bed. Together the sisters took turns helping each other to paint fingernails and toenails, watching with wide eyes as Colleen showed them item after item of delicate sleepwear, lingerie, and under-clothing.

"This negligee is from Laurel Wagner." Colleen removed something white and flimsy from a box.

"Négligé?" Molly frowned. "Isn't that French for neglected?"

"I don't speak French." Colleen chuckled.

"I doubt she'll be neglected in that," Margaret said wryly.

Colleen laughed. "As you girls can see, a negligee is simply a nightgown and robe set."

"But it's so thin and flimsy you can practically see through it," Bridget declared.

"Doesn't look very warm to me." Molly blew on her shining pink fingernails.

"It's for her honeymoon," Margaret declared as if she were the expert, although she'd had nothing like that for her honeymoon. "It's supposed to be flimsy."

Now they all giggled. But as Margaret watched Colleen packing item after item of fine, expensive clothing, she felt herself growing more and more jealous. Finally, she could take no more and, excusing herself to put Peter down for his morning nap, she left.

After the ceremony was over, Molly couldn't imagine a more perfect wedding. Well, unless it was at Old Saint Mary's. But Geoff's church did not disappoint. Even Mam and Dad seemed to be all right about it as they drove to the reception.

"It really was lovely," Mam declared. "Pretty as a picture."

"Colleen and Geoff looked so glamorous. I hope the photographer got some good photos at the church," Molly said from the backseat. She'd offered to drive, but Dad had insisted he could make the short trip to Geoff's parents' home.

"What about those newspaper photographers in front of the church?" Dad said. "Did Colleen know they were coming?"

"I think so." Molly smoothed her satin skirt, marveling at the play of the iridescent colors in the afternoon light. "And Colleen looked so beautiful, I'm sure they must've gotten some good shots."

"You all looked beautiful," Mam declared. "But I was so surprised to see Patrick there. Louise never said a word about that to me."

"Mrs. Hammond had been sworn to secrecy. But she told Bridget and me after the shower," Molly admitted. "It's just too bad Brian couldn't make it, but I'm glad that Margaret wasn't expecting him." She peered ahead to where Margaret and Bridget were driving in Colleen's car—part of the long processional now headed for the Conrad farm.

"Well, it was handy that Patrick could step in for Geoff's missing groomsman," Dad said. "Jack said he got here just in the nick of time too."

"His navy uniform looked perfect with the others," Mam added. "And didn't he and Bridget look sweet together as he escorted her down the aisle! Such a handsome couple."

"I thought I could hear wedding bells for those two." Dad followed the train of cars down the farm's long driveway.

"Wouldn't that be wonderful," Mam said. "And have you noticed that Bridget hasn't spoken of her doctor friend at all? I suspect that's over with now. Maybe she'll see Patrick in a different light. Especially since he's in uniform—and so handsome."

"I expect Patrick is seeing Bridget in a different light." Dad chuckled. "She's never looked prettier. If that doesn't turn the boy's head, well, I don't know what will."

Molly was tempted to express her opinion on this—hadn't Bridget and Patrick already made it clear that they were only just friends? But she knew that wasn't what her parents wanted to hear. For as long as she could remember, Mr. and Mrs. Hammond as well as Mam and Dad had plotted for Bridget and Patrick to marry. As much as Molly hated to admit it, they could all be right. After all, people could change…and Bridget did look incredibly beautiful today…and they did make a very handsome pair.

As Dad parked, Molly felt relieved to get out of the car. It wasn't that she resented her parents' opinions on the matter, but hearing them going on about Bridget and Patrick was deeply disturbing.

Before long, the photographer was lining up the wedding party members for pictures. As Molly smiled for the camera, she fought the urge to sneak peeks at Patrick. As badly as she wanted to see him and talk to him, she was determined not to chase after him. That was for schoolgirls.

And Molly didn't like feeling childish, but she'd been ridiculously jealous to see Patrick as Bridget's escort at the church. Naturally, as maid of honor, Molly was escorted by Geoff's best man, Hank Gardner. Hank was nice enough and, like Geoff, he was a navy pilot—but he was not Patrick. Hopefully she would get a chance to connect with him once the dancing began.

Geoff's mother had told everyone the plan. After the bride and groom greeted their guests in a reception line they would be seated for the wedding dinner in the enormous marquee. Champagne would be poured and toasts would be made and eventually the bridal couple would cut the cake. Finally, Colleen and Geoff would open the floor with their first dance—to their favorite song, *I'll Be Seeing You.* After that, the wedding couple would invite their parents to dance, Hank would invite Molly to dance, and the rest of the wedding party would follow. According to Mrs. Conrad, it was simply how things were done. But Molly hoped and prayed that as soon as all that was taken care of, she would get a chance to visit and perhaps even dance with Patrick.

The reception continued like clockwork and Molly did all that, according to her recent research, a maid of honor was expected to do—mainly to ensure that the bride was well taken care of—but now that the perfunctory dances were complete and everyone seemed relaxed and having a good time, Molly stepped aside to take a little break. Standing on the sidelines, enjoying the spectacle of festivity, she was also trying to spot Patrick, but he seemed to have made himself scarce. And then, just like that, he was standing beside her, smiling warmly down on her.

"Molly Mulligan." His eyes twinkled. "It's so good to see you."

"You too." She suddenly felt shy. "I'm so glad you made it home."

"So am I. It was touch-and-go there for a while."

"And it was great you could help with the wedding. Colleen was so relieved to have you here today."

"Glad to be of service." He saluted.

"It's too bad Brian couldn't make it."

His smile faded. "I don't know what went wrong. I really thought he'd be here. But that's the military for you. Plans can change quickly. You always have to be ready to turn on a dime."

"I'm just glad we didn't tell Margaret. She'd have been so disappointed."

He nodded sadly then seemed to focus on her. "You're all grown-up, Molly." He studied her closely. "Beautifully grown-up."

She felt her cheeks warming. "Thank you."

"So...will you honor me with a dance?"

"I was just waiting for you to ask." She smiled happily as he reached for her hand and led her to the dance floor. As Patrick took her into his arms, it felt magical—almost electric—and completely amazing. So much so that she never wanted the dance to end. To her delight, he asked her for a second dance as soon as it was over, and it was even more wonderful than the first one. Did Patrick feel it too? For a moment, she wasn't even sure that her feet were on the ground. Was she floating? Then suddenly—and too soon—the song ended and Mrs. Hammond stepped in.

"I think it's time for someone to dance with his mother," she told Patrick with a coy smile.

Before Molly could exit the floor, the best man stepped up, insisting on another dance with her. And then after that dance ended, Patrick was pressed into leading Mam around the dance floor. And Molly danced with Hank again.

Midway through that number, several happy shrieks were let out when, to everyone's surprise, Brian Hammond arrived! Molly's heart went out to Margaret when, completely shocked to see her husband, she burst into emotional sobs. Their embrace was sweet and long. Then when Brian met his son for the first time, Molly longed for her camera. But the image of Brian in his army officer's uniform, with Peter in his little blue suit and in his father's arms, was etched into her mind.

Margaret could hardly believe that Brian was really home! As they talked and danced and talked some more, she felt almost perfectly happy. Well, except for one thing...and Margaret was determined not to think about that. For now, all that mattered was that she and Brian were together again. Brian held Peter in his arms between them as they danced and danced. It was so incredible, so unbelievable that Margaret worried it might simply be a dream. And if it were, she hoped that she never woke up.

When Molly interrupted them, explaining it was time to help Colleen get ready for the "big getaway," Margaret protested. "I want to be with Brian," she whispered to her pesky little sister.

"Colleen needs to talk to you," Molly urged.

"I won't be long," Margaret promised Brian with a kiss.

"I'll keep him with me." Brian grinned down at his tiny son. Margaret reluctantly followed Molly into the house and up to the bedroom where Colleen was just changing into her traveling suit.

"We have a proposition for you," Colleen told Margaret as all four of the Mulligan sisters gathered together.

"For me?" Margaret blinked. "But this is your big day, Colleen. Besides, I've already had a delightful surprise."

"It's been a pretty big day for both of you," Bridget told them.

Colleen zipped her pale blue skirt, smoothing it down. "Anyway, I want to offer you and Brian the use of my apartment."

"In Beverly Hills?" Margaret asked.

"Yes. And you can have the use of my car too." Colleen straightened the seams on her stockings.

"And Bridget and Mam and I will take care of Peter while you're gone," Molly said as she helped Colleen into her pendulum jacket. "As well as the store."

"And you will have a real vacation," Bridget told her.

"Or a honeymoon." Colleen winked at Margaret as Molly pinned a rose corsage onto her lapel.

"I don't know what to say." Margaret felt close to tears again.

"Just say you'll go ask Brian about it," Colleen told her.

Margaret gladly agreed, and then they all went back downstairs to where Geoff was waiting to whisk his bride off to the Fairmont Hotel. But first Colleen told the women to gather for the tossing of the wedding bouquet. Standing part way up the staircase, she turned her back and tossed the blooms over her shoulder. Everyone cheered when Bridget caught it. And then, just like that, the bride and groom were on their way.

Some of the older wedding guests were congregating in the

house now, including Mam and Dad. "Let me keep the baby for you." Mam opened her arms. "You and Brian go kick up your heels while you can." Margaret gratefully handed over Peter, but before they joined the younger guests out in the marquee, she told Brian about her sisters' kind offer. "We can even use Colleen's car to drive down there."

"That sounds great, but let's only be gone a few days," he suggested. "That way I can spend some time with my parents and Patrick—as well as our son—before my leave is over." He grabbed her hand, leading her out to the dance floor for a lively swing number.

As they danced, Margaret felt happy about the prospect of a few carefree days in Beverly Hills with her husband. But she also felt uneasy. That nagging sense of guilt was gnawing at her. Of course, she knew that she hadn't actually been unfaithful to Brian. Not really. And yet she knew that if Brian was aware of her time spent with Howard—however innocent it was—he would definitely be hurt. And that hurt her. Deep inside, it ached far more than she'd ever imagined possible.

Molly was about to give up on spending any more time with Patrick when she felt someone tapping her on the shoulder. Turning around and expecting it to be Hank again, since he'd been her most frequent dance partner, she was pleasantly surprised to see Patrick.

"May I have this dance?" he asked politely.

"Of course." She eagerly nodded.

"I heard the musicians are about to quit." He led her to the dance floor. "I was worried I might not get another dance with you."

She slid her hand into his and smiled happily. "I was worried too."

"Every time I made an attempt, it seemed you were already

taken." As he took her in his arms, she sensed that he was keeping a distance between them. More so than he'd done earlier.

"You were fairly busy too." She looked into his face. "A handsome navy officer is in high demand with these ladies."

"Seems you were dancing with a navy officer too."

"Yes, Hank has been quite attentive." She chuckled. "I hope he doesn't think that's his responsibility as best man."

"I suspect it had more to do with pleasure than responsibility." Patrick's eyes seemed slightly sad as he looked down at her. "Molly, I still can hardly believe it. You really are all grown-up."

She felt her cheeks grow warm again but didn't know what to say.

"And yet...you're still the same sweet little girl. I can see that now."

"Yes, of course, I am." She wasn't sure what he meant by that. Was he insinuating that she was still a child? She certainly hoped not. She didn't feel like a child!

"I've said this before, Molly, but I want you to know how much I appreciate your letters. I always look forward to them."

"I feel the same way about your letters." Molly couldn't deny there was a distinct coolness between them. A formality that hadn't been there earlier. As if a small wall had been erected between them. But why? Was Patrick trying to give her a hint, sending her a message? She hoped not.

"I'm so glad that Brian made it home." His tone suggested he was simply making polite conversation with a casual acquaintance. "What a great surprise for everyone."

To fill the space and to distract herself from fretting over Patrick's change in attitude, Molly told him about Colleen's offer of the apartment in Beverly Hills for Brian and Margaret.

"But Brian just got here. When is he leaving?"

"I think they plan to drive down there tomorrow morning."

"I'd hoped to spend some time with him." Patrick looked disappointed.

"He'll be back soon." She explained about the baby and store. "They can only be gone a few days."

"Well, I suppose I'll have to catch up with him when he gets back."

Molly didn't know what more to say, but since the song was ending, she simply thanked him and stood there looking at him. She felt flustered and confused...and indescribably sad. Patrick's expression was impossible to decipher. But before either of them could say anything, Dad was by Molly's side.

"I thought you were tired," she told him. "Shouldn't you take it—"

"I've not had the chance to dance with my youngest daughter yet." Dad turned to Patrick. "You don't mind if I take my baby girl for a little waltz now, do you?"

"Not at all." Patrick politely tipped his head.

Then spotting Bridget nearby, Dad grabbed her hand. "Here." Dad winked at Patrick. "You take this one."

Dad looked victorious as he danced Molly away. "Sometimes young lovers need a gentle little push."

"Young lovers?" Molly questioned.

"Patrick and Bridget." He chuckled.

"Really, Dad!" Molly didn't like feeling this irritated at her father, but she couldn't help it. Why was he being so insistent about all this? "Do you honestly think Patrick and Bridget are young lovers?"

"They could be," he told her. "Oh, sure, he's navy and she's army, but it could work out." He laughed like this was funny.

"I hope you're not overdoing it," she said.

"Not at all," he assured her. "Never felt better."

Molly didn't know what game her dad was playing, but she

suspected it had as much to do with her as Bridget. Dad was probably worried that Molly's young heart was getting too involved with Patrick. Hadn't he suggested as much before? The Hammonds had even questioned her correspondence with Patrick. It seemed everyone, except maybe Colleen, thought that Molly was too young for such feelings.

After the song ended, Molly escorted Dad back into the house. She suspected that Dad would do whatever was necessary—including dancing with her even though he was tired—to protect her from any heartache. The problem was that Molly didn't want protection.

Twenty-Three

Molly had her hands full for the next few days. Tending the store and caring for the baby was demanding work. Bridget had offered to help, but determined that her sister relax and enjoy her last days of leave, Molly insisted on handling it herself. As a result, by the time Margaret and Brian came home from Beverly Hills, Molly had new respect for all that Margaret did.

"There you are," Margaret gushed as she reached for Peter on Wednesday afternoon. "How I missed you!"

"Did you have fun?" Molly asked.

"It was heavenly." Margaret nuzzled her baby. "Sleeping in, eating out, lounging by the pool. Pure heaven."

"Where's Brian?" Molly asked.

"Using the phone in back. Making dinner arrangements with his parents." Margaret glanced around the store, which was free of customers. "Go ahead and leave if you want, Molly. It's almost closing time anyway. I'll take care of it from here on out."

Glad to go home, Molly went for her purse. "Don't forget that Bridget's leave ends tomorrow. You might want to catch some time with her tonight."

"Yes, definitely." Margaret rubbed noses with Peter. "Thanks for all you did while I was gone, Molly. I really do appreciate it."

Molly stroked Peter's round head. "It made me appreciate how hard you work, Margaret. Managing the store and caring for the baby is no small task."

Margaret's face lit up. "Thank you for saying that."

"See you later," Molly called out as she headed out the front door. As she walked home, she felt hopeful. It seemed that the messy business of Howard Moore was well behind them now. That was a huge relief. Still, she wondered...would Margaret ever tell Brian about it? Not that it would do anyone any good. Perhaps some things really were better left unsaid.

At home, Molly went straight to the kitchen to help Mam prepare supper, but when she started to set the table in the dining room, Mam stopped her. "Let's just eat in the kitchen tonight. It's only Dad and you and me—and leftovers."

"What about Bridget?"

"She's going out with the Hammonds."

"The Hammonds?" Molly gathered up the dishes.

"Yes. Jack and Louise are taking Brian and Margaret and Patrick and Bridget to Gionatti's tonight."

Molly frowned. "Bridget's last night here and she's not staying home?"

"Hush." Mam put her forefinger to her lips. "Don't say a word about it. I already told Bridget it was just fine for her to go."

Molly simply nodded as she arranged three place settings on the kitchen table. Fine, she wouldn't say a word about it, but she could wonder. Was this an official date? Was Bridget dining with the Hammonds or was she going out with Patrick? What if Dad had been right about Patrick and Bridget? What if things had changed between them? After all, what with tending the store and the baby, Molly hadn't been home much since Sunday. Who knew what might've transpired in her absence? And if Bridget and Patrick had miraculously fallen in love, well, Molly would be happy for both of them. It wouldn't be easy, but somehow she would manage.

"Don't you look pretty," Mam said cheerfully as Bridget came into the kitchen. And she did look pretty, wearing an aqua blue summer dress that showed off both her figure and South Pacific tan.

"Colleen gave me this dress." Bridget did a little spin, making the skirt swirl out.

"It looks gorgeous on you," Molly told her.

"I still feel bad about not being home on my last night of leave." Bridget slipped a little cream-colored cardigan over her shoulders.

"Don't you worry about it. We've had you almost all to ourselves these past two weeks." Mam patted her cheek. "It's about time you went out and had some fun."

"Well, I still think it would've been nicer if we'd all had dinner together—the Hammonds and us." Bridget picked up her purse. "Like old times."

Mam just shrugged. "I think it's better this way."

"Well, it's such a lovely night, I want to walk over to their house."

After Bridget was gone, Molly tried to act as if nothing was wrong, but as they were finishing supper, her cheerful act began to wear thin. "I think I'm tired," she told her parents. "If you don't mind, I'd like to start the dishes and—"

"No," Mam told her. "I'll clean up tonight. You've had a busy few days, Molly. You just take it easy for a change."

Molly made a forced smile then excused herself, but once she was in the privacy of her bedroom, she burst into tears. She felt silly and childish for reacting like this, but she just couldn't help it. She could blame it on being worn out from the last few days, but the truth was that the mere idea of Patrick and Bridget together was just too much. Still, she knew this was a secret she would have to keep from everyone. And if by chance Bridget returned to her post in the Pacific with an engagement ring, Molly would pretend to be overjoyed for both of them.

"I almost feel guilty for being this happy," Colleen told Geoff as they drove along the coastline toward San Diego. "I don't know when I've ever felt so happy."

"Even better than when your Hollywood dreams came true?"

"Well, it's a different sort of happiness." She pretended to consider this then grinned. "But this is far, far better! To be honest, getting my first movie role felt sort of lonely... Plus, with you out of the picture, well, it was pretty sad." She reached over to run her fingers through his short sandy-colored hair. "In comparison, this is much better."

"You've had a pretty good honeymoon, then?" Geoff's tone was playful.

"Are you kidding?" Colleen threw back her head and laughed. "I never dreamed that my pilot husband was going to fly me off to the Grand Canyon."

"So you did enjoy it?"

"After I got over the shock of flying in such a small plane." She grinned. "Then I loved it."

"Well, I'm glad you arranged for us to use your friend's place for the rest of our time." He parked his car in front of the beach house. "Much more relaxing."

"And the view's not bad either."

"I don't know about you, but I'm ready for a swim."

"Last one in is a rotten egg." Colleen sprinted toward the house, going inside just in time to hear the phone ringing. She eagerly grabbed it up to discover it was Georgina Knight on the other end.

"Oh, darling, it's so good to hear your voice," Georgina gushed. "Laurel told me I might find you at this number. Are you having a perfectly delicious honeymoon? We're all still talking about your wedding. Everyone thought it was perfectly charming. And the publicity you kids got—well, we can't buy that sort of coverage."

"That's great." Colleen kicked off her shoes. "I haven't even had a chance to pick up a movie magazine."

"Of course not." Georgina laughed. "You're on your honeymoon. Anyway, the real reason I'm calling is to tell you the good news. Pinnacle wants you to co-star with Laurel and Barry again. Filming won't start until mid-September, but I just couldn't wait to tell you."

Colleen sat down. "That's great," she said in a less than enthusiastic tone.

"You don't sound very excited, honey. Is anything wrong?"

Colleen thought about the last conversation she'd had with Geoff—trying to make a deal—if he quit the navy she would quit making pictures. So far, they hadn't come to any agreements.

"You're not giving up your career just because you're married, are you? I know some women do that, but I can tell you that most of them regret it. And even if you're considering taking a break, I'll warn you against it. Your career isn't established enough for you to take such a luxury and expect to be welcomed back."

"I guess you just caught me off guard, Georgina. Do you mind if I talk to Geoff and get back to you about this?"

"Of course not. And give that handsome man of yours my best regards. Rory said that if he decides to leave the navy, he could probably make it in films. That is, if he's got any acting chops."

Colleen laughed as Geoff burst out of the bedroom wearing his swim trunks and a victorious grin. "I'll be sure to let him know."

"And don't wait too long to call me back. I promised Pinnacle a quick answer on this. You can just imagine how many other hungry young actresses would be eager to snap it up."

"Yes, I'm sure you're right."

After Colleen hung up, she hurried into her swimsuit and, grabbing a towel, chased Geoff out the door, across the beach and toward the sea.

"Welcome, Mrs. Rotten Egg." He swooped her into a hug, plunging them straight into the rolling surf.

They swam and played awhile and eventually flopped down on their towels in the sun, warming themselves and catching their breath. "Sounded like that was your agent on the phone." Geoff pushed a wet strand of hair away from her face, landing a damp salty kiss on her lips. "Let me guess, they're offering you a new movie contract?"

She sat up and looked at him. "Yeah, pretty much."

"What did you tell her?"

"That I'll call her back."

"Uh-huh?" He waited.

"I said I wanted to talk to you first."

"Yeah?" He nodded.

"So what do you think about it? Are you comfortable being married to an actress?"

"As long as the actress is you."

"But your mom...?"

"We've been over that, Colleen. Like I told Mom, we've got to live our own lives and make our own decisions. No one else can tell us what to do."

Colleen studied his face. She knew what he was saying...what he really meant. "You don't plan to quit the navy, do you?"

He slowly shook his head. "I just can't, Colleen. Every time I listen to the news or read the newspaper, I think about my buddies still over there. I know how badly they need experienced pilots—more than ever right now. I gotta go back. And I hope you'll back me in my decision."

She leaned forward to kiss him again. "You know I will, Geoff. If that's what you really want, how can I stand in your way?"

"How about you? What do you really want to do? You don't have to make movies, you know. I may not make a lot of money in the navy, but it's enough to support a wife who can live within her means. Although I know you've got expensive taste. Not that I'm complaining." He grinned. "But what do you really want to do, Colleen?"

She thought long and hard. "Well, the film I'm being offered would be with Laurel and Barry."

His eyes lit up. "And you loved working with them."

"I did."

"So what do you think?"

"I think I'd love to make another movie." She smiled.

"Sounds like we're set then." He sealed it with a kiss. And, sure, maybe Colleen didn't feel completely supportive of Geoff's decision to return to the dangers of active service, but they'd already gone round and round over it. What good was it to dig in her heels? Just because they were married didn't give them the right to dictate to each other. And hopefully this war would be over soon.

Twenty-Four

Molly had managed to conceal her hurt feelings for the next few days. She even acted like she thought it was great that Patrick got the privilege of delivering Bridget to her base at the end of her leave. But underneath her cheerful comments and sunny smile, Molly was blue. In fact, outside of losing Peter, Molly couldn't remember ever feeling this miserable about anything. And it wasn't just a simple case of jealousy. The most disturbing part of this was feeling almost completely ignored by Patrick. Had she been deluded to believe they were friends? Perhaps the only role Molly had in Patrick's life was being his pen pal. Why had she assumed it was more?

By Sunday morning Molly knew she couldn't continue to conceal her emotions. So she tucked a note into Mam's handbag and slipped out of Mass early. It was a warm summer day, perfect for a nice long walk. Or so she told herself. The real truth was that the Hammonds had invited her family for Sunday dinner—a chance for everyone to say good-bye since Brian and Patrick would be heading back to their military units in the next few days. But, like the note in Mam's handbag said, Molly wouldn't be able to join them at the Hammonds'. She just couldn't.

Molly had never felt so lost and lonely before. Or so hurt. She wondered as she walked and walked and walked, was this what it felt like to have a broken heart? Was that what was wrong with her? Her heart was broken over Patrick? Perhaps this was exactly what Dad—and the rest of her family—had been warning her about. Were they simply trying to protect her from this kind of pain? Perhaps they'd all suspected that she was getting too attached to Patrick. And they probably knew that, thanks to their age difference—or Patrick's indifference—it was hopeless. And foolish. Molly didn't like to think that she'd been a fool.

She longed for someone to talk to. Maybe if Colleen were here, Molly would be able to tell her sister about her broken heart. But Colleen would be on her honeymoon for another week. Besides, Molly decided, this was something she needed to keep from her family. Just in case Bridget and Patrick had truly fallen in love. Molly's feelings would only create problems. No, this might be a secret she'd have to take to the grave.

Feeling warm, Molly unbuttoned the top of her dress to let in some cool air. Then, adjusting the brim of her hat to block the sun from beating down on her, she longed for a cool place to hide out. Checking her watch, she didn't think that Mam and Dad would've left for the Hammonds' yet and she really didn't want to speak to them just now. She considered going to the store, but Margaret and Brian might've stopped by there before going to his parents. San Francisco was usually fairly moderate, but today was a scorcher. Even the soles of her shoes felt hot. As Molly peeled off her gloves, she hoped that Mrs. Bartley would think to water their victory garden.

That's when it hit her—Mrs. Bartley! She would be a sympathetic listener. And her shadowy house would provide a cool sanctuary from the heat. Molly hurried down a backstreet toward her neighborhood and before long was seated in Mrs. Bartley's front room with a glass of sweetened iced tea.

"I can see that something is upsetting you," Mrs. Bartley said with concern. "Do you need to talk?"

Just like that, Molly poured out her sad story. She didn't even attempt to stop the tears as she told all. "I'm just so completely miserable," she finally said as she wiped her tears with her handkerchief. "I don't know what to do."

"Oh, my poor dear." Mrs. Bartley wrapped an arm around Molly's shoulders. "I wish there was something I could say or do to make you feel better, but alas, this may be the sort of wound that takes time to heal."

"So you think it's true? I have a broken heart?"

"It certainly sounds like it."

"What should I do?"

Mrs. Bartley slowly stood. "For starters, I think you should have some lunch." She smiled. "I have some chicken salad in the icebox. Come help me."

As they made sandwiches, Molly waffled back and forth over whether or not she should continue corresponding with Patrick. "On one hand, I'd feel horrible to just cut him off," she said. "He's always saying how much he appreciates my letters. On the other hand, it would be painful to continue keeping up the pretense that we're still friends."

"Then it's probably time to stop."

"But he's a serviceman. Shouldn't I be supportive and—"

"If you want to be supportive, buy war bonds." Mrs. Bartley set the plate of sandwiches on the kitchen table.

"But what will I say if he asks me why I stopped writing?"

"Aren't you still writing to that other young man?" They both sat down. "As well as Bridget? Plus you'll have classes in the fall. And helping at the store. Just tell Patrick you're too busy."

"But I—"

"Think of it this way, dear. You will be freeing Patrick up to write letters to someone else...perhaps even Bridget." Mrs. Bartley bowed her head to say grace.

"I suppose that makes sense. Maybe I can just write to him once in a while." Molly took a bite of her sandwich.

"As harsh as this may sound, I believe your heart will heal more quickly if you make a swift, clean break of it."

Molly just nodded, slowly chewing.

"Do you think that Bridget and Patrick are serious, Molly? Is it possible they will want to marry?"

"According to my parents, it is. At least, that's what they're hoping."

"Then I strongly encourage you to stop writing to Patrick. You will need time and distance from him if they get married." She held up a finger. "And that brings me to another question. I know you're planning to only take part-time classes at the college. Why don't you consider going to school full-time?"

"Mam and Dad need me at the store. And, although Colleen is helping with my tuition, I don't know if it's enough—"

"That is precisely what I want to talk to you about. I want to cover your tuition. All of it. But only if you will agree to be a full-time student."

Molly blinked.

"As you know, I have no descendants. You're such a bright young woman, Molly, and you've been such a dear friend to me. I have given this much thought. I had planned to raise the question with you, but

Colleen beat me to it. However, the more I think about it, the more I feel that you should be in school full-time. Wouldn't you like that?"

"Of course. I would absolutely love that. But there's the store and—"

"That's the other part of my offer. I know some people think I'm too old to be much use, but it just so happens that I'm still good at arithmetic, and thanks to working in the garden, I'm rather spry. I would love to volunteer to help at the store—if it would free you up to full-time studies." She smiled. "Besides, it would give me something to do."

"Oh, Mrs. Bartley." Molly jumped up from her chair to hug the old woman. "You would really do all that? Just for me?"

"Nothing would give me more pleasure, Molly."

Molly sighed as she sat down. "Earlier you said there was nothing you could say or do to make me feel better—but you just did."

"I'm so glad."

"I mean, I'm still sad about Patrick—and my heart still hurts. But you've given me something to look forward to."

"Do you think you'll have difficulty registering as a full-time student?"

"Not at all. Thanks to the war, enrollment is down. There's never been a better time to get into college."

"Perfect."

As they made plans for going to the admissions office together to take care of the details, Molly felt a tiny glimmer of hope growing inside of her. She would soon be devoting all her time and energy to her studies, providing her with a good excuse for cutting back on her war correspondence.

Geoff had only been gone a few days before Colleen grew so lonely that she'd packed up and gone home. The studio wouldn't begin shooting the next movie for a few more weeks, and Colleen hadn't relished the idea of spending it alone in her Beverly Hills apartment. Besides that, she'd been missing her sisters. Now, in order to spend more time with them and allow Mam to remain home, Colleen was working in the store every day.

"You seem different," she told Molly on her third day back, as they were going home from work. "At first I thought it was simply because you're getting older, but now I suspect it's something else."

"Oh?" Molly smiled but didn't really look happy.

"And you've been extra quiet at work. At first I thought it was because Margaret and I have been such chatterboxes. But I was watching you this afternoon, Molly. You hardly ever smile anymore." Colleen frowned as she stopped for the traffic light. "What's wrong?"

Molly shrugged. "I'm probably just preoccupied. You know, with school starting next week. It's pretty exciting."

"Maybe so, but you don't seem excited to me. You seem sad."

"I just have my mind on other things," Molly declared. "I told you how Mrs. Bartley decided I should live on campus—and how she's helping me get into a sorority. Isn't that wonderful?"

"It should be. At least for you. I mean, it's not my cup of tea. But I still think something is wrong. And I wish you'd tell me about it." Colleen glanced over to see Molly biting her lip with a perplexed expression. "In fact, I think you and I should go out together tonight. Let's go home and get all dressed up, and I'll take you out for dinner. We'll give Mam the night off. What do you say?"

"That sounds fun." Molly made what looked like a forced smile. But Colleen was determined. Before the night was over with, she would get to the bottom of this. Something was wrong with Molly, and she intended to find out what!

Molly was trying to appear happy as she and Colleen enjoyed a great seafood dinner at Alioto's on Fisherman's Wharf. It was so sweet of Colleen to bring her here, but Molly was determined to keep her secret a secret.

"Molly, I know you," Colleen said as they waited for their dessert to arrive. "And I know something is wrong." She reached across the table to grasp Molly's hand. "You were my maid of honor, you're my favorite sister—don't tell the others I said so, but you know it's true. Please, tell me what's going on with you."

Molly took a slow sip of her tea, trying to think of a way to avoid this.

"If you refuse to tell me, I'll just have to start guessing."

Molly shrugged. "Guess away."

"Okay." Colleen nodded firmly. "Well, my first guess is Patrick."

Molly tried not to look surprised.

"Ah ha!"

"I didn't say you were right."

"I know I'm right, Molly." Colleen peered closely at her. "So fill me in. I barely remember what went on at the wedding, but I'm sure you were pleasantly surprised to see Patrick there." She waited like she expected Molly to respond.

"I guess so." Molly twisted the napkin in her lap.

"And then Geoff and I were on our honeymoon. So what happened while I was gone? Did Patrick say or do something to hurt your feelings?"

Molly knew it was pointless to hold back on Colleen. "Fine," she said. "I'll tell you. But only if you promise not to tell anyone." She narrowed her eyes. "And I mean anyone."

Colleen held up her hand like a pledge. "Scout's honor."

"You're not a scout." Molly rolled her eyes.

"Come on, Mol. You know you can trust me."

And so Molly told Colleen a condensed version of her broken heart. "But I'm getting over it," she assured her. "And if Patrick and Bridget get married, I'll be very happy for them."

Colleen frowned. "Seriously? You think Bridget is over Doctor Cliff?"

Molly shrugged. "Mam and Dad seem convinced of it."

"Well, that's just ridiculous. We all know Bridget was completely smitten by the doctor. She nearly said as much in her letters."

"She didn't want to talk about him while she was home," Molly reminded her. "It's possible that Doctor Cliff has found someone else."

"Anything is possible. But Bridget and Patrick? Really?" Colleen shook her head. "I'm sorry. I just can't see it."

"But they spent time together. And you said yourself that Bridget had never looked prettier and—"

"Thanks partly to my makeover." Colleen smiled smugly. "But even so, it seems so..."

"Then why were they together so much?" Molly demanded. "No one forced them. And we all know Bridget is strong-willed. She wouldn't have spent time with Patrick unless she wanted to."

"Yes, but—"

"It's okay." Molly attempted a more convincing smile. "I'm going to be fine, Colleen. Already I'm doing so much better. And when school starts I'll be so busy that I won't have time to think about, uh...well, you know."

"Patrick."

"Anyway, I really don't want to talk about this anymore." Molly paused as the waiter set down their desserts.

"Just one last question?"

Molly waited with impatience.

"Did you tell Patrick about this? I mean, about how you feel?"

"No, of course not."

"What about writing letters—"

"That's two questions."

"Sorry."

"I just wrote him a short letter to politely inform him that, seeing how I was about to become very busy with college and being in a sorority...well, that I wouldn't have time to continue writing but that I would keep him in my prayers." Molly felt a familiar lump growing in her throat but, determined not to cry, she picked up her dessert fork.

"Well. Then..." Colleen seemed to be closely studying Molly.

"I do appreciate your concern, Colleen, but even more than that, I'd appreciate you keeping this completely quiet."

Colleen pursed her lips as she picked up her fork.

"And in the event that Bridget and Patrick should get married... well, I never want you to show me the slightest bit of sisterly sympathy. Understand?"

"Absolutely." Colleen nodded solemnly.

"Thanks. Now this looks yummy." Molly forked her lemon cream pie as if eager to partake in the fluffy yellow confection, but the truth was her stomach felt like she'd swallowed a brick. As she took a bite she had to wonder...who was the actress now?

Twenty-Five

By late September, Margaret felt certain of several things. First of all, she desperately missed her sisters. Molly was in college, Colleen was off movie-making, and God only knew where Bridget was stationed. No one had heard from her since she'd returned to the field. Margaret also knew, after one long month, that Mrs. Bartley, although fairly efficient in the store, was no fun whatsoever. Honestly, Margaret did not get what Molly saw in the opinionated old woman.

Last but not least, Margaret felt certain that she was pregnant. And she was not the least bit happy about it. Peter wasn't quite one yet—and quite a handful since he'd just started to walk. But he would probably still be in diapers when Baby Two arrived. She couldn't imagine living in the studio apartment, carrying her babies and water and groceries up and down, cooking her dinner on a hotplate, doing laundry in the downstairs bathroom sink—and worst of all, being alone. She did not need this!

As a result, she'd decided not to tell anyone. Not even Brian. She planned to keep this secret until she was at least three months along or starting to show. Maybe she could put it off until Christmas. Unfortunately, her pregnancy was making her both tired and cranky—so much so that, after chewing out Mam for no good reason,

Margaret was tempted to tell all. But she knew what would happen if she did. Mam would make a big deal of it. She would insist Margaret take it easy. And then Mam would work even harder and would probably start having headaches again, or Dad's health would be impaired. No, this was Margaret's problem, and she needed to just grow up and deal with it herself. At least, that was what she was telling herself.

The only good thing about this pregnancy was that she'd been so tired she'd become neglectful, allowing her appearance to completely go. Her unkempt image made it even easier, the few times Howard had showed up at the store, for her to treat him professionally and impassively. Not that he'd seemed to mind. She obviously offered no attraction to him, dressed in her dowdy shop clothes, no makeup, and tightly pinned hair in need of washing. And, for the most part, she did not care that Howard Moore had stopped coming in. For the most part.

Margaret knew that Brian had returned to active service in Italy and, thanks to Mrs. Bartley, who loved to talk about the news, Margaret also knew that September had been a difficult month in that region. On one day Mrs. Bartley would be telling her good news that some sort of unconditional surrender to the Allies had taken place. But then the next day, she would tell Margaret that the Germans had seized Rome. It was up and down and down and up—and Margaret had never liked roller coasters.

Colleen was grateful to have long days of work to keep her busy—a welcome distraction from worrying about Geoff. Just the same, she did pay close attention to the news. So when she read the headlines in mid-October, she felt sick inside.

"Oh, no!" She tossed the *Los Angeles Times* down.

"What is it, doll?" Stella's hands stilled on Colleen's hair. "Bad news? Not about our boy?"

Colleen attempted a smile. She loved how Stella called Geoff *our boy*. "No, not exactly about Geoff. But it's awful news just the same."

"What happened?"

"The Japanese just executed about a hundred American prisoners of war," Colleen said glumly.

"Oh, dear." Stella shook her head. "That's horrible."

"I'm so thankful that Geoff isn't a POW anymore. I'd really be a mess if I heard that news while he was imprisoned."

"Where did it happen?"

Colleen picked up the paper to see. "Wake Island."

"Where's that?"

"I'm not sure exactly where. I mean, besides somewhere in the Pacific. We need Molly here to tell us where it's located. She's a walking geography book."

"How is Molly?" Stella secured a pin.

"According to her last letter, she loves being in college and living on campus. And it sounds like she's turning into a real social butterfly. Very active in her sorority."

"Good for her."

Colleen almost added that Molly still sounded a bit sad, but she was determined to keep her promise not to mention her sister's broken heart to anyone. Not even Stella. "I'm happy for her," Colleen continued, "but a little sad too. Sometimes it seems like she grew up too fast. She's the baby of the family, but in so many ways, she seems older than all of us. Well, except maybe Bridget. She's always been the most mature of the Mulligan girls."

"What news of your nurse sister?"

"No one's heard from her." Colleen frowned. "And it's got Mam and Dad pretty worried. But Molly keeps assuring everyone that it's probably a glitch in the mail. Hopefully she's right."

"And any news about your other sister? The one who's a mother—I can't recall her name."

"Margaret." Colleen sighed. "I had a long talk with her on Sunday. She sounded worn out and weary. Her little boy just started walking."

"The baby is walking?"

"He's almost one," Colleen told her. "His birthday is next week."

"And what did Auntie Colleen get him?"

Colleen giggled. "Well, I probably went a little overboard. It started out with just a sweet wooden rocking horse. I got it a couple weeks ago and sent it to my parents to hold onto. But then I saw this wooden airplane the other day. It's big enough for a toddler to sit on, and it has wheels that make it go and a little propeller. Well, I knew that Geoff would want Peter to have it. So I got that too. It will arrive there before his birthday."

"I bet you wish you could be there to see his face—"

"As a matter of fact, I plan to go." Colleen explained how she'd splurged on airfare. "I'll be there in time for Peter's party then fly out early the next morning in time for work."

Molly hadn't been home for a couple of weeks, but she was excited to see her family for Baby Peter's birthday. Mam was hosting the celebration, and Colleen had called Molly last night to inform her that she planned to show up. It felt strange to knock on the front door of what used to be home, but it seemed the proper thing to do.

"Molly!" Dad swung the door wide, sweeping her up into a bear hug. "Come in here, stranger."

"I'm not a stranger." She set down the stuffed bear she'd gotten for Baby Peter and removed her coat and hat.

He peered closely at her. "No, I suppose you're not. But I'm glad you're here early. Give us a chance to get reacquainted." He led her to the living room. "Sit down and tell me about your exciting college life."

"Don't you think I should go help Mam in the kitchen?"

"Nah, Margaret's in there with her." He pointed to the chess set. "We might even have time for a game before the Hammonds get here."

As she set up the chess pieces, she gave Dad the quick lowdown on her classes and her roommate. "Margie is a junior, but she pretty much treats me as an equal." She grinned. "Especially when she found out that Maureen Mulligan was my sister. It's surprising the sort of respect that gets a girl—at least in college. For some reason it didn't seem to work like that in high school." She lowered her voice. "Speaking of Colleen, I'm not supposed to tell anyone, but she's going to make a surprise appearance tonight."

"You don't mean it?"

"Yep. Just keep it under your hat." The reason Molly told Dad was because of his heart. She knew he wasn't supposed to have too much excitement and figured it would be best to give him advance notice.

Dad had just taken one of her pawns when the doorbell rang. "That's probably the Hammonds." He started to rise.

"Let me answer it." Molly hopped up. She hadn't seen the Hammonds since Colleen's wedding and hoped Mrs. Hammond wouldn't ask why she'd missed the dinner for Brian and Patrick. But to Molly's pleased surprise it was Mrs. Bartley. "My benefactress!" Molly exclaimed as she led her inside and hugged her.

"I'm so happy to see you." Mrs. Bartley let Molly help her with her coat. "I want to hear all about school."

Molly repeated what she'd just told Dad as she led Mrs. Bartley into the living room, but before they were seated, the doorbell rang again. Continuing to play hostess, Molly let the Hammonds and then Colleen inside. Greetings were exchanged and suddenly the house was filled with noise and laughter and, to Molly's relief, it felt almost like old times. Except that Margaret seemed different. Besides looking tired and not very stylishly dressed, she seemed quiet...and perhaps even sad.

"Why don't you stay out here and visit with the guests?" Molly suggested to Margaret. "I'll help Mam in the kitchen."

As Molly gathered place settings to take to the dining room, she asked Mam about Margaret. "Has she been ill?"

Mam frowned. "Not that I know of. And I've worked at the store twice this week."

"Oh. She just seems different. Or tired or something."

Mam stopped stirring the gravy. "Now that you mention it, I've noticed it too. I haven't wanted to say anything because we all know how hard she works. And Peter is a darling but a handful. But Margaret seems to be letting herself go."

Molly nodded. "I noticed that too."

"Maybe she isn't feeling well."

"I'll go set the table." Molly hurried out. She suddenly wondered if Margaret had neglected her appearance because of Howard Moore. Perhaps she thought if she looked less attractive, she'd be less tempted to spend time with him. In that case, maybe it was a good thing.

"Well, Molly," Mrs. Hammond said as she came into the dining room. "I haven't seen you since the wedding. Where have you been keeping yourself?"

Molly gave her a quick report about college life. "I was sorry to miss your farewell dinner for the boys, but I had lunch with a friend that day." She smiled pleasantly. "And I didn't figure I'd be terribly missed."

"Of course you were missed," Mrs. Hammond assured her. "You're part of the family."

"Speaking of family, what do you hear from your sons?"

"I just got a V-mail from Brian. He sounds well enough. But I haven't heard from Patrick in weeks. I was hoping you could give me his latest updates."

Molly kept her smile in place. "I'm sorry, but I haven't heard from him either."

Mrs. Hammond looked slightly alarmed now. "Oh, dear. Do you suppose anything is wrong? Every time I hear any news about the Pacific front, it sounds worse than ever. I hope Patrick is okay."

"I'm sure he's fine. He's probably just very busy." Molly focused her eyes on the table and getting the place settings just right.

"When did you last hear from him?" Mrs. Hammond pressed.

Molly turned to look at her. "Well, the truth is, I've stopped writing to him."

Mrs. Hammond blinked. "Oh?"

"You see, I've been so busy with my classes and the sorority. I just had to let something go."

"But Patrick so enjoyed your letters, Molly."

Molly nodded nervously. "Yes, but I'm hoping that Bridget will take up where I left off. She's a pretty good letter writer too."

"Oh...yes, well, I suppose that makes sense. Have you heard from Bridget?"

"I haven't, but perhaps my parents have. You should ask Dad." And now Molly excused herself to the kitchen, but as she helped Mam put the finishing touches on supper, she felt uneasy. What if something had gone wrong for Patrick? Mrs. Hammond was right—the war news from that region had been disheartening of late.

What if Patrick was in trouble? What if he'd been captured or injured or worse? She would never forgive herself for cutting him off like that. How selfish she'd been to stop writing to him so abruptly. And, really, what was the harm of sending cheerful letters to a serviceman who was laying his life on the line for his country? Hadn't she sent letters like that to Tommy Foster? And they hadn't meant anything. At least not to her. And even when she'd wanted to slow down her correspondence with Tommy, she'd been careful about it. She'd made sure that he understood. And the last time she'd talked with Prudence, it sounded as if she and Tommy were both quite happy with the arrangement. But when it came to her dear friend Patrick, she'd cut him off completely, no questions asked.

Despite her previous resolve not to, Molly was tempted to rush up to her old room and whip out a letter to Patrick right now. But Dad was calling everyone to gather in the living room to watch Peter open his birthday presents. And, feeling guilty and worried, Molly ran to get her camera and went out to join the festivities. But as she took photos of Peter's first birthday—some with him on the rocking horse, some on the airplane, and some with his cake—she decided that she would get extra prints to send to Patrick. And she would write a letter…and attempt an apology for cutting him off like that. After all, he'd been like a brother to her. Someday he might even be a brother-in-law. Shouldn't they be able to remain friends?

Twenty-Six

By the time Molly got the photographs of Peter's first birthday ready to send to Patrick, the American troops had invaded Bougainville in the Solomon Islands—and according to the news reports, the battles were intense...and brutal. This wasn't only concerning for Patrick's sake but Bridget's as well. More than ever, Molly was praying for both of them to remain safe.

But when she sat down to write what she hoped would be a brief letter to Patrick, she felt torn. On one hand, she wanted to keep that safe distance Mrs. Bartley had encouraged her to maintain. But on the other hand, this was Patrick, and she'd always been honest with him. Perhaps it was time for her to be honest again, even if it was the last time she'd write to him.

As Molly started to write, she realized that if she laid it all out for him, transparently revealing her feelings, he might actually welcome the opportunity to gently move on. It could provide a way for both of them to step aside from a potentially awkward situation...and hopefully remain friends. Somehow she had to do this.

> *Dear Patrick,*
> *I know my last letter was supposed to be just that—*
> *my last letter. But I have to confess that it wasn't a*

completely honest letter. This one will be. My true reason for stopping my letters to you is not because I'm overly busy. It is because my heart has gotten overly involved. I would like to say that I love you as my brother, Patrick. And that is true. But it is also true that I've let my love for you grow into something much bigger than that. I suppose some would call it a schoolgirl crush. And perhaps it is something that simple. Perhaps time will tell. But because I've always considered you my dear friend, I feel you deserve to know the truth. Even if it's embarrassing for me to put this into words. But I believe you'll respect me enough not to humiliate me with my confession. Just know that this is the real reason I can no longer write to you. I need to step back and allow my heart the time it needs to heal. I'm sure you will understand that.

And I want you to know that if you and Bridget ever decide to get married, I will be happy for both of you. I promise I will. And I don't ever want you to feel you are to blame for my heartache. I am the one who allowed myself to fall for you. And like they say, time heals all wounds. My heart will heal too.

On another note, I am enjoying college immensely. My main interest is journalism and photography, but right now I have to take all those required freshman classes. Of course, you know about that. Anyway, I want you to know that I will always love you as a brother, Patrick. And I pray for your safety every day. But this really will be my last letter to you. Thank you for understanding.

> *Sincerely,*
>
> *Molly*
>
> P.S. *The photos are of Peter's first birthday. Your nephew is growing up fast!*

Molly paused from putting the letter and photos into an envelope in order to wipe her tears. She didn't know why this still had to be so hard...and painful. It had been more than three months since the last time she'd seen Patrick. How long did it really take to recover from a broken heart?

It was a few days before Thanksgiving, and Margaret had yet to tell anyone about her condition. By her calculations, she was more than three and a half months pregnant—although she still hadn't been to her doctor. So far Mam seemed none the wiser, but nosy Mrs. Bartley seemed a bit suspicious. She was always making comments about Margaret's health, even suggesting she should take iron shots.

"Look at me," Mrs. Bartley had said to Margaret a few days ago, shortly before closing time. "I can tell what's wrong with you by reading your eyes."

"That's ridiculous," Margaret told her.

"No, it's not." Mrs. Bartley peered into Margaret's eyes as if she knew what she was doing. "My father was a physician, and he taught me a thing or two." Mrs. Bartley took Margaret's chin between her fingers, turning her head from left to right to catch the light. "Just as I thought."

"What is that?" Margaret pulled away from her, reaching for the broom.

"You are with child."

With her back to the old crone, Margaret forced what she hoped sounded like a genuine laugh and vigorously swept in front of the counter. Then, squaring her shoulders, she turned to face Mrs. Bartley. "You seem to forget that my husband has been overseas for nearly two years."

"He was here for Colleen's wedding."

"That was last summer." Margaret rolled her eyes. "If I were pregnant, wouldn't I know that by now?"

Mrs. Bartley seemed to consider this but still didn't look convinced.

"I am simply a worn out." Margaret went over to the playpen where Peter was pounding a wooden toy against the wall. "Caring for a toddler and managing the store is tiring." Then, eager to escape Mrs. Bartley's overly discerning eyes, Margaret had asked her to lock up and excused herself to go upstairs.

She hated to admit it, but Mrs. Bartley was excellent help at the store. Sure, she was overly bossy sometimes, but her ideas were usually good. And although she was an old woman, she seemed to have more energy than Margaret these days. But then, Mrs. Bartley didn't have a child to care for—and she wasn't expecting. Because Margaret's confidence in Mrs. Bartley had increased these past few months, and because she needed her, she'd given the old woman keys to the store and even called her the assistant manager to the part-time employees, Jimmy and Dirk.

So when Margaret woke up feeling weak and sluggish on Monday, instead of calling Mam to come in and help out, she called Mrs. Bartley. "I know you weren't scheduled to come in until noon," she told her, "but I wondered if you could come in this morning."

"Are you sick?"

"No, not exactly. But I don't feel, uh, quite right."

"Is your mother coming today?"

"She wasn't scheduled. But Dirk will be here at eleven to help unload the shipment. And Jimmy will be here later for deliveries. I just need some help first thing this morning."

"Well, fine, I'll come in. But only if you promise to make an appointment with your doctor. I must insist that you call him today. I'm certain that something is wrong and—"

"Fine," Margaret declared. "I'll call my doctor today."

"Good. I'll be there in time to open."

As Margaret dressed Peter, she knew that it was time to let the cat out of the bag. Besides calling the doctor today, she would call Mam. "Well, Peter," she said as she buttoned his coveralls. "How do you feel about having a baby sister or brother?"

He grinned happily.

"You'll be a good big brother." She kissed a chubby cheek. "Maybe you'll have a sister." For the first time since discovering she was pregnant, Margaret thought it might be fun to have another baby. Especially a little girl.

Still wearing her nightgown, Margaret set Peter in his highchair and began spooning food into his eager mouth. She wasn't completely sure why she hadn't wanted anyone to know she was pregnant. Probably because she'd been wishing she wasn't. By ignoring the situation, she might've deluded herself into believing it would go away. But it was not going away. It was time Margaret admitted as much.

Using his bib to wipe Peter's mouth, Margaret decided that she would make her big announcement at Thanksgiving this week. The Hammonds were hosting this year. She would have both sets of grandparents as well as Molly and Colleen to make the announcement to. They would all be so happy. It would be quite the celebration. Maybe Molly would want to be the godmother for this baby. She would make a good one.

As Margaret lifted Peter from the highchair, his shoe got stuck. She tugged and pulled and finally wrestled it free, but when she set him on the floor, she felt a cramping pain in her abdomen. Sitting down in the kitchen chair to catch her breath, she watched as Peter toddled over to the wooden airplane Colleen had given him. He'd already figured out how to get on it without help and was doing so. Another pain made her double over, clutching her middle and groaning in agony. Something was wrong.

When the pain subsided, she looked at the clock to see that Mrs. Bartley was probably already here. Slowly making her way to the door, she opened it and called out in a weak voice. But then, seized by another pain, she let out a loud cry, collapsing onto the floor.

"Margaret!" Mrs. Bartley's eyes grew wide to find Margaret on her knees.

"You were right," Margaret sobbed. "I am pregnant."

"Oh, dear girl." Mrs. Bartley bent down to help.

"No, don't hurt yourself," Margaret warned and, grasping the doorframe, she worked herself to her feet.

"Do you want me to call your mother?"

Margaret tried to think. This would be so upsetting to Mam. "Not yet. Call my doctor first. Dr. Groves. His number is in the book downstairs."

"Let's get you to your bed first." Mrs. Bartley took Margaret's arm, guiding her across the room and gently helping her to lie down.

"Thanks." Margaret felt tears coming.

"I'll go call Dr. Groves," Mrs. Bartley said. "I'll close the door so Peter can't get to the stairs and then I'll come right back up. You stay here, Margaret."

Margaret whispered her thanks and then closed her eyes, moaning in pain that was so intense she felt like she was dying. Maybe she deserved to die.

When Margaret opened her eyes again, she was in a hospital bed with Mam standing over her. "Oh, Mary Margaret." Mam reached for her hand. "I'm so sorry."

"Sorry?" Margaret tried to remember. "What happened?"

"You...you lost your baby." Mam wiped her red-rimmed eyes with a hanky.

"I lost the baby?"

"I'm so very, very sorry. But why didn't you tell me, Margaret?"

Margaret closed her eyes, feeling hot tears seeping out from the sides.

"I had no idea you were with child, Margaret. Why didn't you say something?"

"I—uh—I don't know," she said in a raspy voice. "I was getting ready to...for Thanksgiving."

"Oh, darling." Mam wrapped her arms around Margaret. "I'm so sorry."

Colleen had been looking forward to reuniting with her family for Thanksgiving, but as she drove to San Francisco on Wednesday, she knew that it would a somber gathering. Molly had called her on Monday night with the sad news that Margaret had lost a baby. Colleen tried not to feel indignant that no one had bothered to tell her about Margaret's pregnancy, but Molly quickly clarified that it had been a shock to everyone.

Glad that her film had just wrapped, Colleen had been looking forward to some downtime, but after hearing about Margaret, she'd quickly volunteered to lend a hand at the store. "Until Margaret's back on her feet," she'd assured Mam on the phone last night. But then a telegram had arrived from Geoff this morning, announcing that he would have a week of leave, starting on Saturday. She wired him back, explaining the need to go home and help with her family, asking him to meet her there.

After a warm welcome home, Colleen went straight upstairs to check on Margaret, who was still confined to bed rest. Not surprisingly, she looked incredibly sad. "Oh, Margaret." Colleen went over to hug her. "I'm so sorry."

Margaret just nodded, sniffing back tears. "Thanks."

Colleen looked around the room. "Where's Peter?"

"Napping, I think. Mam's taking care of him for a few days."

Colleen pulled a chair close to the bed and, peeling off her driving gloves, she peered at her sister. Margaret looked like a shadow of her previous self. "How are you feeling?"

Margaret shrugged. "I'm not in pain. I actually think I could be out of bed, but the doctor said not until—"

"I don't mean physically. Although it's good to hear you're better." Colleen tapped her chest. "How are you feeling inside?"

Margaret's chin trembled. "Uh, well, pretty bad."

Colleen reached for her hand. "I'm here if you need to talk."

"Talking won't help." Margaret sadly shook her head.

"How do you know?" Colleen persisted. "Have you really talked to anyone yet?"

"What do you mean?"

Colleen studied her closely. "Did you tell Brian yet?"

Margaret's eyes opened wide. "Tell him what?"

Colleen waited. Although she'd meant about losing the baby she knew Margaret was thinking about something else. Perhaps she should let her sister broach the subject. But when Margaret said nothing, Colleen decided to press a little harder. But first closed the door.

"Margaret," she said gently, "you look absolutely miserable. I don't know how it feels to lose a baby, but—"

"I didn't want the baby," Margaret whispered in a desperate tone.

Glad for her acting skills, Colleen acted completely nonchalant. "That's not so surprising."

Margaret looked shocked.

"You already have one child, you're working hard at the store, your husband is far away... Why would you want to add another helpless baby to the mix?"

"But—I—I—"

"You don't have to pretend with me."

For a long moment, neither of them spoke. Then Margaret began. "I feel so guilty, Colleen. So guilty it feels like it's killing me. I doubt you can even imagine how horrible it feels to harbor such guilt."

"You forget that I felt terribly guilty when I thought Geoff was dead. I blamed myself for writing those silly letters, imagining that my careless words resulted in him being careless in the skies. I blamed myself for—"

"Perhaps you do understand. But you were never unfaithful to him." She looked up with frightened eyes. "I mean, I wasn't completely unfaithful. But, well, you know what I did."

"I know." Colleen nodded.

"And you never wished a baby away, Colleen. That is unforgivable."

"Why is it unforgivable?"

Margaret folded her arms in front of her. "It just is. It's horrible. I am horrible. A horrible wife—a horrible mother. It's unforgivable."

"So you say it's unforgivable. Have you gone to confession? Have you talked to Father McMurphey?"

"No, of course not."

"Well, I'm not one to talk, but maybe you should consider it. If anyone can tell you whether you are unforgivable or not, I expect it would be Father McMurphey."

Margaret locked eyes with Colleen. "What do you think? Do you think it's unforgivable?"

Colleen pursed her lips. Talking about religious things wasn't exactly comfortable for her, but perhaps this was necessary. "I believe in a God who will forgive anything...if we ask him."

"Really?" Margaret blinked. "You really truly believe that?"

Colleen nodded somberly.

"Well, then I guess you really are a good godmother for Peter."

Colleen couldn't help but smile. "Who would've thunk?"

Margaret's brow furrowed. "Colleen?"

"Yes?"

"Do you think God is punishing me?" she whispered.

"Punishing you?"

"For spending time with Howard. Do you think that's why he took my baby?"

Colleen considered this. "First of all, I don't believe God took your baby. Not really. I think it just happened. The same way other bad things happen. Like Peter dying at Pearl Harbor. Or Dad getting sick. Or Geoff being captured last year. It just happens. And I don't believe God was punishing any of us with those things. But it probably feels like it sometimes."

"Yes...it does."

"And, sure, maybe we bring hard things on ourselves sometimes, by being stupid. Believe me, working in Hollywood, I've been seeing plenty of stupid. And I'm trying to learn from it. I never want to make the same mistakes I see other actors and actresses making. But I also don't want to judge them." She sighed. "It feels like I'm preaching a sermon here. Sorry."

"No, go on," Margaret urged. "I think I need it."

"Anyway, I don't think God is punishing you, Margaret. But I think he might be trying to teach you some things…about life."

"You're probably right." Margaret slowly nodded, closing her eyes. "I just hope I'm smart enough to learn."

Twenty-Seven

Although Colleen worked at the store on the Friday after Thanksgiving, she knew that with Geoff coming home tomorrow, this was all she could offer. And so, with Mrs. Bartley watching, Colleen asked both Jimmy and Dirk why they only worked part-time. "Is it your choice?" she asked. "Or simply that Margaret hasn't offered you full-time work?"

"I'm taking bookkeeping classes," Jimmy explained. "So working part-time is best for me."

"I have to work two part-time jobs to make a living," Dirk explained. "But I'd rather be working just one."

"Meaning that you're interested in being a full-time employee here?"

His eyes lit up. "Sure."

"Then you're hired." As Colleen reached out to shake his hand, Mrs. Bartley actually clapped.

"It's about time," Mrs. Bartley declared.

"What about Margaret?" Dirk asked with a worried expression.

"I'll handle Margaret," Colleen assured him.

So that evening, when Colleen went home, she explained her plan to Margaret. "If the store can't cover the extra expense, I will," she assured her. "I've been offered another movie contract. According to my agents, it'll be my best one yet. My first starring role. And although it's not a big film, it sounds like it'll be solid—and the pay is good. If I can't help my family some, then what's the point of being rich and famous?" She laughed.

"I should argue this with you." Margaret slowly shook her head. "But I don't even have the strength. So thank you."

"But here's the deal," Colleen clasped her sister's hand. "You must promise me that you will work less now. You need to spend more time with Peter—and take it easier. Will you agree to that?"

"Sounds good to me."

"One more thing." Colleen held up a finger. "Promise me you'll go to confession as soon as you're on your feet."

"I promise." Margaret sighed. "Although it's hard to believe that you're the one telling me to go."

"Speaking of going, I need to tell you good-bye."

"Good-bye?" Margaret sat up in bed. "But you just got here a couple days ago."

Colleen explained about Geoff's leave. "He arrives in San Diego tomorrow. I plan to leave early in the morning to meet him. Geoff doesn't know it yet, but I just signed an agreement to purchase Laurel Wagner's beach house."

"You're kidding!" Margaret's eyes grew wide. "You really are becoming rich and famous, aren't you?"

"I don't know about that, but Laurel wanted to sell it, and it seems like a good investment. Geoff and I can use it when he's in San Diego. And we'll loan it out too. Next time Brian has leave, you're welcome to use it. It's a sweet little place. And maybe Geoff and I will even live there when the war ends."

"Well, as usual, I'm jealous." Margaret scowled. "But I'm glad for you too. I really am. I hope you and Geoff have a good time."

"And I hope you get well soon." Colleen squeezed her hand. "And go to confession. And take it easier." She leaned down to kiss her sister's cheek. "Remember, this war won't last forever, Margaret. Someday we'll all look back on these days, and hopefully we'll just remember the good times."

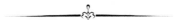

Molly still hadn't heard back from Patrick. According to his parents, they hadn't received any letters either. It was worrisome, but everyone tried to act as if he was simply too busy to write. And based on the news of the Pacific front, everyone stationed there was busy. It brought some comfort that Bridget finally sent a letter home. Although it was vague, as usual, regarding her whereabouts, it was encouraging to hear that she sounded fulfilled in her work. But there was not a word about Doctor Cliff.

On December 7, after her last class, Molly braced against the chilly fog to trek over to the National Cemetery, laying a single white rose by her brother's memorial stone. It was hard to believe it had only been two years ago since the attack on Pearl Harbor had taken Peter from them. It felt like another lifetime in a different world. As she walked back to campus, Molly wondered what Peter would think of his grown-up baby sister. Hopefully he would be proud of her, just like he used to be.

Finals week was coming to an end, and Molly eagerly anticipated Christmas break and being at home. She was on her way back to her sorority house, where she planned to grab her already packed bag and make it home in time for dinner tonight. She was halfway across campus when she was surprised to be stopped by Professor Blackstone.

"Molly Mulligan," he cheerfully declared. "I am so glad to see you. How are you doing?"

"I'm fine, thanks." She smiled brightly. "It's good to see you too, Professor."

"Are you a full-time student here now?" He kept stride with her as they walked across the lawn.

She nodded. "I just finished my last final, and I'm happy to say I think I did all right."

"I'm not the least bit surprised." He glumly shook his head. "Although I am sorry you haven't been in any of my night classes this term. I could've used your enthusiasm."

"Do you only teach night classes? I don't recall seeing your name on the roster of history classes I had to choose from."

"Unfortunately, I'm not tenured at the college yet. They only let me teach at night." His mouth twisted to one side. "So I'm forced to keep my day job."

"Really? What is your day job?"

"I'm a reporter for the *Chronicle*. Current events."

She turned to stare with wide eyes. "Really? You work at the *San Francisco Chronicle*?"

"Yep." He nodded. "Been doing it for years. That's how I put myself through college. But my first love is history. My dream is to be a full-time professor here."

"My dream is to be a journalist," she eagerly told him. "I can't believe you work for the *Chronicle*, and you don't even seem to like it."

"Oh, I like it well enough," he explained. "It's just that I'm ready to move on. I love history, and I love teaching."

"I love history too," she confessed. "But I also love writing and photography. And I would love to work at the *Chronicle*."

He rubbed his chin. "Have you ever considered an internship?"

"I would love to be an intern. But what about my classes here?" She paused in front of her sorority house.

"You can work your class schedule around it. Plus you can get college credits for interning."

"Really? And do you think the *Chronicle* would actually consider me?"

"Of course." Professor Blackstone checked his watch. "I'd love to tell you more about this, but I'm on my way to talk to the chancellor right now. Working on an article about the college for the Sunday edition."

"Oh, yes, of course. I don't want to keep you."

"But if you'd like to meet up later, maybe grab some coffee?"

"I'd love to. Anytime."

"Well, we should probably do it soon. In case you want to try to set something up for winter term. I don't work on Saturday. How does tomorrow sound?"

"Tomorrow is fine," she said eagerly.

"Let's meet at the Coffee Pot at nine."

She thanked him then hurried into her sorority house, using the payphone in the lobby to call Mam. She quickly explained her change in plans to come home tonight, apologizing for missing dinner.

"But I invited the Hammonds," Mam said with disappointment. "And Margaret and the baby will be here too. We wanted to celebrate your homecoming—and that you finished your first term of college."

"I'm so sorry, Mam. But this opportunity is too good to pass up." The truth was Molly wasn't overly eager to see the Hammonds. Not that she didn't love them. She did. But she was worried they'd raise the topic of Patrick and Bridget, speculating on their romantic ties. She just didn't need that.

"Louise made a pie."

"Maybe you could save me a piece," Molly said. "But really, it doesn't seem worthwhile for me to run home tonight when I'd need to be back here first thing in the morning." She went into a little more detail, explaining about the professor and the possibility of doing an internship.

"You say he's a professor, but he works for the newspaper?" Mam sounded confused.

"Yes. I had Professor Blackstone for a night class last year. He's a wonderful teacher. But it's really exciting to think he can connect me with someone at the newspaper. Imagine me working for the *San Francisco Chronicle*, Mam. It's a dream come true."

"Well, we will miss you tonight."

"I'm sorry. Give everyone my love."

"Yes, and I'll tell them your news, Molly. I'm sure Dad will think that's very exciting. After all, it's his favorite newspaper."

Molly considered trying to set Mam straight—that she didn't actually have an internship yet—but she didn't want to put another nickel in the pay phone, so she simply said good-bye.

Colleen knew the letdown of saying good-bye to Geoff was directly related to the fabulous days they'd just enjoyed together. It had all been so wonderful and good and fun and right. And then, just like that, they were forced to part ways. She also knew that each time they said good-bye could possibly be the last time, so she did not take their farewells lightly. Just the same, she didn't like them—and she usually spent the next few days trying not to wallow in self-pity.

To distract herself from missing Geoff this last time, she'd thrown herself into cleaning, changing, and rearranging the beach house that she had recently purchased. It was rather amazing to actually own a sweet place like this. And it had been pure pleasure to transform it into a place that really felt like home. She and Geoff had brought all their wedding and shower gifts with them, but she'd yet to fully unpack and put them into place. As she put new sheets on the bed, new towels in the bathroom, and pretty dishes and things into the kitchen, she could imagine the two of them happily living here, in their little love nest. As long as Geoff came home. Colleen wasn't sure what she would do if he didn't.... She didn't want to think about that.

After she got the beach house into perfect order, she drove back to her Beverly Hills apartment and then, a few days later, packed her bags and headed north to San Francisco. Her next movie wouldn't begin until the end of the month and, in the meantime, she looked forward to being home with her family in the few days before and after Christmas. She was curious to see how Margaret was faring and how Molly's first full-time term at college had gone. Also, she planned to spend some time with Geoff's family. Then it would be back to work—on her first starring role!

It was just getting dark when Colleen slipped into the house, which seemed quiet. The blackout curtains were already up and Molly was sitting alone at the kitchen table with a bowl of half-eaten soup.

"Colleen!" Molly leaped to her feet. "I thought you weren't coming until Christmas Eve."

Colleen dropped her cosmetics case and hugged her sister. "I finished putting the beach house together sooner than expected, and I couldn't wait to get home." She looked around. "Where is everyone?"

"Mam and Dad went to the Hammonds' for dinner. And Margaret and Peter moved back to the apartment over the store."

Colleen peeked at the pot on the stove to see there was more soup. "Mind if I help myself?"

"Let me get it for you," Molly insisted.

Before long they were both seated at the table with Colleen grilling Molly for all the latest news. "Is Dad worse?" she asked as she broke a piece of bread. "Is that why Margaret went back to the apartment?"

"Not at all. Dad actually seems better. Margaret has gotten better too. I think she just felt too cooped up here. And Peter's been getting pretty rambunctious lately. Margaret might've been concerned that he was too noisy for Mam and Dad. But mostly I think she wanted some independence."

Colleen grimaced. "She's not seeing Howard again, is she?"

"Oh, no, I really don't think so." Molly chuckled. "It probably helps that Mrs. Bartley is around. She keeps a pretty careful eye on Margaret."

"And has anyone heard from Bridget?"

"I just got a letter from her yesterday. She sounded good. They're getting another leave in New Zealand for Christmas. It's summer down there."

"And you?" Colleen studied Molly closely, trying to discern if she was still suffering from her broken heart. "How was school?"

"I love school," Molly proclaimed. "And you won't believe this, Colleen. I've been offered an internship at the *Chronicle.*"

"*The San Francisco Chronicle?*"

Molly nodded eagerly. "It's so thrilling! I've only been doing it a few days, but I'm loving it. I'm assisting Mick Blackstone. He's a part-time history professor at the college, but he's been with the *Chronicle* for about ten years. I go along with him to get the story. Just current events. But I take photos and make notes and Mick even

272

let me write my own article yesterday." She laughed. "Not that he'll use it. But he said it was good."

"That sounds exciting." Colleen dipped her spoon in the chowder, keeping her eyes down. "Any news from those Hammond boys?"

"Margaret thinks Brian is in Italy. I don't tell her the latest news when I hear it. It's been pretty rough in Italy these last few weeks."

"I think it's been rough all over," Colleen said somberly. "The Pacific front sounds like a powder keg right now."

"I know." Molly nodded. "Ever since our allies have been going full force in the Solomon Islands. Seems like one day they have a victory and the next day...well, you know how it goes."

"Geoff seems to thrive on the drama." Colleen tried to sound light. "He loves flying right into the thick of the battlefield. Like it's some kind of game. I suppose that's what makes him such a great pilot. He's fearless." She set her spoon in the empty bowl and looked at Molly. "How about Patrick? Any news from him?"

"Mrs. Hammond got a brief note. Mostly saying he was busy and unable to write much, but that he was okay."

"Well, that's good." Colleen peered at Molly. "And are you getting over it...I mean, him?"

"I think so." Molly sighed. "I still get sad sometimes. But then I remind myself that Patrick is my brother—and it might sound corny, but it actually helps. I mean it's bad enough to feel hurt like...well, you know how I was. But it would be even worse to completely lose his friendship too."

Colleen sighed as she picked up their empty bowls. "I'm guessing Christmas will be a rather quiet affair this year. All the fellows and Bridget overseas...along with all the other servicemen and women."

"At least we've got little Peter." Molly smiled. "He's really growing up fast. He's into everything and even saying quite a few words. He ought to liven things up."

"Wait until you see what I got him for Christmas." Colleen set their dishes in the sink. "Which reminds me, I should probably go unload my car."

"Not without me."

As Molly helped Colleen lug bags and boxes into the house and up the stairs, they laughed and joked just like they'd done as little girls—and Colleen decided that, despite the heaviness of a horribly cruel war, some things would never change.

Twenty-Eight

January 1944

Margaret's friendship with Mrs. Bartley had improved significantly in the last couple months. Ever since that awful day. Oh, certainly, Mrs. Bartley could get irritating at times—especially when she got bossy—but for the most part, Margaret was glad to have her around. Not just for the help, but for companionship too.

"It's so slow this afternoon," Margaret told Mrs. Bartley, watching as Peter rode his airplane down the canned food aisle, making sound effects for the engine. "Feel free to go home if you'd like."

"I'd just as soon be here." Mrs. Bartley expertly flipped the feather duster over the pyramid stack of canned corn. She smiled sadly. "It's a bit lonely at home. Especially in winter when the nights are long."

"I'd think you'd enjoy the peace and quiet." Margaret hurried to stop Peter from removing a can from the bottom of a stack before the whole thing tumbled. Lately he'd been acting like the cans were his building blocks.

"I'm happy to stay until closing. In fact, if you and Peter want to go upstairs, I can finish up down here. And there's Dirk in the backroom if I get busy."

Margaret scooped up Peter. "Then I'll take you up on that

generous offer." She smiled at Mrs. Bartley. "I don't know if I tell you how much I appreciate your help here, but I do."

Mrs. Bartley patted Margaret's cheek. "You tell me that all the time, dear."

"I suppose I'm trying to make up for how cranky I used to be to you."

Mrs. Bartley just laughed. "I suspect you and I are similar in many ways, Margaret. We can both get a bit cantankerous at times. I believe it's simply because we are both strong women."

Margaret considered this as she balanced Peter on her hip. "I'd like to be a strong woman, but I'm afraid I've mostly shown a lot of weakness." She looked down at Peter's scuffed walking shoes. "I'm certainly not proud of my behavior this past year."

"Pride is highly overrated."

Margaret looked curiously back at Mrs. Bartley.

"The Bible says that the proud will be humbled." She put a hand on Margaret's shoulder. "And lucky are the ones who get their humbling done while they are young."

"The Bible says that?"

"Well, I made up that second part, but I believe it holds true."

"Do you think that's what happened to me? I got my humbling done while I was young?"

Mrs. Bartley laughed lightly. "Well, I doubt we're ever done. At any age. But I do believe you've made real progress, dear."

Margaret thanked her and, as she carried Peter upstairs, she hoped the old woman was right. The past year had been rough... she'd made mistakes...had regrets. Mostly she was glad that it was over with. She just wished the war was over too.

After just a month of filming, Colleen felt unexplainably weary. It wasn't just because the script was a bit weak or that her costars seemed inexperienced, although both were true. It was simply that Colleen was tired. Naturally, she had to keep this to herself. After a particularly trying scene, she flopped into the hairdresser's chair with a loud sigh.

"Are you okay?" Stella asked as she began to restyle Colleen's hair for the next scene.

"I'm fine." Colleen sat up straighter. It wouldn't do for the star of this film to appear out of sorts...or as sluggish as she felt.

"Seems to me you're worn out," Stella declared.

"I'm a little tired," Colleen admitted.

"These long days take their toll."

"That's true. But at least we'll be finished soon. I just heard Leon say we're going to wrap early. If all goes well, this might be a six-week movie."

"That's because we're on a six-week budget." Stella spun the chair around to work on the front of Colleen's hair.

"Meaning this is a B movie." Colleen had suspected as much, although so far no one had actually said so.

Stella shrugged. "You never know...sometimes a B rises to an A."

"Well, just the same, I'm thankful." Colleen forced a tired smile.

"Thankful and worn out." As she secured a pin-curl, Stella looked closely at Colleen. "Say, doll, is there any chance you could be pregnant?"

Colleen felt a wave of panic, but keeping her expression placid, she lowered her voice. "I, uh, I don't think so."

"But you don't know so?"

Colleen glanced around to be sure no one else was listening.

"So you've got your suspicions," Stella said quietly.

Colleen just nodded.

"Well, don't worry about it, doll. Lots of actresses make movies while they're expecting. And you can schedule a break when the baby comes." She patted Colleen on the back. "Won't it be exciting to have a little one? You'll make a beautiful little mother."

Stella's words sent an uneasy chill through Colleen. She and Geoff had agreed to wait a few years before having children. What if she really was pregnant? Without warning, Colleen's eyes filled with tears, and she choked back a sob.

"Oh, dear." Stella grabbed some tissues. "Diane?" she called out. "Makeup over here."

Diane, carrying her portable case, rushed over in time to see Colleen's eye-makeup running down her cheeks. "What on earth?" she demanded as she leaned down, trying to remedy the situation. "What did you say to her, Stella?"

"I didn't say anything. Well, except..." Stella leaned over to whisper in Diane's ear. "But keep it under your hat, you hear?"

"Are you certain?" Diane asked Colleen.

"Of course not," Colleen mumbled. "This is Stella's idea."

"Well, if you think it might be possible, I can give you the name of a good obstetrician." Diane used powder to repair a cheek. "My sister Lydia just had a baby, and she says Dr. Albert is the best OB around. I'll call her and get the number while you're doing your next scene."

"Better yet, why don't you call the doctor for her, Diane?" Stella suggested. "Make Colleen an appointment."

Colleen considered protesting but realized these women were probably right. Whether she was pregnant or not, it would be better to know.

So it was that a little over a week later, sitting in Dr. Albert's paneled office, Colleen's fears were confirmed. The test results from last week's exam were back. She was expecting.

"I asked the lab to put a rush on this." Dr. Albert tapped the file on his desk. "I knew you were feeling rather anxious."

"Yes, I've been a little worried. You know, due to my work." She tried to look more confident than she felt. "So when is my due date?"

"Around the end of August," Dr. Albert declared.

"August...?" she said the word slowly, trying to absorb this information.

"These are the prenatal vitamins I recommend." He shook a sample bottle. "And this pamphlet will tell you what you can expect," he said, chuckling, "while you're expecting."

"What about my work?" Colleen had already told him about her concerns for her career.

"Many actresses continue throughout their pregnancies. Well, as long as their general health is good. But most of them quit by month five or six. I'm sure that's partly because the camera might be too revealing. But in my opinion, that's a good time to take a break. So I'd recommend you slow it down starting in, say..." He checked the calendar. "Early June."

Colleen considered this. "So maybe I can get in another movie... or maybe even two...before that."

His gray brows arched. "You mentioned feeling tired. Two movies sound demanding. Are you sure you have that much energy?"

She forced an uneasy smile. "I'm not sure of much of anything right now, doctor. My head is spinning."

"Will your husband be happy to hear your news?"

"Now that's one thing I can be sure of. Geoff will be thrilled." Her smile became genuine. "In fact, I think I'll go send him a telegram right now."

"Congratulations to both of you." He handed her the vitamins. "Hopefully these will put some spring back in your step." And then the pamphlet. "Pay close attention to the nutrition section in here. I know how you young actresses try to live on salad greens and air. This is not a time for dieting."

"I'll keep that in mind." She thanked him. As she went outside, she considered all that Dr. Albert had told her. She liked the idea of being able to eat again, but she had no appetite. It was still hard to believe that she really was pregnant. Up until the doctor announced the news, she'd been telling herself she had a stomach bug. That was why she hadn't been hungry and had felt tired. It was the excuse she gave the director for going to the doctor last week and leaving work early again today.

But as she drove to her apartment, stopping to post a telegram to Geoff on her way, she realized that—despite her reservations—it was rather exciting to think that she and Geoff were going to have a baby…and be a family. Somehow they would muddle through. She just knew it. And so the telegram she sent Geoff was joyful and celebratory. Hopefully her news would make his day.

With that taken care of, Colleen went home to her apartment, took a vitamin with a glass of orange juice, and just slept.

Whether it was the prenatal vitamins or accepting the fact that she really was pregnant, Colleen felt better the next day. Really, being pregnant was not the end of the world. Lots of actresses had babies and continued their careers. Of course, they depended on baby nurses or helpful family members, but somehow they managed. And she would too.

The next day, toward the end of a long afternoon, everyone was on break when a loud voice made Colleen almost fall from her chair.

"Delivery for Colleen Mulligan. Is Colleen Mulligan in the studio?"

"You mean Maureen Mulligan," Stella corrected. "That's her there."

The young messenger handed Colleen a long white florist's box then held up a card with a flourish. "I'm supposed to sing this."

"Really?" Colleen chuckled. "A singing telegram?"

"That's right." He cleared his throat and, as she opened the box to see a dozen gorgeous, long-stemmed red roses, the young man began to sing, using the tune from the *Happy Birthday* song. "Happy baby day to you. Happy baby day to you. Happy baby day, dear Mommy—happy baby day to you. From your loving husband, Geoff."

Everyone clapped for him, gathering around Colleen to see what this was all about. "You're pregnant?" Leon demanded with a furrowed brow.

Colleen took in a deep breath, looking directly at him. "Yes, I am. But be assured, it will not affect my performance. Not in the least."

He frowned. "It better not."

The response from the others was a mixed bag. Some seemed genuinely happy for her. Others acted concerned, as if she were putting the entire film at risk. And so she assured them, again and again, that she was going to be just fine and, if everything went as planned, they would be wrapping in a couple of weeks anyway. But by the end of the day, she realized that Geoff's congratulatory message had just complicated her life considerably. It might even nix her chances of getting another film contract.

During the next few days, Colleen knew that having the whole studio aware of her delicate condition had raised the bar for her. She had to give more than a hundred percent now. And so she gave it all she had—and then some. When she went home each evening, she felt completely drained. It was all she could do to get something to eat and fall into bed. But it worried her...and it reminded her of what had happened to her sister last fall. She'd never questioned Margaret about her last pregnancy or what had caused her to lose the baby, but now Colleen was anxious. What if it was from being overworked? Wasn't that what everyone had assumed? Wasn't that the reason they all wanted Margaret to take it easier? What if Colleen was making the same mistake?

It was late February and an unseasonably warm morning when Margaret decided to make the most of it by taking Peter out in his stroller. "I don't think you'll be too busy while I'm gone," she told Mrs. Bartley. "And you've got Dirk here today. Plus Mam will be in at eleven. And Jimmy at two. Although I'll be back long before that. I just want to run a few errands, enjoy some sunshine."

"Go, go." Mrs. Bartley waved her toward the front door. "Some fresh air will do you both good."

But Margaret was barely to the door when she froze in her tracks. A uniformed Western Union boy was just leaning his bike against the building then reaching into his messenger bag. She waited as the boy pushed the store's front door. As the bell jangled, he glanced around. "Telegram for Mrs. Hammond."

Margaret's voice stuck in her throat, but she wanted to tell him that he was at the wrong address, that Brian's mother was not here. Instead, she raised a hand. "I'm Mrs. Brian Hammond," she said in a trembling voice.

"Mrs. M. Margaret Hammond?"

"That's me." Margaret stepped past the stroller with shaking knees.

"Oh, dear." Mrs. Bartley was by her side now, putting a comforting arm around Margaret's shoulders. Several customers in the store were clustering nearby, quietly whispering amongst themselves—everyone thinking the same thing.

"This is for you, ma'am." With a furrowed brow, the boy handed Margaret the yellow and black envelope and then without giving her a chance to respond, hurried back out and onto his bicycle.

Margaret felt dizzy as she turned the strange paper around in her now-trembling hands. It seemed a foreign object, and she couldn't make sense of how to open it. Finally, she handed it over to Mrs. Bartley. "Will you?"

"Yes, of course, dear."

As if in a dream, Margaret followed Mrs. Bartley over to the counter, watching as the old woman slit it open and unfolded it. She turned to Margaret. "Do you want me to read it to you, dear?"

"No." Margaret took the lightweight paper from her.

"It might not...might not be bad news," Mrs. Bartley said in a way that wasn't convincing.

"Yes...maybe not." Margaret attempted to focus her eyes on the capitalized bold type, slowly reading the words aloud for Mrs. Bartley to hear.

WUX WASHINGTON DC 1005AM FEB 16 1944

MRS M MARGARET HAMMOND
1452 CHURCH STREET
SAN FRANCISCO CAL

THE SECRETARY OF WAR DESIRES ME TO EXPRESS HIS
DEEP REGRET THAT YOUR HUSBAND FIRST LIEUTENANT

BRIAN J HAMMOND HAS BEEN SEVERELY WOUNDED
IN ACTION ON 15 FEBRUARY IN ITALY. HE IS BEING
TRANSPORTED TO ENGLAND. FURTHER INFORMATION
AND DETAILS TO COME.

R L PARKER THE ADJUTANT GENERAL
1045AM

Margaret turned to Mrs. Bartley. "He—he's only wounded. Brian's
not dead." She felt tears of relief filling her eyes. "He's alive!"

"Yes, he's alive." Mrs. Bartley walked Margaret over to the
straight-backed chair beside the counter. "Thank the Lord, Brian
is alive."

As Mrs. Bartley wheeled Peter's stroller closer, Margaret reread
the message. "But it does say he's severely wounded." She looked
up to see not only Mrs. Bartley but several store patrons looking
on with such compassionate expressions that a few pent-up tears
slipped down. "I wonder...what does that mean?"

"My sister's boy Gerald was wounded in battle," Mrs. Spencer told
Margaret. "I don't recall what her telegram said, but the boy made
it safely home, and he's not in too bad of shape. Gerald claims our
stateside military hospitals are the finest in the world. And the best
part is that Gerald will never return to active service."

Margaret blotted her tears. "So my Brian is coming home."

"Yes," another woman assured her. "Your man is coming home,
dear. You can be assured of that."

"So, really, this is—is good news." Margaret heard the tremble
in her voice.

"Yes, in a way...it is," Mrs. Bartley told her. "Brian is coming
home!"

MELODY CARLSON

Even as Margaret told herself that Brian was not dead, the words *severely wounded* seemed to be screaming inside of her. She suddenly imagined her handsome Brian, twisting in agonizing pain on an Army stretcher. *Severely wounded.*

As a child, she remembered being frightened by veterans from the previous war—disfigured men with missing limbs and empty eyes. Her parents had explained they were war heroes, but to her they were lost, lonely monsters. Was that how Brian would return to her? Margaret could hold it back no longer. Covering her face with her hands, she crumbled into loud sobs.

"Go ahead and cry," Mrs. Bartley gently told her. "Get your tears out, dear. But then you must remember that Brian is alive. And perhaps he's not even in such bad shape. We don't know anything for sure. And we shouldn't jump to conclusions. We must hope for the best."

"And we'll all be praying for Brian too," Mrs. Spencer assured Margaret. The other ladies chimed in, sharing various hopeful stories of soldiers who'd made it home, reassuring her that it was always darkest before the dawn and promising to keep Brian in their prayers.

But even as Margaret dried her eyes and thanked the kind women, she wondered...could their prayers actually change anything? Why would God even listen? It seemed obvious to Margaret, despite what Colleen had told her, that God was punishing her. He was repaying Margaret for her unfaithfulness. And the truth was Margaret deserved punishment. She knew she did...but Brian did not.

Twenty-Nine

Early March

Production for Colleen's movie wrapped later than the director had hoped for, but not because of Colleen. As Leon told her on the last day of shooting, she'd been a trooper. On the following day, she'd met with Georgina, preparing herself for rejection since word of her condition had spread fast. But to Colleen's relief, Georgina remained hopeful about her future in film.

Just the same, Colleen felt uncertain as she drove to San Francisco the next day. Despite Georgina's optimism, it was entirely possible that this pregnancy would derail her career. She knew better than anyone that she was not established yet. The general public didn't recognize the name Maureen Mulligan...perhaps they never would. Even when the film with her first starring role released this summer—and she could just imagine herself showing up at the premiere looking like Humpty Dumpty—there'd be no guarantee the film would succeed. For all she knew, this baby might be the perfect excuse to bow out.

And right now, she wasn't sure she cared one way or the other. Besides feeling utterly exhausted, she was terribly worried about Margaret. That was the primary reason she was headed home so soon after finishing the film, even though her obstetrician had recommended she take a couple weeks to rest and recover. Hopefully, she could do that at her parents' house.

When Colleen had called home last night, planning to share the good news about her pregnancy with her family, she never got the chance. Before she could let the cat out of the bag, she'd been shocked to learn that Brian had been wounded in action. According to Dad, her brother-in-law was coming home minus his right leg.

"Not the whole leg, mind you," Dad had said in a matter-of-fact tone. He was obviously trying to keep the subject light. "There's enough upper leg that they'll be able to fit him for a prosthetic device."

"You mean a wooden leg?" Colleen had momentarily imagined Brian dressed like a pirate.

"Molly said it's called a prosthetic. She did some research and even found photographs of some fine modern models. She feels Brian will be able to live a fairly normal life."

"How is Margaret handling it?"

At that point, Dad had handed the phone over to Mam, and Colleen had learned that Margaret was not taking it well. "Margaret and the baby moved back home a few days ago," Mam had explained. "But Margaret has taken to her bed."

"Is she sick?"

"Sick at heart." Mam's voice had cracked with emotion. "For some reason, she blames herself for Brian's injury. It makes no sense. But no one can convince her otherwise."

As a result of this sad news, Colleen had decided to postpone sharing her own good fortune—but she'd longed to get home as soon as possible. And so no one was more upset than Colleen when a technical glitch caused the studio to lose more than a week's worth of film. Highly motivated for a wrap, Colleen worked harder than ever to re-shoot all those scenes. It was exhausting, but now that it was behind her and she was almost home, she pondered over what she could say or do to encourage Margaret. A part of her just wanted to shake her sister and tell her to straighten up. But she knew that wouldn't help. Poor Margaret!

Molly knew it was no coincidence that Patrick would be on leave during the same time Brian was coming home. He obviously wanted to be here to lend support to his wounded brother, the same way Colleen and Molly had been trying to support Margaret during her dark time. Molly couldn't have been happier for Colleen's homecoming last week—and to hear her good news! She'd hoped that, of all people, Colleen might be the one to get through to Margaret. And so far, it seemed to be working. At least Margaret was getting out of bed now, and caring for her child. That was progress.

But today was the big day. Brian had been transported by train to San Francisco and was supposed to have been admitted into Letterman Army Hospital earlier. She hoped it had gone well. But since it was once again finals week, Molly had remained focused on her studies, as well as her intern responsibilities at the *Chronicle*. It was actually a relief to have these distractions to keep her busy during this difficult time.

Molly's heart ached for Margaret...and for Brian. But she also knew that, besides praying, there was little she could do for either of them at the moment. And so when no one remembered her birthday—yesterday—she pretended not to notice. After all, she was eighteen now—an adult. Birthdays were for kids. Being completely overlooked almost seemed like a rite of passage. Someday she would laugh about it.

"How'd your last final go?" Mick Blackstone asked as Molly entered his office to see what assignment was waiting for her.

"It seemed okay." She unbuttoned the top of her coat.

"I'll bet you aced it."

"I hope so." She glanced at the corner of his desk where he usually kept a pile of work for her, frowning to see the basket was empty. "No assignments?"

"Not today."

She frowned. "I'm sorry I couldn't come in yesterday. I had—"

"Yes, yes, I know this is finals week, Molly. You were excused. And that's not why you don't have an assignment today."

"So you're not firing me after all?" she teased.

He laughed. "Hardly. In fact, I can name several editors ready to bribe you away from me."

"That's nice to know." She put her hands on her hips and frowned. "Maybe I should go ask one of them for an assignment."

"No, don't do that." He grinned. "It's just that I think you deserve a day off."

She frowned. "But I don't want a day off."

"Don't you know what they say about all work and no—"

"It might make Jack dull, but Jill likes the challenge."

He chuckled and set down his pencil.

"So if you don't have anything for me, I have an idea I'd like to run past you—if you can spare the time."

"Hold on." He stood.

"It'll only take a minute to tell you about it. It's something I can do independently and—"

"Not right now." He led her to the door, holding it open. "First I want to take you to meet someone." As he led her through the building and down several flights of stairs, her curiosity grew. Before long they were in the photography department. She'd only been here a few times, to deliver negatives or pick up photos, but each time she'd longed to linger and see more of the inner workings of this mysterious area.

Mick knocked on an office door and was soon introducing her to a middle-aged man named Jim Hampton. "Jim's our photography editor. He's in charge of all the photos that make it into the *Chronicle.*"

"It's an honor to meet you," she said as they shook hands.

"You too, young lady. I've seen some of your work. Not bad."

She felt her cheeks blushing. "Thank you very much."

"I understand you're interning with Mick, but I want to extend an invitation to my department too. Mazzie Proctor is one of my best photographers. She's out on assignment right now, but I told her about you. Someday when you've got spare time and Mazzie isn't too busy, she can show you around the department."

"That sounds wonderful. Next week is spring vacation, so I plan to be around quite a bit."

"You're not taking time off to do something fun?" he asked.

"I think it'd be more fun to be here," she admitted.

"Well, make sure you get together with Mazzie."

"Thank you so much, Mr. Hampton."

"No problem. When we get an intern with real talent and a good work ethic, we try to make them part of the family."

She thanked him again and then, interrupted by his secretary, she and Mick made their exit. "That was so wonderful," she quietly told Mick. "Thank you for arranging it."

"Better than an assignment?" he asked as they went upstairs.

"I'm still disappointed that you don't have any work for me," she confessed. "I don't know what to do with myself now."

"You mentioned a story idea?"

"Do you really want to hear it?" she asked hopefully.

"Could we discuss it over an early dinner? I worked through lunch today and I'm absolutely ravenous."

"I missed lunch too," she confessed.

"Shorty's is nearby, and they have a great blue-plate special on Thursdays. Let's go there." He paused by the editorial department. "Let me finish up some things in my office then I'll meet you down in the lobby."

"Would anyone mind if I used the phone?" she asked. "My sister's husband was supposed to come home today."

"The soldier who was injured?" he asked with concern.

She nodded. "I just want to be sure he made it okay."

"By all means, use the phone. I'd like to hear how he's doing."

So Molly stopped by her little desk, just outside Mick's door, to use the phone. To her relief, Colleen answered.

"Brian arrived at Letterman this morning," Colleen confirmed. "Mam watched the baby, and I took Margaret over this afternoon. Brian was in surprisingly good spirits."

"That's good to hear. How did Margaret do?"

"She was okay. I mean, sure, she cried some. Who could blame her to see him like that? But mostly she did just fine. I left them alone for about an hour. Then the Hammonds showed up—and Patrick too."

"Patrick's here already?" For some reason it was slightly unsettling to think of Patrick being in town. Probably because he'd never responded to her confession letter. Not a word.

"Apparently he came to Letterman straight from the ship. And I must say, it was touching to see the brothers reunite. But I'm afraid Brian got a little overwhelmed with all of us there. Finally, the nurse shooed us out, saying Brian needed his rest after the long trip. She said no visitors tomorrow, and after that no more than two at a time. So we came on home."

"Well, I'm glad to hear Brian was in good spirits. And it's not surprising he's worn out. Poor guy."

"So Mam is asking when you'll be home for supper? She's got an enormous roast in the oven and the Hammonds are already here."

Molly quickly explained her dinner plans then listened as Colleen relayed this information to Mam, overhearing Mam's complaints in the background. "Tell her I'm sorry," Molly said.

"So you're having dinner with Mick tonight?" Colleen's tone was laced with what sounded like insinuation—or maybe she was just teasing.

"To talk about work," Molly firmly told her.

"Uh-huh..." She sounded doubtful.

"It's true, Colleen."

"Mam is not pleased with your decision." Colleen declared this in a way that suggested others were listening. "She says you should tell Mister Mick that you're needed at home with your family tonight."

Molly considered this. "I'm sorry, Colleen, but I've already agreed to dine with Mick—to talk about a project. And I really should go now. Tell Mam that I'll be home tomorrow."

"Okay then." Colleen giggled. "Have fun, sweetie."

Molly pushed down feelings of guilt as she headed to the lobby. It wasn't that she didn't love her family—they all knew she did. But sometimes...well, they needed to understand that Molly Mulligan was entitled to a life of her own. She settled into one of the big leather arm chairs in the lobby, picking up the evening paper and skimming the front page. Although it had ended nearly a week ago, the headlines were still about the recent victory in the battle of the Bismarck Sea. As she studied the photographs, Molly wondered if Patrick had been there for any of that battle. Perhaps if she was forced to spend any time with him in the next few days, she could ask him about it. Not that he'd be inclined to reveal any real information. But at least it would show him that she still followed current events.

"Ready to go?" Mick smiled down on her.

"My stomach was just rumbling." She laid down the paper and stood.

"Do you like swiss steak?"

"Sure."

"Shorty's makes a good one. That's their blue-plate special on Thursdays."

As they walked, Molly told him as much as she knew about Brian. "I was glad to hear he's in good spirits, but I'm sure he wanted to appear strong for everyone. That's what I guessed he would do."

"That's understandable." He shook his head. "My heart goes out to the guy. I've suggested doing a story on some of our wounded servicemen, but Marty keeps shooting it down."

"Because it doesn't help war morale?" Molly had been with the paper long enough to pick up on their managing editor's unspoken rules.

He nodded grimly. "I suppose that's true. Folks at home don't need that kind of discouragement right now. But it's also true that a lot of these young men are coming back with some serious injuries and life challenges. Seems we'd all be better off to be up front about it instead of hiding the poor fellows away."

"I don't think Brian will want to be hidden away."

He shrugged as he opened the door to Shorty's. "Time will tell."

After they were seated and had placed orders for two blue-plate specials and two cups of coffee, Molly brought up a topic that had been bothering her for months now. "You told me your age." She remembered her surprise to learn that he was only thirty-two—she'd assumed he was older. "But I've wondered why you're not in the military." She smiled apologetically. "I hope you don't mind me asking, but my boss has encouraged me to be a nosy investigative reporter."

He chuckled. "A fair question. In fact, I was thinking about this very thing when you first told me about your brother-in-law's misfortune. You see, I injured my knee playing football in college. Unfortunately, that rendered me a glorious 4-F when I registered for the draft." He glumly shook his head. "I'd rather have been injured serving my country. But alas, it was running a pigskin down the backfield."

"Well, you can't help that. Besides, you have other talents that help the war effort."

"Speaking of age...a little bird told me that someone just had a birthday." His dark eyes twinkled.

"What?" She feigned ignorance.

"Sharon in Human Resources informed me that it was your birthday yesterday." His brows arched. "But, Molly, I had no idea you're only eighteen. I assumed you were in your twenties. I was still in high school when I was your age."

She smiled sheepishly. "I graduated early. That's why I was in your night class last year."

"And here I thought you were a motivated young career woman just trying to improve her mind."

"Well, I did want to improve my mind," she declared.

After they finished their blue-plate specials, which were surprisingly good, Mick insisted on ordering dessert. "Their berry pie à la mode is legendary, and we can say we're celebrating your birthday."

As they lingered over pie and coffee, Mick asked about her story idea.

"It's just a little idea," she admitted. "I'd like to do a story on small family businesses in San Francisco and how they've been impacted by the war. Whether it's from rationing or members being gone... or whatever."

He slowly nodded. "I like that. And you even have your own family business to draw from."

"Yes, but not only that." Now she began telling him about some observations she'd been making, how some businesses had vanished and others had flourished—all as a result of the war. "I thought I could get photos and do a short piece. Maybe two or three hundred words?"

"Sounds doable. That might be a nice feature for the Human Interest section of the Sunday paper...someday. Go ahead and take a stab at it and see how it goes. I can always lend a hand if you need it."

"That sounds great." She smiled. "You're such a great journalist, Mick. I honestly don't understand why you'd want to give it all up just to teach history."

"Because I love history."

"Someday this will be history," she declared. "People will look back on our generation, and they'll marvel that we—I mean all the Allied nations, our people on the home front and our men serving overseas—they will be amazed how we were able to stop the evil forces that threatened to overcome the world."

"Well said, Molly." His expression was somber. "I'd like to believe that."

"I believe it."

"I just hope our descendants will gain some valuable insight from what's happening now." Mick frowned. "But unfortunately, history teaches us that we don't always learn from the past. The human race continues to make similar mistakes...generation after generation." His smile seemed apologetic. "Forgive me for turning into the longwinded professor again. You see why I probably should be teaching full-time?"

They continued to visit, and by the time they finished the last of their pie, it was a little past seven and starting to get dark outside. Because Mick still had an unfinished article, Molly assured him that she could get back to campus just fine on her own. But not long after they'd parted ways, she heard footsteps trailing her. Feeling a bit uneasy on the darkened street, she paused by a coffee shop and peered through the dusky blue light to see a sailor approaching. She was about to duck into the coffee shop when she recognized his dimly lit face.

"Patrick Hammond!" she exclaimed. "You scared me half to death."

"I'm sorry," he said quickly. "You probably thought I was stalking you."

"What are you doing here?"

"Stalking you?" He chuckled.

"What—?"

"Oh, Molly. It's so good to see you." He reached for her hand, tugging her toward the coffee shop. "How about we go in there to talk?"

Thirty

After they were seated in the coffee shop and Molly was sipping on what had to be her fourth cup of coffee this evening, Patrick explained overhearing Colleen on the phone earlier. "I knew you were having dinner with some guy named Mick," he confessed. "I had to see for myself."

"But why? And why were you trailing me like that?" She stared evenly at him, trying not to get pulled in by those clear blue eyes, that sweet smile, his big-brotherly charm...and feeling completely chagrined that he was still so darned attractive to her! His handsome officer's uniform wasn't helping much either.

"Well, you know how I've always been a little protective of you." He stirred sugar into his coffee. "So I thought I better make sure you were all right." His smile faded. "As it turns out, I'm glad I did."

"Why?"

"Well, for starters, I don't like seeing you out by yourself on the streets at night. Especially with blackout going on. Do you really think it's safe? And why didn't your fellow see you safely back to campus and your door?"

"Mick still had work to finish at the newspaper."

"And who is this Mick anyway? Colleen said he's your boss, but when I saw you two in there together just now—"

"You were spying on us at Shorty's?"

"We call it reconnaissance." His smile looked slightly sheepish.

"Really? And what did you learn while doing your reconnaissance?"

Patrick's brow creased. "For starters, he looks too old for you. And he looked more interested in being your boyfriend than your boss."

"He is not my boyfriend, Patrick. And he's not actually my boss. I'm only an intern at the newspaper. Mick is my supervisor and... my friend."

"Ah ha!" He held up a finger. "That's a flag."

"A flag?"

"When a man wants to befriend a beautiful woman, there is usually more than just friendship on his mind."

Slightly taken aback by the *beautiful woman* bit, Molly couldn't quite think. "Well, I don't know about that, Patrick Hammond, but I can assure you that Mick is not my boyfriend."

"Not yet." He frowned. "How old is he anyway?"

"Thirty-two."

"So a thirty-two-year-old man is preying upon a seventeen—"

"Eighteen." She bristled.

"Yes, I know you're eighteen now. But you weren't eighteen last week and I'll bet he was—"

"Patrick, I don't want to offend you, but your big brother act is starting to wear on me. In fact, it's becoming rather aggravating. I'm an adult and perfectly capable of taking care of myself now. You need to accept that Mick is my supervisor and my friend...but he is not my boyfriend. Furthermore, I have no interest in him becoming my boyfriend."

"But I saw him looking at you. A guy knows when another guy is interested in a girl for more than just friendship. This guy Mick had that look in his eye. I saw it myself." He sighed. "I don't even blame him."

"Mick is a good, decent man. I've known him for more than a year now, and I have no reason to believe he's anything but a gentleman." Now she told him about her work at the newspaper and how Mick just introduced her to the photography department. "I don't know why you're acting like this, but it's making me uncomfortable." She locked eyes with him. "I'd like to know what's behind it."

Patrick ran his fingers through his short-cropped hair and, for the first time, Molly didn't see him as the man who was so much older. Suddenly he seemed like a young man...or even a boy. A frustrated boy. "It's because I care about you."

"I care about you too." Molly watched as he folded and unfolded the paper napkin. Was Patrick nervous?

"I owe you an apology, Molly," he said quietly. "You are a grown-up, and I shouldn't be spying on you like that. But, honestly, it's only because I care about you." He made a crooked smile. "Will you forgive me for overstepping my bounds tonight?"

"Of course." She smiled warmly at him.

He slowly shook his head as if he was disappointed in himself. "This isn't at all how I'd hoped this evening would go."

"What do you mean?"

He looked directly into her eyes. "That letter you wrote me. Did you mean what you said?"

"Which letter?"

"The last one."

"I did mean it...at the time."

"But you don't now?"

"I'm not sure. I can't remember everything I wrote. It's been awhile. And you never wrote back." She studied him closely.

"For starters, I didn't get that letter right away. We were, well, out of range...not getting mail. Anyway, I got the letter and was going to write back, but I kept hoping I'd be getting leave time. I really wanted to talk to you face-to-face. But the fighting's been pretty intense over there. I barely got leave to come see Brian, and I'll ship out again on Saturday."

"Just two days?"

"So...anyway, I was really hoping to see you tonight. Your family said you were coming home for dinner. Your mom even made you a cake. But then you went out with this Mick fellow instead. Well, I suppose I got a little jealous."

Molly didn't know what to say.

His mouth twisted to one side. "Truth is I was a lot jealous."

"Jealous like a big brother?"

"No," he said firmly. "That's what I wanted to talk to you about. First of all, I don't know how you ever got it back into your head that I was seriously interested in Bridget. Like I told you a long time ago, Bridget and I are just friends and—"

"You just said not to trust a man who wants to befriend a beautiful woman."

Patrick laughed. "Just one of the things I love about you, Molly. You're a good listener with a sharp mind. But, honestly, in this case, Bridget and I really are only friends. Ask her if you don't believe me."

"I do believe you." She frowned. "But I felt hurt last summer. It really seemed you preferred Bridget to me. When we danced that night at the wedding...well, I felt like we had something special. And then just like that, it was gone."

"Don't you know why?"

"Why?"

"Your parents and my parents—all four of them—one by one,

took me aside and spoke directly to me. They were all sending some pretty strong clues, reminding me that you were still a girl—that you were only seventeen, that I was almost twenty-four—warning me not to get too involved with you."

Molly nodded. "I wondered about that. And you listened to them?"

"They're our parents. They were all saying you were off limits, and because you were still seventeen, well, I decided they were probably right."

"I'm not seventeen now." She smiled shyly.

"I know that." His eyes lit up. "That's why I wanted to see you tonight. I know your birthday was yesterday. I'd hoped to be here in time for it, but we didn't get in until this morning."

"You actually remembered my birthday?"

"Of course." He nodded. "It's been on my calendar for quite some time."

"Really?" She felt that warm feeling buzzing through her again, similar to when they were danced at Colleen's wedding. "No one else seemed to remember...well, except for Mick." She smiled. "He made me have pie to celebrate."

"I understand your aggravation toward me tonight. And I'm sorry for spying on you. I'm sure your friend Mick is a perfectly good guy." He paused. "Although I will stick to my suspicion that he thinks you're a lovely girl and that he'd like to know you better. And it's understandable. Can you accept that?"

She shrugged. "Maybe. At least I'll be more aware since you mentioned it."

"Because you are a beautiful woman." He leaned forward. "But more than that, you are an intelligent woman. And best of all, you are a goodhearted woman."

"You're calling me a woman now? You called me a girl last summer," she teased.

"Like I said, our parents had a lot to do with that." He smiled. "Although would you fault me for thinking of you as a girl? A sweet girl that I've known and loved for years."

"As a little sister?" She arched her brows.

"Maybe at first...but not lately." He reached inside his uniform jacket, pulling out a long thin box covered in dark blue velvet. "I got this for you overseas. I actually got it some time ago. I nearly sent it to you a time or two, but I was concerned that you were too young. And when I got that letter where you informed me you weren't going to write again..." He grimly shook his head. "That was a dark day."

"I'm sorry, Patrick. I was just so hurt, so certain you loved Bridget."

"I know that now. But it cut to the core at the time. And how I missed your letters after that—it's like they say, you don't know how good something is until someone takes it away from you."

"I know." She nodded. "I felt the same way."

"So when I got your next letter, well, I knew I needed to see you. And I hoped I'd get to do that on your eighteenth birthday."

"So was your leave for my birthday? Or for your brother?"

"I'd been trying to make it for your birthday, but it wasn't going too well. Then I heard about Brian, and my superior pulled strings to get me over here. Unfortunately, I'm needed back almost at once." He held the box out to her. "Here, please, open it."

She lifted the lid to see a beautiful strand of graduated, gleaming white pearls. "Oh, my...it's beautiful, Patrick." She looked up at him. "But it's such a precious gift. Are you sure—"

"I'm absolutely certain, Molly." He picked the strand out of the box and then moved over to her side of the booth. "You should wear them."

"Oh, but I'm not dressed up or—"

"The little lady who sold them to me in Honolulu said you should wear them as often as you like. She said pearls need to be worn. They get more beautiful and lustrous by rubbing against your skin."

"Really?" Molly felt slightly breathless now. Was this really happening? Or was it just a wonderful dream?

Patrick sat next to her, holding the strand up to the light. "I made up a little story about this string of pearls," he said quietly. "Want to hear it?"

"Of course."

He pointed to the largest pearl in the center of the strand. "This big pearl symbolizes us, Molly. And the ones on either side symbolize our parents...and this one is your brother Peter and this is Brian. And these are your sisters and these will be their spouses and children, and other relatives and friends, and the people we've yet to meet. I imagined all of us being strung together like this string of pearls. Even though we might be far apart at times, we're still connected. And the string that binds us and holds us together, no matter what comes, that's God's love."

"I love that image, Patrick."

He pointed to the large pearl in the center again. "But this one is us, Molly." He looked into her eyes. "Does that make any sense to you?"

Molly nodded with wonder. "Perfect sense."

His smile seemed relieved. "Can I help you put them on?"

"Please do." She leaned her head toward him, lifting her hair and waiting as he clasped the strand behind her neck. But before he took his hands back, he held her face in his hands, looking intently into her eyes. Without questioning herself, Molly leaned toward him, and they kissed. It was magical and perfect and far better than Molly had ever imagined.

"Okay, you two," the waitress called out in a teasing tone. They both looked up to see the matronly woman pushing buttons on the jukebox. "This song's for you kids."

Glenn Miller's "String of Pearls" filled the room. Patrick stood, reaching for Molly's hand. And there, in the small, deserted coffee shop, he took her into his arms and they danced...and danced.

Other Books by Melody Carlson

THE MULLIGAN SISTERS
I'll Be Seeing You
As Time Goes By

DEAR DAPHNE
Home, Hearth, and the Holidays
A Will, a Way, and a Wedding

SECOND CHANCES
Heartland Skies
Built with Love
Shades of Light
Thursday's Child
Looking for Cassandra Jane
Armando's Treasure

WHISPERING PINES
A Place to Come Home To
Everything I Long For
Looking for You All My Life
Someone to Belong To

CPSIA information can be obtained
at www.ICGtesting.com
Printed in the USA
LVOW12s1001251017
553713LV00001B/16/P